The

in the

Snow

by

Christoph Fischer

For Eddie

with lots of love

Chris

Create Space ISBN – 13: 978-1537329765

Create Space ISBN – 10: 1537329766

Cover design by Daz Smith of nethed.com

Dedicated:

to the lovely people of Llandeilo

for their warm welcome and their kindness.

And to Cosette and Gareth Newman

for their help in getting us settled in so quickly.

www.christophfischerbooks.com

Table of Contents

Prologue: February 2012

Snow crunched underfoot with every step that she took as she squinted to see through the wind that howled around her sending snow swirling in the night sky. The hamlet in west Wales was silent. Its occupants huddled in their homes as winter clawed at windows and loosened roof tiles. The wind ripped through the trees, their snow-covered branches quivering and creaking beneath its onslaught, adding to the noise that raged. But that was good. It meant she didn't have to be so careful – nobody would go out to investigate in this weather, even if they did hear something suspicious.

Her heart pounded with excitement, so much so that she didn't feel the cold on her flushed face. She crept closer. The anger gave her the physical strength and mental resolve to keep going. She wouldn't be treated like a fool . . . talked down to and toyed with – too many people thought they could simply walk all over her these days. Now even practical strangers were doing it. Well all that was ending right here. She was reclaiming her life, and this would be the first step. She paused in front of the house to look back at her footprints in the snow on the driveway, wondering how quickly they would be obliterated. Suddenly she sensed movement and turned. She gasped. There stood the cause of her pain, with a shovel in hand, poised to strike.

"You wouldn't dare," she said, her words dragged from her mouth and lost in the howling wind.

"Try me!" came the confident response.

She took a small step and spat: "I'm going to make you pay for what you did." She hesitated and took another step back, careful not to slip as she contemplated the best escape route. But it was too late for escapes. Before she could say any more, the shovel came swinging down.

The body fell to the ground, enveloped in the dense surrounds of a snow bank.

The wind howled wilder and the ice crystals fell more rapidly as though the heavy flecks wanted to conceal the lifeless body as quickly as possible. The killer let out a heavy sigh and watched as blood from the gaping wound seeped into the pristine whiteness.

How stupid . . . to threaten someone who was carrying a shovel.

Chapter 1: The Snow - Eight Days Earlier

Bebe

"...and now for the weather: In the West and North of Britain we are currently seeing the worst snow falls in over twenty years. All roads and motorways have been closed. Road services are working around the clock to restore normal transport conditions but with so many areas affected it will mean that some communities will be isolated for some time to come.

Most airports and railway stations are closed, too. Please check with your local news and council websites for exact details. People are advised to stay indoors and make only essential trips while the snow is still falling so heavily. Please remember to stay safe.

In other news, Cheryl Cole has been replaced on the X Factor panel by Bebe Bollinger. The industry is in shock over this surprise choice, apparently this is Simon Cowell's dream cast ever since the beginning of the show. Younger people may not be aware of Bollinger's singing career in the 1980s but the move is rumoured to be part of a wider comeback plan of the retired singer..."

Bebe Bollinger was torn from her magic dream by the piercing sound of her alarm clock. She swiftly switched the thing off and rolled back on her pillow, smiling and indulging herself for a few more moments at the idea of a return to the limelight. The mere thought gave her a surge of energy, she bounded out of bed and her knees immediately let her know that bounding was now not a good idea. "Dreams can come true," she hummed as she paraded through her bedroom. As she pulled back the curtains she saw that at least one part of her newsflash dream had come true: she looked with amazement at the snow-covered landscape. It was just as the announcer in her dream had foretold. She could hardly even make out her car beneath the huge amounts of snow. Trees, bushes and fields were all only vaguely distinguishable, and the snow kept falling in heavy flurries.

For more than twenty four years Bebe had lived in the hamlet of Llangurrey and not once had there been bad weather like this – there had to be at least a metre. Everything had turned into a winter wonderland, but as beautiful as it looked, there were practicalities to be considered. She and her neighbours were cut-off from the world. With snow this high, no regular car would be able to drive the few miles to the main road, and it was too far to walk to the rest of civilisation.

There had been weather warnings on the radio, but Bebe had heard such grim predictions many times in the past and nothing had ever come of them. Only the day before, the teller at her bank had told her that it might be as severe as the winters of 1947 and 1963. She had gasped at the impertinence of the woman for implying that Bebe should have first-hand knowledge of those years. Yes, she had been around in '63 but liked to pretend that she was younger than she was. Anyway, for Llangurrey such conditions were totally unheard of. No one could blame her for being surprised that this time the weathermen had actually been right.

The phone rang. Bebe sighed. This had to be Bryn, her hairdresser, to cancel their appointment. He was one of her biggest admirers. Not in a sexual way, Bryn was gay as the proverbial goose although he still pretended to be in the closet at the age of 65. He was an incredibly talented stylist, though.

"Yes," she said abruptly into the receiver, trying to sound busy.

"Bebe my darling, please tell me that you're alright," Bryn sang into the phone. "My sister said that the road to Llangurrey is completely snowed in. I take it our hair session today won't be happening if that's the case. How will you cope?"

"Bryn I'll be just fine," she said. "Don't worry about my hair. I'm not likely to see anyone until this snow is gone. I might as well look scruffy, nobody will care."

"That is exactly the moment when some paparazzo will get you and write a nasty 'where-are-they-now-article' about the retired singing legend Bebe in the gossip magazines," Bryn said. "And people will think like that it was all my doing."

Bebe rolled her eyes. Bryn was such a drama queen.

"Tell me, do you have enough food for a few days?" he asked, his voice panicked.

"Of course I have darling, please don't worry," she reassured him. "There is plenty in the freezer, and a little diet will do me good, if the worst should happen and I'm stuck for longer."

"But there is nothing of you," Bryn said.

Bebe perked up at the compliment.

"Sweetheart, I need to go," she said, wishing to examine the situation outside first hand. "I've literally just woken up."

"No problem Bebe. Look after yourself and call me if there is anything I can do," he said.

"Thank you. I promise I will."

She hung up. Bebe had to come to rely on Bryn over the years for a weekly ego boost, but wouldn't dream of relying on him for anything else. He was good for make-up advice and for sourcing the right chemical peels, but he would be the last person capable of rescuing her from the snow.

If she had known that this amount of snowfall was a real possibility then she would have joined the panic buyers at the supermarkets and petrol stations over the past few days. After the incident with the bank teller, she had walked the aisles of the local superstore and had been disgusted by the scramble for goods. Manic people were pushing in her way, rushing from shelf to shelf and taking as much as they could get their unwashed hands on, probably without even knowing if they needed it or not.

When Bebe had gone shopping in Carmarthen a few days earlier, there had been an end-of-time atmosphere in the store that Bebe could only ridicule. Even if there were no supplies for a few days, no one would starve. This wasn't a war zone, and the major supply routes would be re-opened in no time even if they ever would have to be closed temporarily. Yet here were barbarians hoarding the few remains on the shelves as if their survival depended on it.

Bebe had been surprised to see that even her usually laid-back neighbour Dora had filled one of the large shopping carts to the very brim with long-life milk and other emergency provisions; at least that's how it seemed from the safe distance Bebe had been keeping. It was hard to tell through the huge '70s-style glasses that Bebe wore in public as a disguise from potential autograph hunters. Whether the glasses did their job well or whether it was just a lack of demand for her signature was debatable. As far as chit-chat with Dora was concerned there was certainly no need for it here in the cereal aisle. The two women rarely spoke to each other anyway.

Bebe refused to be seen pushing towards the emptying shelves. She only bought a few essentials and left as soon as she could get out via the self-service check-out. Having to scan her own shopping was a little beneath her but on a day like this she really did not want to speak to anyone.

Now that she was actually snowed in, it looked as if she would be stuck with the little provisions she had brought home that day. Bebe's larder was filled with snacks, so she wouldn't starve, although theoretically she had planned to go on a diet in the New Year — always ready for that return to the musical stage — she had just not got around to starting it yet.

Llangurrey consisted of an old abandoned farm and three country cottages, tucked away in a small valley, several miles away from the nearest town. Fields and a little stream acted as natural borders and a narrow country lane ran through the hamlet, rather close to the houses. Petite front gardens served as buffers from what little traffic that passed.

The idyllic but remote setting in west Wales had attracted her to the place. Her singing career had just come to an unexpected halt and this cottage — a listed building with a large thatched roof — shielded her from the press and paparazzi eager to pursue the small-scale scandal about the end of her marriage. The break-up had heralded her unexpected departure from the recording studios of London, leaving her resentful and suspicious of everyone who tried to come close to her and ask questions.

After years of fame and socialising with the rich and powerful, the last thing she wanted was to be plagued by a group of nobodies, so she avoided the farmer and her neighbours. Thankfully, the farmer had moved on and now it was just the other two houses in the hamlet that Bebe had to avoid. Haunted by the scandal she would rarely answer her door when anyone knocked and she always made sure she looked busy. The other households soon completely ignored her in the same way as she did with them.

Her main connection to the outside world remained her daughter Helena, who, unlike her mother, spoke to everyone and probably had told the nosy people everything there was to know, judging from the gossip her child related to her on the rare occasions that Helena would invite herself over for dinner. The longer Bebe lived on her own the more she succumbed to a vague curiosity about what was going on outside her front door and, when inspiration was lacking, she had become partial to keeping an eye on her neighbours from behind the safety of her curtains.

From her window she could see that her neighbour Ian had already tried to get out of the hamlet with his car. His Rover had been meticulously freed from snow and ice. Bebe could make out tyre imprints that showed he had attempted, albeit unsuccessfully, to make his way through the meter-high drifts. If he with his superior car and driving skills had failed then there was no hope for Bebe. Her brand new Nissan might look like a 4x4, but it was of no use in this weather.

She almost rejoiced in the drama of her situation. Without even noticing she started to hum the theme of *Love Story*, which had also had such a beautiful winter setting in the film. Only when she started to lilt the words "Where do I begin?" did she remember that Shirley Bassey and Nana Mouskouri had both covered the Andy Williams song and that was enough to stop her in her tracks. A wave of envy rushed over her: Those two women had managed to make it big in a small market that should have belonged exclusively to Bebe.

She decided to go outside and examine the situation first hand. She put on her big mink coat, her Russian-style hat, also made of fur, and the warm leather winter boots. She adored the look. In her mind it was the perfect cross of *Dr Zhivago* and *Sex and The City* and she looked herself up and down in the mirror before making for the door. A former publicist had been so bold as to call it the 'Babooshka' look. Bebe found the word distasteful. It rang too much of Kate Bush, another musician whose guts she hated, and because the remark put her prematurely in the casting category of older women and mothers. It was no wonder she let said publicist go.

Bebe stepped outside her front door. She felt clumsy and unwieldy in the winter clothes. Since she was neither tall nor slim she feared that, despite the glamour factor, these big coats might also give her a square and disadvantageous figure, even though Bryn assured her that it was not the case.

Wrinkles could be painted and operated away and hair could be bleached, but few fabrics and styles could cover up the results of comfort eating.

The truth was that Bebe was far from being fat. At close to sixty she was entitled to a little bit of extra weight. For someone with such a dislike for physical activity she had a fantastic body. With the right dress her large chest could distract from her expanding belly and her bottom could pass as curvy and voluptuous. Or so she told herself successfully on a good day, and Bryn said so every time they met.

She studied the snow-bound hamlet: only a snowplough could free them from isolation. Given that there were so few inhabitants along this insignificant loop of a lane, Bebe knew they would not be a priority on the council's list of rescue missions.

As she stood outside her cottage she heard a door open nearby. Bebe turned as quickly as she could on the icy ground without losing her balance and hurried towards her house. She was not in the market for pleasantries, nor interested in other people's stories, yet didn't want to appear rude or ignorant.

As she turned around to close the door behind her, she could just about make out Dora standing in her garden only wearing winter boots and a pink morning gown. What on earth was this woman doing outside dressed so sparsely? She must be catching her death, never mind about the rudeness of it. Bebe rid herself of the warm winter clothes and went upstairs to have a look into Dora's garden from her window.

Her neighbour had wiped the snow off her bird bath and had hung up some bird feeders in the trees. That woman seemed to love animals more than humans, talking to cats and feeding squirrels and birds the way she did. On the single lane road that led to their hamlet Dora never showed consideration for other drivers. It was always they that had to reverse to the nearest widening in the road so that the cars could pass each other. And yet, she would almost certainly brake for a mouse or a bird on the road. Bebe shook her head at her eccentric Portuguese neighbour.

Dora was about ten years younger than Bebe and – the singer hated to admit it – was a stunning beauty. And that was not just down to her age. With her long black hair, which she wore in various styles and with colourful outfits she made a big impression, although it was not one Bebe thought as being classy and age appropriate. In Bebe's eyes, some of the dresses were nothing short of tacky.

Dora had moved to Llangurrey, a hamlet a few miles east of Carmarthen, after divorcing Dylan Jenkins. His family had money and education and was well known in Wales: they were often pictured in the local papers. Although Bebe had never acquainted herself with the provincial gentry she had observed them from a distance and knew a fair bit about them.

To ignorant people like Dora, there was no real difference between the genuine aristocracy and 'new money' but to Bebe and the Jenkins family themselves such distinctions had always been most important.

Bebe knew all about how the unlikely match between Dora and Dylan had come about. She had never asked Dora one personal question but Bebe's daughter Helena had quizzed the newcomer relentlessly and between those snippets of news and the gossip column of the local newspaper it was easy to paint a picture.

Dora had come to Britain to learn the language, and worked as an au pair in London. During the last week of her stay, she'd decided to treat herself to the luxury of a once-in-a-lifetime dinner at the Ritz. And this was where she met Dylan. Stunned by her beauty and taken in by how unimpressed she was by closed upper class circles he fell head over heels for her.

She extended her stay in the UK to improve her language skills, especially as she could live rent-free in his London studio apartment. He proposed, she accepted; then came the wedding, the children and the years of house arrest in their country mansion with lots of staff and the dos and the don'ts and tedious family intrusions into their private life. Eventually it ended in divorce.

On her arrival in Llangurrey three years earlier, Dora seemed to have taken Bebe's abruptness and rudeness in her stride. Bebe assumed she had scared the newcomer into submission, but she was sorely mistaken as she came to discover one memorable day. Bebe was in the garden sunning herself when Dora suddenly blasted out one of Bebe's least flattering recordings, the tune of a children's TV programme, over her sound system, and replayed the song for over an hour. Bebe was fuming, but wouldn't give Dora the satisfaction of knowing that, so instead she forced herself to sit in that lounger for another hour before finally going inside, her face flushed red with mortification. She never forgave Dora for the affront.

Chapter 2: The Happy Divorcee

Dora

During her marriage to Dylan Jenkins, Dora had endured enough snobbery to last a lifetime. For years she had been confined to a stiff life in a manor house near Abergavenny, with staff who knew more about etiquette than she did and in-laws that were so lifeless and disapproving that Dora felt she was always doing everything wrong before she even moved or opened her mouth. With all that she had heard about the warm and welcoming nature of the Welsh, Dora, unfortunately, had landed in a cold and xenophobic island within the community.

Had it not been for her two daughters, Isabella and Julia, Dora would have left that life behind ages ago, but she'd persevered, sticking with the patronising Jenkins family until her girls were old enough to cope with their parents' divorce.

Dora had not fought Dylan for custody; she knew that her children would be much better off getting their education under the tutelage of her ex-husband and his family. The girls knew the door was always open, and came to her whenever they needed a loving warm mother.

Dylan had behaved like a gentleman during the divorce and, despite being at a loss as to why Dora had decided to leave, he was happy to provide her with a generous alimony so the mother of his children would not, as he advised his own fuming mother, "look like a complete hwran (slag)".

Dora had moved in to this cottage because it was merely a ninety-minute drive to her daughters' boarding school in Monmouth, but still far enough from her ex-husband's family in Hereford. She had deliberately chosen a home that was less grand than Dylan had suggested, in the hope that the lower property prices in Llangurrey would bring with them a friendly social environment, free from the snobbery she had experienced. Alas, that was not to be.

Three years living side by side had barely softened the strained relations between her and her neighbours, so when Dora came out to feed the birds that snowy morning and noticed Bebe standing on road in her furs, she cursed her bad timing. Had she known Bebe would be there, she might have waited a little bit longer to come out but she cared for the birds and she could not punish little innocent creatures for the presence of that ego-inflated woman. Such chance meetings, albeit harmless, were almost always unpleasant. So much was conveyed without words. The hasty exit of the singer was an insult. Dora had no intention of engaging in conversation; a polite 'Hello' was all they would have exchanged anyway.

Dora knew that her wearing a bathrobe would be yet further proof of inappropriate behaviour in the eyes of her judgemental neighbour. She knew that in Bebe's book Dora was no better than the people that appeared on the Jeremy Springer TV Show. Dylan had accused his ex-wife of paranoia when it came to other people's opinion about herself, but how could Dora ever be sure, living in a foreign culture? When it came to Bebe, however, Dora knew she was not being paranoid. Just the other day she had seen her neighbour in the supermarket in Carmarthen. While mothers and entire families desperately tried to prepare for the looming weather catastrophe, Bebe had flounced through the aisles with her little hand basket, casting dismissive glances left and right at those who had more shopping to do than her. The singer then had pretended not to have seen Dora and walked twice in the opposite direction just to avoid having to say a friendly word.

At least fame seemed to have waned enough for the former legend if she had to do her own shopping.

Dora busied herself with hanging the feeders. She was appalled that nobody else in the hamlet bothered to put out food for the birds.

Did they not care for those lovely creatures that enriched everyone's life with their beauty and their songs in the mornings? Why were these people living in the countryside? Didn't they love nature?

Dora went back inside and turned on some bossa nova to cheer herself up. She began to water her indoor plants, picking dead leaves, talking to the plants and telling them all about her beautiful home city of Lisbon. When she got to the plants upstairs she saw that her neighbour Ian had scratched his car, probably in a vain bid to reach the main road. She guessed his wife Christine was away on business again and stuck on the other side of the snow. How marvellous.

Ian was friendly and gregarious. Christine on the other hand rarely spoke to people, and if she did it was always in the most awkward manner. Usually, she talked to complain about something.

The first time the two women had met was when Dora had put the waste bin outside a day too early by mistake. New to the area, jet lagged from a holiday, confused and tired she got rudely dragged out of her sleep by the doorbell ringing incessantly. In front of her stood a slender, middle-aged woman in a grey suit and heels, with flustered cheeks, a nervously shaking leg and arms crossed over her chest.

"Hi, I'm your neighbour Christine Morris. Would you awfully mind pulling your rubbish bin back onto your property?" Christine had said with steely politeness.

"Dora Jenkins," Dora had replied, sleep-drunk and confused and had stretched out her hand.

"So, would you mind?" Christine repeated her request, not opening her arms to return the gesture.

"I beg your pardon?" Dora had asked.

"Your bin is out early," Christine said, enunciating every word. "Council regulations clearly state that refuse bins must not be on the road until the day of collection between 7am and 7pm."

"So?" Dora asked.

"So, please comply with the rules. Pull the bin back onto your property and put them out tomorrow morning, like everyone else. Bins out overnight are a feast for rodents and wildlife and the lane really isn't a pretty sight when the bins are out. It's rubbish, for crying out loud. We need to reduce that to the least possible hours, wouldn't you agree? We don't want to look tacky, do we?"

Dora's mind had been too slow to compute the insults. She didn't want a fight on her first encounter with this woman, so she had pulled the bin back and then, as what had happened began to sink in, slammed the door shut noisily. She had regretted her weakness and the lost chance to stand her ground.

Another time Dora's solicitor had parked on the lane but, according to Christine's assessment, it was too close to her and Ian's house, leaving not enough space for their own potential visitors. Within minutes of the solicitor's arrival, Christine had stormed to Dora's door.

"I'm sure you can see that this is a really inconsiderate way of parking," Christine said. "Let's have that error corrected right now and we'll speak no more of it."

"In all the time I have been here you haven't had one visitor," Dora had replied, "and there is space for several cars on your driveway. Are you expecting anyone right now?"

Dora was unwilling to ask her lawyer to move his car, so she added: "If you do, there would be plenty of space by the farm, too, if you haven't noticed."

Christine pursed her lips.

"That's not how we do things here," she insisted. "There are certain unwritten rules."

Dora's solicitor by now had come to the door and had overheard some of the conversation. He re-parked his car immediately.

"Thank you," Christine had said with exaggerated humbleness.

The next day, Christine marked the curb with a few yellow dots on the tarmac to divide the parking.

Dora was fuming and waited for Christine to come up with another complaint. She would tell her neighbour what she thought of the unwritten rules. As if she knew she had pushed the boat out too far, Christine kept a low profile in the following weeks and the next time she complained she put it in writing, avoiding direct confrontation with the neighbour. She suggested Dora cut her hedge and even advised on how much to cut. She complained that the planned wild-flower meadow would attract weeds that would send their pollen across the lane towards Christine's pristine garden and 'strongly suggested' that Dora take care of it.

But Dora did nothing of the sort. Weeks passed without any drama until Christine showed up on her doorstep once again. Dora didn't even wait for her to say what the problem was and simply slammed the front door in the bossy neighbours' face.

"Go to hell," Dora had shouted through the door.

Christine stood there in stunned silence for several minutes until Ian came and took her home.

Dora liked Ian. He was rather handsome for a middle-aged man. Hardly a swelling around the hips, tall and broad shouldered, he had still a lot going for him. Dora wasn't attracted to him, partly due to his poor body posture and his hanging head (a side effect of his marriage, no doubt), but there had to be plenty of women – much nicer than Christine – who would want to take care of this otherwise handsome and masculine man. How he had ended up with such an unattractive, unfriendly and controlling woman was beyond her.

Dora and Bebe relied on Ian when machinery broke down or other physical tasks needed doing, but they always checked if Christine's car was parked outside before approaching him. On his own he was a totally different person.

What luck Christine was not here right now, Dora thought. She wondered if Ian was alright without his wife. Did he have enough food? She went downstairs to put trash into the shed where she kept the rubbish bin, cursing under her breath at how cold it was.

Dora took her boots off and put on her slippers, went to the kitchen and had some breakfast. She turned the heating to the hottest setting but she was still not toasty enough, so she decided to have a hot bath while watching the mid-morning television in the other room through the open bathroom door.

She had just sunk into the hot water when the doorbell rang unexpectedly. She hurried down and opened the door, again only in her bathrobe. It was Ian.

"Bom dia, neighbour!" he called, giving the Portuguese greeting, as he approached.

"Bom dia, muita obrigada (much obliged)," she replied, pleased at the kind gesture.

"I tried to see if I could reach the main road earlier with my Rover but there's no way of getting out," he said. "Christine is stuck in Scotland. She sends her regards and asked me to borrow some pasta and cream off you," he said shyly.

"Oh no, no, no," Dora said, "I need to eat myself, why don't I just cook something for both of us and we share it. There is no point at all in you making a mess in your kitchen, no!"

"That's terribly sweet of you," he said, blushing, "but I know Christine wouldn't like it much if I did that. She has her own little system for the food in the house. We have condiments and vegetables that would go off if I didn't cook today. She's very good at planning things like that and knows exactly what food expires when."

"Now don't be silly," Dora said animatedly. What had this man called his wife? Good at planning? Obsessed and dominant was more like it. She felt that his eyes lingered that little bit longer than was necessary as she stood there in her bathrobe.

"Bring your 'condiments and vegetables' Ian and I will cook them for you. Don't you have work to do? It would make perfect sense for us to pool our resources. Who knows how long we will be stuck here? Have you not heard the news? Half of the country is snowed in and there are not enough snow ploughs to go round. Our three houses won't be the first to be rescued. Get real and tell your wife she can resume control when the crisis is over."

"Oh, no, no," Ian said quickly. "She wouldn't like that."

"Fine, if you think she is going to air-drop an emergency supply over the hamlet then go ahead. I'll get cream and pasta for you. Penne or tagliatelle?"

"Oh, any will do," Ian replied embarrassed.

"Why don't you come in?" Dora asked him. "It's cold outside."

"Oh I better wait here," he said evasively. "By the time I got my boots off you should have found the cream."

Dora rolled her eyes and left him standing outside her door. Ian must have worried that Bebe would see them together, especially with Dora again wearing only her bathrobe. Looking at her wristwatch Dora realised that was unlikely at this hour. Around this time Bebe usually locked herself in the basement and dedicated herself to her recordings. Quite often the postman left deliveries for her with Dora because Bebe didn't answer her door.

But why did everyone always assume that just because a woman was comfortable in her body and was wearing little clothes that she was trying to seduce men? Dora was not in the least interested in a man right now. After her dreary marriage she really just wanted to be left alone. Did she have to run around like a nun just to assure everyone of that?

She grabbed a package of penne and a small pot of cream and took it to the door.

"Here you are," she said, a little less friendly since she felt she had just been insulted. "You know where I am if you need any more food."

"I still can't believe this weather," Ian remarked.

"Oh, well," Dora replied. "We kind of knew that this would happen, they've been warning us for days. If you need anything I have a full fridge."

"Truth be told, I am a little short," Ian admitted. "I didn't think it would get this bad so quickly. Christine was due back from a work trip this morning and she would have brought the weekly shopping with her."

"I'm sure the lane will be clear by midday or tonight at the latest," Dora said, trying to sound hopeful.

"We'll see," Ian said. He went to his driveway, grabbed a snow shovel and started to clear a path between the houses.

Dora closed the door and returned to her bath. She hoped her invitation had not implied to him that she was up for anything else but cooking food together. It was time she repaid him for the many occasions when Ian had helped her with her car or with plumbing problems. What was the big issue about a shared meal, particularly when Christine wasn't even here? Well, if he had to be as distant like that then so be it.

She wondered what Bebe would do if she ran out of food. After all, the woman had exuded huge confidence in the supermarket that she needed nothing but a loaf of bread and some milk. Dora would love to see the 'star' come to her door begging for eggs and sugar.

Dora sighed. She had not expected to be so isolated in Wales. TV programmes often idealised rural settings and made one think that here the world was a simpler and harmonious place. She had falsely assumed that in the countryside everyone would be much nicer. The narrow lane dividing the front gardens was only a small barrier between the houses, a constellation which made for an intimate and close knitted setting. Dora had not expected such complicated politics and so little mingling amongst the few inhabitants of Llangurrey.

The only friendly person was Ian and so Dora was pretty much on her own here; which was not all that bad since at least she had now time to rediscover her hobbies. She took up painting again and, equipped with a satellite dish, she started to watch a lot of soap operas and other shows – pastimes that had not fitted into her married life. The Jenkins family had frowned on the common nature of TV and spoiled it for Dora with their disapproving looks. Even her painting didn't escape those disdainful remarks. Her style of art had been too abstract for her mother-in-law and had earned Dora a lot of criticism.

Now that was all behind her. Whenever her daughters came to visit they marvelled at the transformation their mother had made, from shy wall flower to independent woman. They had not been aware how much she had sacrificed in those years just to keep the peace and protect them from a childhood tainted by arguing parents. Now that that phase was over, Dora was never going back. She couldn't lead a life like Ian, oppressed by a strong-willed partner. Never again would she allow someone to treat her like a door-mat.

Chapter 3: The Handy Man

Ian

Ian walked slowly back to his house. He was not remotely cold after all the shipping of snow that he had done. He worried a little that what Dora had said might be true and that he might be cut off from civilisation for longer than just a few hours. Christine would go absolutely mad with worry.

He wished he could have taken Dora up on her offer to cook for him. He hated preparing even the simplest dishes and was notoriously prone to ruin perfectly safe recipes. With all the chaos caused by the snow, it would have been nice for him to have some company, too. Ian had married when he was over forty. Prior to that he used to have a very busy social life but gradually Christine had angered most of his friends with her difficult manners. Moving to Llangurrey sealed his fate. A graphic designer by profession, he used to travel a lot, and had met Christine over ten years earlier, when she had commissioned some work for her events management company. That and some other steady clients provided him with his income ever since and, with the advancement of the internet, he mostly worked from home, seeing few clients in person.

After their wedding he and his wife initially lived in the centre of Tenby, a beautiful historical town by the sea, but Christine wasn't happy. They hadn't anticipated how busy it could get with tourists and how noisy the roads became at pub closing time. And parking was a problem there, too. After a few years of trying to get his wife used to the situation, they finally put the place up for sale and moved to Llangurrey. He warned her right from the beginning that the close-knit nature of this mini hamlet would bring unwanted intimacy with the neighbours, but Christine had fallen in love with the cottage and wouldn't listen. Despite his misgivings, though, Ian thought that he would make it work.

He enjoyed the odd chat over the garden fence and would have liked to be on friendly terms with Dora, but Christine and her endless list of unwritten laws had rendered that a virtual impossibility. Ian often found himself caught in the middle of her many disputes with their neighbour. The rules that Christine imposed were often illogical, but she was his wife, so he backed her up in her squabbles and endured the consequent distance from an otherwise charming and kind neighbour.

Christine got on better with the pretentious Bebe. Since Bebe rarely left her home, conversations were limited, a fact that was very much to Christine's liking. Furthermore, the two women shared an equally snobbish attitude when it came to Dora, who was always sitting in her front garden, sunbathing, embarrassing her neighbours with her tiny bikinis in the summer and annoying the women with her continuous presence on the road that made it so darn hard to ignore her.

He wasn't so bothered about that; often defending Dora by pointing out that gardens were meant to be used when it was warm.

In his opinion Christine should just go and make peace with Dora, then the moments when their paths crossed would not be so unpleasant.

It was Bebe who really set Ian on edge. He actually liked her singing, but her behaviour had put him off so much that he no longer listened to the three CD's of her music that he owned.

He sighed in frustration at the thought of the perilous state of his neighbourly relations. It was all an unnecessary distraction and all this snow wasn't helping matters. It prevented him from focussing on his work, as did all the constant phone calls and texts he was receiving from Christine or her secretary.

As he entered his home the landline rang. That had to be Christine again.

"Yes, hello?" he answered.

"Oh thank god you're in," Christine said on the other end. "My secretary just called the council and they estimate the plough won't get to our lane until tomorrow afternoon. You'll have to go to the freezer and get some of the Tupperware out of the lower compartment, or else you won't have enough food for tomorrow."

"Alright. Are the boxes labelled?" he asked, looking for pen and paper so he could write down her instructions.

"I've sent you an email already. You do have internet, don't you?" she asked, the panic clear in her voice.

"Of course we do. What about you? Are you still stuck up in the conference centre? When is the plough coming to get you out?"

"We're snowed in just as bad as you and we are probably going to be stuck here a little bit longer. The place is even more remote than Llangurrey. We're lucky there's on-site catering. We've supplies for weeks. It's you I'm worried about."

"Well don't. There's plenty of food here, too," he tried to calm her down.

"Ian, I have done the shopping. I know exactly how little there is. The forecasters are saying this is not just a minor snowfall. This could go on for much longer than a few days," she said in a condescending voice.

"I'll check your email and mail you back," he replied.

"Of course you will. Now, did you get cream and pasta from Bebe?" she asked.

"Bebe didn't answer her door," he answered, sheepish.

"Oh, you haven't asked that Dora, have you?"

"She was the only one I *could* ask."

"How many times have I told you that we have to stay clear of that woman," Christine said, launching into a familiar sermon. "You give these Southern European people your small finger and they take your entire arm. You have just given her an excuse to come round to ours and ask for favours, and before we know it she'll be knocking on our door every day. That woman is lonely and desperate for company. Oh, I don't know what you are thinking sometimes."

He knew there was a little bit of truth in his wife's hysterical ramblings. Dora was keen on establishing more contact with her neighbours and even though she had issues with Bebe and Christine she would probably be the first one to kiss and make up and try to establish good relations. He doubted however that Christine's fears of being overrun were realistic. Dora also seemed to be very independent.

"Don't be jealous," he said.

"Jealous of that trollop? You *are* kidding me!" Christine barked down the phone.

"I'd better go," Ian said quickly. "I've been shovelling snow; I'm quite sweaty and need to take a bath. I'll speak to you later, OK?"

"Fine, but don't ask any more favours of the neighbours."

He hung up and ran himself a bath.

The snow just kept coming.

The next morning, news reports stated that due to heavy falls, large parts of the country were snow covered and major disruptions could be expected in affected areas.

Many roads were closed as the what few snow ploughs there were struggling with the workload. The government and the army were drawing up emergency plans, but there was still hope amongst some weather forecasters that the cold front over Britain might move away and give everyone respite.

Ian started eating his way through the emergency supplies in the freezer as laid out in the daily food roster emails sent by Christine. Following the strict instructions by his wife he had established a system of defrosting and cooking the dishes she had prepared and saved for a snowy day over the months. However, not even her bleakest and most pessimistic estimates matched the worst case scenarios laid out by the TV programmes. Ian had a long way to go before he would run out of food, but Christine was panicking and scolding herself for having not bought more imperishable or canned goods.

In her worried state she even had enquired about hiring a helicopter to get her out of Scotland but the only ones available came at an astronomical cost, she told Ian on the phone. The roads from the conference centre to the nearest town had eventually been cleared and she could make it as far as Edinburgh where she booked into a hotel. Against official advice, Christine drove further south but she was now stuck in a motorway motel. The snow came down particularly heavily around Dumfries and there were frequent crashes. Now, the motorway was closed and she had to wait until it was reopened. Ian was charmed that she wanted to be with him but worried at the risks she was taking.

He was not one for television and was starting to get bored. He'd often wished to have more freedom for himself, away from work and his wife's demands. Those dreams would have included the chance of going on long bicycle tours and working in the garden, both of which were impossible in the current cold climate. Deprived of company, apart from Christine's frequent calls, he was finding the evenings long and lonesome.

When Christine was on her business trips he would normally go to the local pub a few miles away, to have dinner. Sometimes, he would visit business partners and have human contact that way. He was not cut out for being alone for such a long stretch of time and was starting to get cabin fever.

And so it was a welcome surprise to hear music travelling across the winter landscape . . . even if it was from Bebe. She may have been annoying but her vocal efforts were better than many of the electronically altered voices of current artists, he grudgingly admitted.

Chapter 4: The Diva

Bebe

Bebe was oblivious to the world outside. She had been busy in her basement which served her as a recording studio. It wasn't quite industry standard but it was most certainly good enough for the purpose of working on new material as well as her back catalogue in preparation for a return to the limelight. She was determined to make it happen before she turned 60, and for that she was running out of time.

Producing music was not the same as in the good old days. She had to do both the recording and the singing, but once she got started she felt like she was back in the heyday of her success. She could lose herself in the past for entire days. A small cupboard with snacks 'to keep her going' prevented her from having to walk up the steep stairs to the kitchen continuously, something rather important when you had creative juices flowing and the muse whispering into your ear.

In the basement, Bebe re-lived her glory. She rehearsed her large repertoire, wrote her own compositions and practised songs which she thought would sound so much better in her voice.

She was particularly jealous of Norah Jones, Amy Winehouse and Adele, all of whom were nothing but younger incarnations of herself, she felt. If only the record-buying audience could give her another chance to prove how much more soul and class her voice had compared with those amateurs. Why had there been a need for them when she was so perfectly capable of singing those songs just as well? Why did it always have to be someone new and younger? Why did composers and producers stop giving you their greatest work when you had the audiences ready?

Right now, however, none of that mattered, and neither did the snow. Bebe had suddenly been catapulted into her private showbiz heaven. In a TV talent show, the magnificent Will Young named Bebe as one of his favourite British artists. She could hardly contain her excitement and ran around her cottage like a headless chicken. There was just so much to think about. She could do a duet with the young man. He could invite her to be on the show? She'd always thought that Will Young and maybe Michael Buble were her natural male equivalents in the music industry. She could do well using either of them as a vehicle back to stardom. Admittedly, Buble, being Canadian, might not even have heard of her. But Will Young! What a joy! Her gays - her true and loyal admirers, would just love that. Oh how pleased she was that she had kept relations to their community amicable.

Overly excited, she went wild downloading music and instrumental versions of duets she thought would be candidates for a cover version between her and Will. Oh she was so pleased that he had won that talent show back then and not the other boy. Will Young was a godsend.

Bebe was so focused on her new project that she completely forgot to eat or worry about the snow. Motivated more than ever to be ready for that phone call to bring her back to the biz she started to use her Wii Sport, a Christmas present from Helena. Of course it had been a present meant to hurt her feelings but as it turned out it was another great piece in the jigsaw puzzle. Stuck indoors, Bebe had plenty of time to figure out how this thing worked and she practised plenty. She could feel an instant effect and felt years younger and slimmer already.

As soon as the snow was gone she would take up singing lessons again. She had set her eyes on a few difficult numbers, like *I Feel Love* and *It's a Heartache*. Bonnie Tyler and Donna Summer were high on her list of artists whose repertoires could be sampled. Bebe had just about the vocal range to pull it off; the songs were well known and yet could easily be transformed in to the Jazzy funky new image that she envisaged for herself. All she had to do was take the big fog-horn parts out of the songs and make them sound hurt and soulful. She could do that, she had experienced enough pain to pour it into the new arrangements.

Helena did have the courtesy to telephone and enquire about her mother in the middle of the snow catastrophe.

"How sweet of you to call," Bebe said, still high on her Will Young rush. "What a pleasant surprise."

"Of course mother," Helena said. "Listen, you haven't heard from Aidan, have you?"

"No," Bebe said, bemused. "Your lovely husband, unfortunately, never calls me. Is he alright?"

"Well," Helena said, "if he does call, can you please tell him that I'm staying with you?"

"Why, where the devil are you, you naughty child?"

"Stuck in the snow," Helena said sheepishly.

"Oh darling, please say it's not with another man?"

Helena kept quiet.

"Oh Helena, what have you been up to now?" Bebe asked. "How do you always end up in so much trouble? You've only been married for a year and already you're going astray and risk being caught in the act? The snow was forecast. Could you not have thought of that before going to some guy's house?"

"Will you cover for me or not?" Helena asked.

"I don't know," Bebe said, "Aidan's such a nice man."

"There's no point in making things worse by telling him the truth."

"OK," Bebe sighed. "I suppose you're right there."

She wrote down the exact times that Helena had claimed to be with her and left the note by the phone to make sure not to mix things up if caught off guard. If Aidan should call, Bebe would know what to say.

She almost didn't blame her daughter for her troublesome character. Richard, the absent father, had behaved appallingly throughout her entire life and with his constant neglect and unkindness he'd made Helena easy prey for unworthy men who promised her the world for a little attention and a quick fumble. Bebe tried to do her best for her daughter by enrolling her in renowned boarding schools, where such nonsense should have been educated out of the girl. It clearly hadn't worked.

It was lucky that the snow was blocking the road to Llangurrey, thought Bebe. If things got nasty between her daughter and Aidan, and Bebe sensed that this would be the case sooner or later, Helena was bound to arrive unannounced seeking shelter from her jealous husband, and right now the singing mother had much more important tasks at hand than to save a marriage that had been doomed long before the 'I do'.

Wary of exposing her throat to the cold air and getting laryngitis, Bebe had not set foot outside. She found a lot of food in the freezer and long-life rice and soya milk that Helena had once bought when she thought she had a dairy intolerance.

In her hopeful new state, Bebe continuously tried to contact Bertie, her current agent. They were not on good terms with each other ever since she berated him last year over Amy Winehouse's death. How he had managed to miss the boat to get Bebe on the tribute album was beyond her.

"I was the obvious choice to cover at least one of those tracks," she had told him.

"The world and his brother tried to get on that bandwagon," he'd replied. "A lot of people got refused."

"You keep dropping the ball, Bertie," she scolded him. "That Emma Bunton song, *Maybe*, should have been mine, too. You call yourself a friend of that record producer and let him slip the song to a Spice Girl?"

"It's a better marketing spin to have a song with a Sixties sound sung by her than by someone who already sang those kind of songs for real," Bertie said.

"That song screamed for a singer like me and you know it."

"If you agreed to build up publicity by going into the Celebrity Big Brother house or went on Strictly Come Dancing, like I always tell you to do, then producers would be keener," he'd retorted.

She hated the idea, but she was getting desperate.

"Maybe I can come round to the thought of considering these options," she said.

"Too little too late," Bertie said. "This year's shows have already been filled. We missed the deadline because of your false pride. There are plenty of people interested in these kinds of shows. We'll have to apply next year."

"To think that I should be forced to *apply* to be let on something of such a dubious reputation really scares me, Bertie. My name has to count for more than that. Can't they find me a TV show for music off the beaten track?"

"I'll see what I can do," he had said, which was his usual response when he'd had enough arguing. She knew it meant nothing.

He was not in his office today; either that or he was screening his calls. She also called his mobile but it went straight to answerphone. She left him several messages about her many ideas for a duet with Will Young, but Bertie didn't get back to her. While she was waiting she plunged herself in the living room sofa and listened critically to the music she had recorded during the day of the big snow.

Bebe had been rather confident about the high quality of the finished product but now she was feeling less sure of herself. Bertie's behaviour reminded her of just how little she was currently valued in the music world and it put her in a rare mood of self-doubt.

Her hearing was slowly going and although she never missed a note and never sang in the wrong key she sometimes missed her cue and came in too late. Bebe put the volume up higher and higher so she could hear every little detail, noting all mistakes or suggestions for her next session. She knew that the noise was likely to travel to the other houses but she didn't care. The world might as well know that Bebe Bollinger was ready to take centre stage again.

Chapter 5: The Blackout

Dora

Dora on the other hand did not want to hear what was being screamed across the hamlet. *Something Stupid, Je T'aime, Crazy in Love, The Time of My Life* . . . who did that deluded Bebe think she was? Beyonce? She turned up the volume on her own bossa nova CD to blank out her neighbour.

After a few hours, Bebe seemed to have hung up the mike and all that Dora could hear was a little piano music. That was the kind of thing Dora liked so she switched her CD player off. She could live with this sound.

If Llangurrey were full of people like those of her hometown in Portugal, the neighbours would go through this snow catastrophe together, supporting each other. Dora would cook, Bebe would entertain and Ian would do the manly things. They could have a great time. She knew large parts of Wales had similar close-knit communities, just not this hamlet.

Later that day Dora was watching a romantic comedy on TV while hoovering, when there was a power cut. Thank god it happened during the day when everyone could see. She chided herself for not being prepared for such an event and not having a torch or candles nearby wherever she went.

Llangurrey had been without electricity several times in the past couple of years. The power lines in the surrounding countryside were gradually being upgraded, which frequently led to blackouts, announced and unannounced. Every time, Dora swore she would keep torches in prominent places but would forget her pledge as soon as the power was back.

She had a lot of candles left over from Christmas and started to dot them around the house. It was already getting darker outside but she could see enough to cover all areas. Then she realised that her heating and everything else would now be switched off, too. She rang the number of the power company.

The lines were busy and after negotiating complex customer options and listening to recorded announcements about the affected areas, Dora finally spoke to a real person who took her complaint and promised to call her back as soon as the problem was investigated.

The darkness was closing in and the room was freezing cold. The power company had not known anything about a cut in Llangurrey and with so many affected areas mentioned in the pre-recorded message there was little hope for a quick solution.

The sound of a snow plough outside, clearing the lane lifted her bleak mood. Dora quickly grabbed her purse and the car keys, blew out the candles and ran outside. She knocked enthusiastically on both, Ian's and Bebe's doors to tell them the lane was clear, but nobody answered. She got in to her car and drove to the supermarket in Carmarthen. Her headlights cut through the falling darkness, highlighting the swirling dense snowflakes that danced in the air. It was pretty, but it was dangerous, too. Negotiating the roundabouts felt unsafe, even though everyone drove very carefully. She felt lucky, though, to have heard the snow plough in time to make full use of her freedom. Things always seemed to work themselves out. Her home may be cold but she was able to re-join civilisation. That was a good trade-off for now.

Carmarthen was close to the major road network, so Dora was surprised to find the supermarket shelves were almost empty. Milk and bread were all gone. She was after fruit and vegetables and of course batteries and candles now. She bought five electric torches and several bags of groceries, then she rushed back home so she would not get stuck in the next snowfall. Although the road had been cleared it looked as if the continuous snow might soon render the efforts pointless.

The hamlet was in complete darkness when she returned. Torchlight guided her to her front door. Inside, the temperature was very low.

It took her ten minutes to store her groceries, as her breath fogged on the air and she shivered in the damp chill of her kitchen. Sod those reserved British, she thought, packing the final item away and headed straight over to Ian's and knocked loudly on his door.

After a long time she could hear him slowly coming down the stairs.

"Oh, Dora," he said, surprised. He stood motionless in the door, dressed in cosy cotton pyjamas and a white bathrobe, like a schoolboy ready for bed. "Is everything OK?"

"I'm afraid not," she replied miserably. "I'm getting cold without heating. Do you have a wood-burner?"

"I do," he said. "But I don't think it's worth bothering with it. The power must come back on anytime soon. I was having a hot bath when it happened and I'm still warm."

"I rang the electricity company and they didn't even know about us. I think half of the country is affected."

"Oh dear," he said quietly. "I've got a little diesel generator. I can connect it to your heating pump and get your house warm that way. Don't you have a fireplace in your living room?"

"I took it out because of the draft it caused. I replaced it with an electric one. I've been so stupid!" she scolded herself.

"You could still get into town and buy a generator yourself, if you wanted," Ian offered. "I could come with you to pick one out."

"I don't trust the weather," Dora dismissed his idea. "Look at the snow. The road is going to be covered again in no time! They haven't put down salt or grit either, have you noticed?"

"Oh, you're right," he said. "Well, maybe you could go to Bebe?" he diverted the discussion. "She has this fantastic fireplace."

"OK, but you come with me," Dora insisted.

"Fine. Let me get changed," he said and invited her in, at last.

"I wonder what Bebe does without electricity," he said when he came back down the stairs.

"She's playing the piano with candlelight, wearing her fur coat," Dora told him. "I saw her through the window: Very *Dr Zhivago*."

"That's perfect," Ian said and his face lit up. "We need some entertainment. I hope she'll play for us."

Bebe

Bebe opened the door reluctantly. She, too, had heard the snow plough and feared the arrival of her tearful daughter in flight from her angry husband. Seeing Ian and Dora with their torches outside her front porch she was relieved. She had some heat from her Aga but could do with Ian getting the fire in the living room going like he had done for her in the past when she couldn't get it to work on her own.

"Maybe we could do a deal," Ian proposed. "We were just saying how wonderful it would be if you could play your music for

34

us. We need entertainment and we both heard you rehearsing on the piano this afternoon and thought it was lovely."

Dora quickly added: "I could cook for the three of us."

Bebe's face beamed. "You really liked my music?" she asked.

"We adored it!" Ian said. "I have several of your albums by the way."

"Come on in," Bebe said, "and let me take your coats." She ushered them through the dark hallway into her living room. A large concert piano was in the centre of the room. Pictures of Bebe with celebrities adorned the stone cottage walls, and comfortable sofas piled with cushions made up the rest of the room.

Bebe leaned in close. "It really is still a secret between me and my agent," she said. "You can't tell anyone about this, but I'm planning a new album. I mustn't jinx it by telling you any more!" She held her hand in front of her mouth like a shy Japanese schoolgirl, excitement oozing out of her every pore.

"Of course you mustn't jinx it, my darling," Dora said encouragingly. "I love the thing you do on the piano."

"I've been recording Jazz numbers all my life. There's talk about a very famous singer doing a duet with me," she said. "Did you hear the music I did without the piano today? Do you think I have the voice for them?" she asked, carried away by her flow of thoughts.

"Well darling, of course you have the voice for it," Dora said. "The songs are just not 'You', that's what I am thinking. But what do I know? Ian is the British person here; he can tell you more what the public in this country want. I shall go and fetch some food for us and cook it on your Aga."

With that she made a hasty retreat. Bebe beamed.

"Truth be told, you sound terrific," Ian said. "They should have brought you back a long time ago. Now, where's the wood?"

"Somewhere under the snow," Bebe said sheepishly. "I forgot to get it ready for the winter. I entertain so rarely that I rely entirely on the main heating."

"I'm going to get some from my garage," Ian said, heading back out.

Bebe was suddenly excited. An evening with a private audience! She had not done something like this for a very long time. Her daughter, the main visitor, was not in the least interested in her music. Unless Bebe would be singing a duet with Madonna, Lady

Gaga or Eminem, Helena wouldn't approve. As a matter of fact she remembered how much her daughter hated Will Young for winning X Factor and always slagged his music off. Bebe anxiously peered out the window.

"Please let us be snowed in before that devil girl messes up my comeback!" she prayed.

Ian got the fire going quickly. Dora brought lots of food with her and prepared a proper feast while Bebe took position at her piano.

"I'm so sorry I can't play half as good as I should," she said, fishing for compliments. "I normally never get to practise. My musical partner Maurice usually accompanies me."

"You are being too modest!" Dora called from the kitchen. "Just play, darling!"

And Bebe did. Shyly at first with such an unusual audience around her in her own living room, but then she lost herself in the music and forgot all about her nerves. Without her glasses, of course, she could see little. She had removed them before opening the door and had not wanted to put them back on now that she was in performance mode.

"Can you play *Cabaret*?" Dora asked her.

"Oh sweetheart, I hate show tunes," Bebe replied.

"You did them so well, you must have liked some," Ian insisted.

"Musicals were the reasons I got started out in my own little niche market," Bebe explained. "If I had liked that sort of thing I would have been stuck in the West End for the rest of my life, maybe even on Broadway, but it's not fulfilling for me as an artist. I know I owe Andrew Lloyd Webber a lot but ever since Alison Moyet appeared in *Chicago* I feel I'm done with that world for good. Even that beau from *EastEnders* played in it; that entire genre is becoming cheesy."

"Harsh words," Ian said, "and yet you do it so well. Do it for your fans!"

"I want my fans to follow me to different shores, Ian," Bebe said dreamily. "Everyone sings show tunes as album fillers. I'm after more substance, and I'm sure my fans can get used to that. They don't need me to sing *Cabaret*!"

36

"We would still like to listen to it," Dora called over, "but please play whatever you prefer."

Bebe sang a jazzed-up version of a George Michael song and then some Burt Bacharach. The cracking sounds of the fire and the low lights added to the cosy atmosphere. Her voice was full of emotion. It had never let her down. Bebe's chest swelled with pride as she mastered difficult nuances of mellowness and high notes easily.

Dora had prepared a lovely Portuguese stew and as her audience shared a bottle of wine with her they listened to the stories of her former glory and her hopes for a comeback.

"Your voice sounds a lot like Annie Lennox these days," Ian said beaming with admiration.

"Oh, that witch!" Bebe blurted. "She had a career in pop. Why couldn't she stay there and let me have my market niche to myself. I worked very hard to get to where I was before her and that Alison Moyet thought they had to become serious singers. Don't tell me that I sound like 'her'."

Bebe got up and had retired to a little pouffe next to the fire.

"I'm sorry, Bebe," he said. "I think Annie Lennox has a great voice; that doesn't mean you're imitating her. There are a lot of great voices out there that have a similar range and quality. Whitney Houston and Celine Dion had similar voices," he went on. "Not too alike, but their range and their strength were very alike."

Bebe ignored him completely, fuming at being compared to anyone. Admittedly, the reference to the superstardom of a Celine and a Whitney flattered her a little more than being mentioned in the same sentence as Annie and Alison. But there was only one Bebe Bollinger and she needed no peers in her category.

"Play us some more, Bebe, please!" Ian encouraged her. "Don't listen to an ignorant fool like me. Sing your original music."

Bebe launched in to a rendition of her big hit, *Losing My Mind*.

"Tidy!" Ian applauded her.

Bebe rolled her eyes at the patronising tone she thought she detected. She didn't need Ian to validate her talent.

"I'd better make a move," he said when the song had finished. "Christine will be wondering where I am. The poor thing will be worried sick. I forgot to bring my mobile. Good evening, and thank you so much for a lovely time dear ladies," he said, making for the door.

"You are very welcome!" Dora called after him.

"I shall be going too," she said. "Thanks for letting us stay, Bebe. I hope we will have our heat back tomorrow."

Bebe showed her to the door and then she put more logs on the fire. The evening with an audience, however small, had made her hungry for more.

Chapter 6: The Light at the End of the Tunnel?

Ian

The next morning the power was still off, but for now it seemed possible to reach civilisation. Despite the further snowfall overnight the roads were negotiable, at least for cars with four-wheel-drive. Without wasting any precious time, Ian drove to the supermarket in Carmarthen for provisions.

The shelves were being restocked. Christine, unfortunately, was still stuck up North. She had sent him a lengthy text with instructions on what to buy. Well, she could do that all she liked, he thought. There just wasn't the kind of broad choice available that she had had in mind. He got what he felt was reasonable. Secretly, he hoped that Dora would offer to cook again tonight. He had enjoyed last night.

On the way home he stopped at a hardware store and bought a snow shovel and a small diesel generator for Dora.

"Thank you, she said when she opened her door and saw what he brought. "I don't think I could have coped with the cold for much longer. "I was contemplating asking my ex if I could stay with him. And that's saying something."

"You could always go over to Bebe," Ian suggested with a grin.

"Did you not see that her car is gone?" Dora asked. "She rushed off first thing this morning. I woke up from the engine revving. It sounded so bad; I got up to see what was going on. Did you not hear that loud noise?"

"Oh me, you know, when I sleep, I sleep," Ian said. "What time was that anyway?"

"Seven. I went back to bed after. I doubt it would take her that long to shop. She must have gone away somewhere. Funny that she didn't mention anything about it yesterday. Do you think it has to do with her *comeback*?" Dora wondered.

"Well, she would have mentioned that to us in the mood that she was in," Ian observed. "Her career was all she could think and talk about."

"If you can connect the generator to the cooker then I can make us some breakfast," Dora offered.

"No," Ian said. "I think we better use the power for the heating pump!"

"You can't have eaten breakfast already?" Dora asked. "Connect my cooker first and when we've eaten, then we think about the heat."

Ian was quite hungry and so he let her fry him up a delicious breakfast before they got the heating going.

"How is Christine?" Dora asked politely, clasping a mug of hot chocolate in her hands, her elbows planted on the kitchen table. They both had stayed near the cooker to make the most of the heat it had generated but gradually the central heating system warmed up the room. Despite her Mediterranean background, Dora seemed to cope with the cold remarkably well, Ian noted. If only Christine could show such relaxed pragmatism, too.

"The way she always is," he replied. "Busy, nervous and anxious to come home. The motorway ahead of her is still shut. She's trying to find a route that is free but until she gets off that M74 there's nothing for her to do but wait. The snow is much worse up north; she is really unlucky. It is killing her, I can feel it."

"Has she got electricity and heating?" Dora asked.

"Luckily, yes. She's in a motel and well looked after — comfortable and lacking nothing but being in her own house."

"I'm glad she's fine as she can be," Dora said. "What are you doing with your time? You must be getting itchy feet. I always see you getting out and about. Now you're stuck indoors."

"It's not too bad. I have my home gym, shovelling snow keeps me busy and I even started watching a bit of TV."

"Darling, come round if you are bored. That was lovely yesterday at Bebe's. I don't mind my own company but when one is stuck in the snow it is good to know that one has neighbours and a community . . . even if we don't normally mingle with each other."

"Thank you for the offer," Ian said. "I'm better off at home. If power comes back I have some clients calling me on Skype and then I'll have a lot to do."

"I'll be eating dinner at seven, if that is not too late for you," she said at the door but got no response from him.

Dora

She was sure he had registered the time and would be round. Until then she would get busy with her painting.

As she was searching for a new motif amongst the snowed-in landscape outside she saw a little red Mini park at Bebe's house and a young woman step out of the car. She looked a little like Helena but Dora could not be entirely sure. The woman stormed to Bebe's front door and rang the bell, knocking loudly and repeatedly. When there was no answer she looked through the windows and made her way round the garden, knocking on windows and even trying to get in via the back door, but no to avail. Nobody answered.

The woman returned to her car and tooted the horn several times. When there was still no answer her head sank on the steering wheel and her shoulders shook as if she was sobbing.

Dora put her winter coat and boots on and walked over to the car.

"Darling, there is nobody home," she said. It was not Helena as she had expected but a redheaded woman in her mid-twenties, roughly the same age as Bebe's daughter. "Are you OK?"

"I'm looking for Dominic," the woman said. "I'm his wife, Ellie. I think he's hiding in there."

"Look for yourself," Dora said. "There are no cars here. No one is around. We're having a power cut and we've been snowed-in for several days. Whoever you are looking for isn't here. You better hurry and get home before more snow falls and you get stuck here."

Ellie took a while to take this in and then she nodded vacuously. "I see. Yes, you're right, I better get home. Dammit. Where is that bastard?"

"Not here," Dora said. "Good luck dear, and let me tell you one thing: A man who does not want to be found, leave him be. He's not worth it."

That set Ellie off and she cried out loudly with her head banging against the steering wheel. "But I love him!" she screamed.

"I would ask you in but we have hardly any electricity right now," she said apologetically. "You need to get going."

"I don't have anywhere to go," Ellie said, sniffling.

"You must have a home. If you have a husband you must have a place together. Go there and wait for him. He is bound to come back home some time."

"He's with that woman!" Ellie screamed and started sobbing again.

"But not at your place, I guess, if you are looking for him here. Go home," Dora said. "You must have some friends that can take you in, maybe your mother?"

"My mother said he'd be cheating on me. She never liked him. She's going to have a right laugh at me if I come to her. I could never do that!" Ellie replied.

"Then why not go home? There is nothing to do for you here. The woman who lives in that building left this morning and I can assure you that she is not sleeping with your husband. If he did, you'd be more amused than upset about it."

"It's her daughter he's sleeping with."

"How can you be sure of that?" Dora asked, guessing this was a case of mistaken identity. Helena was a wild girl but her mother valued her privacy and couldn't possibly be listed in any public register.

"I know from his credit card bills that he's been in this area several times in the past few weeks. According to the electoral role this is where his tart used to live with her mother. Dominic and that homewrecker must be coming here and I'm going to wait for them," she threatened.

"You'll probably die before that happens," Dora said coldly. "Woman, have some dignity. You don't need a cheater in your life. Why waste your energy on someone who's not worth it? Go and find someone else, have some fun of your own. There is nothing more boring than a cheated housewife."

"But he's my husband!" Ellie cried.

"If that didn't stop him from sleeping with some woman, why should that stop you from living your own life from now on? Come on, start the engine and get out of this miserable place before the snow buries you alive!"

"No, I'm going to stay here and wait. I can feel this is where they are going to be."

"Darling you seem a little unstable," Dora said, "So I'm going to love you and leave you. Good luck, and think about what I said. People die in this cold."

Ellie just let her head sink and rested it on the steering wheel, sobbing silently. The snow kept falling and the conditions on the road were becoming critical. It would be quite a spectacle later should Bebe come home and find Ellie still waiting. Dora worried for her and since she couldn't get the woman to leave the hamlet, she invited her in for a cup of tea.

"Just to warm you up while you're waiting for him," Dora said.

Ellie nodded and slowly got out of her car. Tears streamed from her face.

"You've got to let go of that man," Dora implored as they sat in her kitchen drinking tea. "You're better off alone," she added. "Trust me. There is no point in making big scenes. My ex-husband and I split amicably. It made things easier. And make sure he never sees your tears."

Ellie put her cup down and stared angrily at her hostess.

"I can see that you're happy on your own," Ellie said full of venom. "You're an old spinster, a cat lady who lives on alimony, isn't that right? Never had career ambitions or any bigger plans, I take it?"

Dora couldn't believe her ears.

"I'm only trying to help you, my dear," she said, telling herself to remain calm.

"Screw your help and your patronising attitude," Ellie shouted. "I know what's best for my marriage. If you knew anything you wouldn't be living by yourself. Something's obviously wrong with you."

"You can insult me all you like," Dora said and put her cup down. She went over to the sink to put her empty cup down and added: "It won't make him any more faithful to you, that's for sure."

Ellie shot across the room and slapped Dora hard in the face, one of her rings managing to scratch her cheek and lip, drawing blood.

"Get out," Dora hissed, while holding her face. Who on earth did this little tramp think she was? Dora had learned to control her fiery temper in the years she had lived with Dylan and his family. Inside she was fuming though and she had to get her ungrateful visitor out before her anger would get the better of her.

"Happy to," Ellie snapped and slammed the door as she left the cottage.

Dora locked the door for good measure and then saw to her wounds in the bathroom. It didn't hurt too badly but anyone would be able to see the remains of the slap on her face.

Around lunchtime, she went to feed the birds again. She had calmed down somewhat and hoped that by now the Mini would have left, but sadly Ellie was still parked there. Dora heard another car outside Bebe's cottage, car doors being opened and slammed shut, followed by shouting and screaming in high-pitched voices. That did not sound like the return of the Diva. All that Dora could make out from her side of the fence was that a car was started and left the hamlet in a hurry. She went to the front of her garden and saw Ellie jumping into her Mini and racing down the lane behind the other car. The pursued vehicle was not the colour or make of Bebe's – that much Dora could see. She suspected it was Helena or her lover, which would explain the screaming.

Dora watched as the Mini slid off the road and into a ditch. The other car hadn't bothered to stop. Dora ran towards the Mini, only to see Ellie climb out of it and run after the other car. The cheated wife had left the car door open but held on to a small satchel as she ran as fast as she could on the icy road.

"Don't be stupid, you'll catch a cold or break your legs!" Dora called after her, but to no avail. She had a good mind to leave the quarrelling woman to it, but she had to make sure that Ellie was alright, however much she detested her for the blow to the face.

Dora raced home, got into her car and followed the lane towards the main road. Ellie was still running, even though it was clear she would never catch up.

"Get in the car!" Dora ordered. "I will give you a lift into town."

Ellie got in without saying anything, just staring into empty space, tears pooling in her pain-filled eyes.

"Now you see what a coward he is," Dora said, trying to make the woman see the writing on the wall.

"Oh shut up," Ellie spat.

Dora got angry again but didn't say another word. She dropped her passenger in Carmarthen, where she hoped Ellie would be able to get a taxi, a cashpoint and a hotel room. When the emotions had run themselves tired Ellie surely would regain her grip on life. Dora was too concerned about the continued snowfall and its effect on the roads to help this ungrateful woman any further and wasted no time in driving back home.

She had only just returned when she saw the same car from earlier park up at Bebe's. It was Helena with a very tall and attractive young man. They tried to get into the big cottage but had the same result as Ellie.

They seemed to be looking in all the usual places for a spare set of keys; under the doormat, in the flower pots and around the dustbins. Compared to Ellie, however, the couple were relaxed. They giggled, touching each other and kissing like two people who were madly in love. Dora watched with pleasure. Bebe would hear about it when she next dared to shun Dora for her 'indecent behaviour' or dresses. She couldn't wait to remind the singer about her not-so-classy family connections should the subject come up.

Eventually, Helena and the man went to the back of the house, smashed in the back door window and let themselves in. Bebe would go mad when she found out.

Dora soon lost interest in the drama next door, though. She had been drawn into this mess more than she would have liked already. She went to the living room and started to prepare for a candlelit evening. She set up her old battery-run CD player, and listened to Enya and Deep Forrest, the kind of New Age music she loved on days like this. It felt like an extra-strong connection to nature. If only the generator was not so noisy and smelly. It was like having a car run in the back garden.

Fortunately, the power was restored just before dark. Ian immediately came round to help her to unhook the generator and sort out the heating. This time she made him promise to come for dinner as a thank you for all his help.

At Bebe's, the return of electricity was celebrated with noisy music and outrageously loud carnal noises. If Dora had not heard about Helena's loose reputation and had seen the two lovers outside the house she would have been inclined to go next door to make sure that no one was being murdered. Luckily, that could be ruled out and the exhibitionism reminded Dora to switch on her TV and catch up with a few episodes of the soaps she had missed.

Ian did come round at seven and they had dinner in her rustic kitchen. She preferred having dinner guests here, so she didn't have to leave them alone in the dining room while the food needed attention. It was much nicer to prepare the meal and be able to chat at the same time. Pans and cooking implements were hanging from hooks over the central kitchen unit, which doubled as table.

"Thank you for sorting out the heating, Ian," she said after they had finished eating. "I don't know what we would do without you in the hamlet."

"My pleasure," he said shyly. "It's a nice change from all the time I spend on the computer. I used to work as a printer and typesetter but that profession has died a long time ago. It was lucky I got the hang of the desktop publishing and graphic design when the technology advanced, but I miss more physical work. Did you ever have a profession?" he asked.

"I did go to art college in Lisbon," Dora said. "After that I took private lessons in the UK. I was living already with the Jenkins family, and Dylan wanted me to be near him. Instead of letting me study in London, he insisted to bring London to our home. I had a studio in a building on the grounds. I wish I had met more artists at a college or university, but I have had some fantastic teachers over the years. It is, of course, not the same kind of profession as yours. I'm not earning any money from it, but then, I don't have to. Do you think I should work?"

He smiled. "We have enough unemployed people in the country. Why should you work if you don't need to? Leave the jobs for someone else who needs them more."

"Helena once said that your wife is earning so much money that you could stop work, too," Dora said.

Ian laughed.

"I know, but if I did I'd be like throwing away a lot of money that I can use. I don't have too long until my retirement. If I stopped now my pension would be ridiculously low. No, I'm quite happy to have something to occupy my mind."

Dora made coffee and served it in the living room. Her cottage was similar to Bebe's but this room had been decorated in a more modern style. The stone walls had been plastered and the walls were full of Dora's paintings. Thick velvet curtains kept the warmth in and gave a more closed-off feeling.

"Could you not just work for Christine?" Dora picked up the previous conversation.

"A lot of what I do is for her firm, anyway," he answered evasively. "She would happily support me, but we've got a big mortgage to pay off. We never had children, so why not work? It keeps me out of trouble. You must miss your kids."

"To be honest I never saw much of them when we lived under the same roof," Dora admitted and lit a few scented candles. She enjoyed setting the scene for guests and making them feel relaxed in her home. "Between school, tutoring, tennis lessons and seeing their friends I got to spend hardly any time with them. Now they are at one of the country's most prestigious boarding schools. I remained a distant confidante. I think I have a better connection with them this way than I would have otherwise."

"I'm sure you are a better influence on them than Bebe ever was on Helena," Ian said with a broad grin.

"Yes, did you see the drama this morning?" Dora asked bemused by the reminder.

"No," he said, so Dora told him about the jealous wife in the mini, the slap, the arrival of the lovers and the chase down the lane.

"I can hear what's going on over there now," he said. "Bebe coming home right now would be a great spectacle." He grinned. "I wouldn't mind seeing that."

"Be glad that your wife isn't here to witness it all," Dora pointed out. "Helena has parked miles into the lane for a start..."

"Oh yes, Christine is spared some troubles here," he said. "That's true, but she's going mad in the hotel room as it is. I couldn't tell you what would be worse."

After Dora served dessert they watched an old Western classic on her large-screen TV, then Ian had to take his leave and return the many phone calls his wife had left on both of his lines in the interim period.

Dora was pleased. She had needed this to get over the unpleasant encounter this afternoon. The evening with Ian had gone very well, they'd enjoyed each other's company and it had been more fun than she would have thought. He could be very serious at times but the absence of his wife made him more fun.

Ian

When he left, Ian felt warm and touched. Dora was certainly mad and extravagant but she was neither as common as Christine and Bebe made her out to be, nor was she as forward and outrageously shocking. She might be a little lively and impulsive but not without restraint and boundaries. If anyone needed proof of this, they just had to see how calm Dora had reacted to the physical assault by

47

some common hussy inside her own home. Ian could tell from the way Dora related the story that she was furious but she had shown enough restraint to do the right thing and drive the strange woman to Carmarthen. He didn't think his Christine would have been so accommodating and helpful. No, that Dora was something else.

He dreaded going back to his place to be told off by Christine for socialising with the neighbours. He wished she wasn't so jealous. Yes, he was very attracted to Dora but his wife had nothing to fear. He wouldn't allow himself to jeopardise his status quo. He was too old for a mid-life crisis and all that came with it, he told himself. In his youth he had done some stupid things and jeopardised his position for a fling. He was above those temptations now. He was pleased to find that there were no messages when he got home. What a relief.

Not that he had a problem with his wife or had fallen out of love with her. She had put up with a lot for him, especially at the beginning of their relationship when he was not as committed as she was. Christine had given up her home in London and moved to the countryside with him. He had always adored her strength and determination, loved her cooking and he knew her reasons for acting strange well enough to cut her some slack for her obsessive streak. Life was simpler and easier when she was here with him; he could calm her down at home where she had her routines. All the travelling she had to do for work did her nerves no good. He wished she would be able to relax in that motel, read a novel and have a hot bath . . . do nothing and stop herself from calling him every ten minutes. That was the extent of Ian's grievances with her.

He heard loud music from Bebe's cottage. He had only enjoyed a few years of Helena living in the hamlet before she had moved away, but those had not been very easy ones. To have her back was very bad luck, as was the love triangle that she had apparently brought with her.

The woman with the red Mini made him laugh. Young and passionate love – it was something he could only vaguely remember. The follies of untamed hearts and hormones had caused Ian a few aches and pains in his days but now he had settled with Christine and their union was solid and he wouldn't change it, however difficult life with her sometimes became.

He wondered where Bebe was. Had she deserted the place ahead of Helena's feared arrival? She had mentioned something like it in passing the night before, but it surely was a joke, wasn't it? Or, had Bebe chosen to stay somewhere with guaranteed heating and electricity?

Chapter 7: Comic Relief

Bebe

The truth about Bebe was that she had received a call from her agent Bertie who had gotten her a gig with Jennifer Saunders and Joanna Lumley. They had written a piece for *Comic Relief*, the marathon charity TV show, which included a scene with an old crooner. Their first candidate to fill the slot was now apparently in secret negotiations for Eurovision and would no longer be available for the sketch. The scene had been rewritten to fit Bebe. Could she come and read for the part as soon as possible at the BBC headquarters in London?

Could she? Bebe was on the way to her car before Bertie had rung off. The timing had been impeccable: The road was clear and her home was cold. Talk about meant to be . . .

During the long drive to London, the Diva was thinking of the many stars that had become household names again after shows like *French & Saunders* or *Ab Fab* had brought them back on the TV: Lulu, Emma Bunton, even Joanna Lumley herself if you came to think of it, June Whitfield – the list was never ending. What a fantastic opportunity!

On further thoughts during the drive, however, Bebe came to the conclusion that she didn't want the part of a has-been who was handled by that PR character Edina in the show. She would prefer to portray a more grounded persona who humours the more trashy main characters; something more subtle that would allow her to show off her likeability? Get her away from being a Diva and help her become a woman liked for her character and great voice.

Then she almost veered off the motorway when she remembered how Bananarama and Jennifer had had a Number One for Comic Relief. Was that what it might be about? Had she been chosen for one of those benefit re-make songs that almost never failed to reach *Top of the Pops*? And she might produce a video? Oh, that Bertie had been so vague about the idea but the potential of the entire set-up made her dizzy.

Bertie met her at the producer's waiting room. He was constantly on the phone. Only 35, wearing those heavy black-rimmed glasses that Gok Wan had made so popular. Short, chunky and –

unlike Gok - always misguided in the designer labels he picked, Bertie was as lovely as he was flaky.

"Darling," he said when he had finished the call, "you look stunning."

"Thank you," Bebe said flattered. "I had hardly time to choose something special. I jumped straight into my car."

She told him about her ideas for jazzing her role up.

"Listen, darling," Bertie said uncomfortable. "The producer is a huge fan of yours and we are all relying on your good sense of humour here."

"I don't like the sound of that!" Bebe said, taken aback. "What have you gotten me into?"

"Honey, being a good sport is much better publicity than getting a little airplay for an old song," Bertie said. "The role is for a huge faded star, it's just a laugh for charity and that will earn you a lot of kudos and goodwill."

She couldn't believe her ears. Her worst nightmare had come true.

"I'm not going to let you parade me on TV like that, for Jennifer Saunders or anyone else for that matter!" she said stubbornly. "I'm hurt you would even consider such a low offer."

"It's far from being low," Bertie insisted. "It's an old trick: if you allow people to take the Mickey out of you, it takes the wind out of their sails. They will all say: 'Hey, that Bebe doesn't care what people say, she cares about charity. Good on her.' When you release your Best-of-Album a few months later they are more likely to buy it and remember you fondly. Everyone in the industry knows how this works. Darling, be a professional!"

"Who was that woman that I'm replacing?" Bebe asked.

"I can't tell you, darling. It's all top secret. There'll be an announcement next week about Eurovision. Then we will all know for sure. It might all fall through, as it so often does with that song contest."

"Have you read the script?" Bebe asked.

"I have. I spoke to Jennifer's assistant about it and we have a few ideas how to make it even funnier and better suited to you – but only if you're totally on board. I think it is hilarious. Jennifer has such a great sense of humour, but you mustn't get too high on your horse. You need to let her go all the way. I want you to think very

51

carefully about this. *Comic Relief* is huge and you could reach more people in one night than you did in years."

"Give me the script!" Bebe ordered. She knew she wouldn't like what was coming, but Bertie was right: this was a great opportunity, so if it was at all possible she should try and do it.

The scene was a small dream sequence in which Jennifer's character ran madly through a large corridor, like Mia Farrow in *Rosemary's Baby,* and entered several rooms full of haunting experiences. The soundtrack was Bebe's big hit *Losing My Mind,* but sung by a different singer and there'd be many Bebe look-a-likes in one room, all imitating her trademark stare until the right Bebe came out with a voodoo doll of Alison Moyet.

"I just don't see how that could be perceived as funny!" Bebe said soberly. "I don't mind doing it, but are you sure that this is really the best that they can come up with? I'm rather disappointed, I have to say!"

"Darling the humour often comes from the make-up artists and the ambience set-up. Jennifer has a top team working with her. They've won awards. Of course it'll only be funny if the characters and costumes are. They have fantastic ideas and you're the star that will make it a success."

"Who is doing the benefit song this year?" Bebe asked. "Couldn't I be working on that?"

"They won't use the song to bring someone back to the music scene. They need to raise cash, so it has to be someone who currently already sells songs by the bucket load."

"Who is it? Please say it's not Adele?"

"I don't think she is. But listen, after the show there'll be a few breakfast TV appearances and radio interviews," Bertie consoled her. "That will bring airplay. All of this is invaluable for you right now. All you need to do is to put on a brave face and laugh about yourself."

Bebe sighed and handed him back the script.

The meeting with the casting director, a bossy little Asian woman in her forties, went well. Bebe had hoped for a little more brown-nosing and star treatment but the team was rather business-like as they discussed the details. Bebe managed to maintain her fake smile when she heard that the other rooms of the dream sequence were currently under discussion but it had been considered to have Nana Mouskouri look-a-likes in one room and probably Lulu shouting in another. No one would dare offer such a role to Shirley Bassey or Bonnie Tyler, would they?

Bebe was reading the lines and showed her trademark look, then she did the scene a few times. She found it rather easy to do, although her heart wasn't quite in it. The casting director got on her nerves, especially whenever she made suggestions like:

"Darling, you have to go a little over the top in your acting to make it obvious that you *are* acting and not just being you!"

Bebe fumed hearing this but she obliged and the casting director eventually nodded.

"I love this!"

Of course it wasn't hard to do her trademark slow walk – after all, Bebe wasn't wearing her contacts or her glasses and so found it naturally hard to see anything. To say her lines she had brought along 'reading glasses' but she wouldn't wear them in the scene.

"That's a wrap," the casting director said and Jennifer and the rest of the team rushed out of the room. Bebe felt like crying.

Disillusioned but clinging to the potential silver lining of future radio airplay, she agreed to come back in two days' time and film the sequence. On the drive home she so wished she could speak to her pianist Maurice and ask him for advice. He was much more in touch with the current trends and able to judge what was funny or acceptable these days. Maybe she could reach the ship he was working on, but she'd have to find out first where he was and which ship. She suddenly wondered why he hadn't left the details with her for an emergency. Had he lied to her and was in fact not on a gay cruise but on a concert tour with that Jane MacDonald? The mere thought of it drove Bebe mad. She remembered the time when she had been offered to go on a cruise and become the entertainment there. She had naturally refused the offer and fired the agent, only to find a few years later that a singer from those ships had been chosen for a fly-on-the-wall documentary and consequently – the said Jane MacDonald – had sold albums and concert tickets by the truckload. That could have been Bebe. She made a note to herself to try and record that *Should Have Been Me* track, by Yvonne Fair. The way she was feeling, she certainly had the right frame of mind to sing it.

Coming back to her more recent past, Bebe reflected on the session with the casting director and Jennifer Saunders. That woman was a wit but who could say whether this dream sequence was really going to be a success for Bebe or a complete disaster at her own expense? There was always a risk that it would remind the audience only of the negative aspects of Bebe's broken career, like the rivalry with Alison Moyet and the so-frequently-joked-about stare. Was national television worth the risk?

"Who am I kidding?" she spoke to herself. "Of course it's worth the risk. I'd kill to get my career back."

That journey started out back in 1967, when the singular child Barbara Bolton was just thirteen years old. A friend of her father's was working for a record company and told her over Sunday dinner that Cliff Richard was looking for a quiet little girl to record a duet with, a pretend father-and-daughter song for Mothers' Day – just perfect for her.

She auditioned and made the shortlist. At the last minute, however, Cliff's management decided against the idea and chose a different direction for the star. Her parents were distraught and cheered when the very next year Cliff Richard missed out on victory in the Eurovision Song Contest. That would teach him for snubbing her, they all had thought.

The song she had auditioned for was given to a different singer and a different girl but the producers had noticed Barbara's memorable voice and took her under contract, not yet as a recording artist but as a performer at Sunday tea dance events. Her voice was very distinguishable and perfectly suited to convincingly cover the songs of Clodagh Rogers, Sandie Shaw or Lulu. Innocent looking as Barbara was, she presented no distraction to the regulars of those dances and blended perfectly into the low-key set-up which the conservative organisers of such events tried to achieve.

Her family invested in a vocal coach and soon she was contributing handsomely to the family's finances with regular engagements on weekends and on some weekday nights. Her father would accompany her to the events to make sure that, despite her young age, she was able to perform in clubs and bars.

She was gradually allowed make-up, new glasses, modern hairstyles and outfits that showed her as a grown-up instead of the choir girl image she so despised. Her mother made sure, though, that Barbara remained a sexless and conservative version of Lulu and Olivia Newton John.

In 1971, a talent scout for Andrew Lloyd Webber hired her to perform in West End shows but after a few years of this, by the mid-Seventies, Barbara was fed up with the repetitiveness of her singing life and with the boring roles she ended up with. She longed for something outrageous and lively and some original material to sing, preferably outside the world of stage.

She observed how back-stabbing and bitchiness had brought less talented women than her to the public eye. By keeping quiet and doing as she was told she was missing out on the opportunity to become a big star. The audience had failed to single her out. Barbara was in danger of becoming a regular side-kick.

"Daddy, I can't bear this boring music anymore," she complained at the kitchen table one evening. The family ate usually early so Barbara could go to work on time and that day was a special occasion because her agent had confirmed that the contract with the musical company was going to be renewed. Her mother had prepared a big roast as celebration and was expected to serve it any minute now.

"What are you talking about?" her father had asked, surprised. He put his newspaper and reading glasses aside and folded his hands over his swelling belly. "I've sacrificed so much time and money for your career. What on earth do you want to do instead?"

"I want to sing real music, Daddy," she said, passionately. "The show tunes are a dead end. The times are changing. Just listen to the Beatles, Abba, Donna Summer, pop music and disco. Don't you recognise the change?"

"That's all just a phase," her father had said, his eyebrows narrowing. "Show tunes are eternal."

"Look, Daddy," she had insisted. "Even at Eurovision miserable chansons lose out to upbeat pop numbers, these days. Abba, The Brotherhood of Man … they have real hits. There is a career to be made out of this trend."

"Everyone needs to know their place in life," her father said dismissive, giving her an affectionate pat on the arm. "Not everyone can be a Barbra Streisand or Dionne Warwick, you know. Be content with the career you have. Others would be happy with that. As a singer, a steady income is hard to achieve. You did very well for yourself," he smiled, picked up his reading glasses and his newspaper and waited for his wife to serve the food.

When her manager repeated the same sentiments, she took a gamble by not renewing her contract with Lloyd Webber and descended into London's nightclub scene, where she covered songs by Gladys Knight and Dionne Warwick. She became a moderate success there but was still stuck at the easy-listening end of the musical spectrum.

Barbara's thick glasses were a problem as they provoked too many comparisons with Nana Mouskouri. After a few months of singing in a popular jazz club, a handsome record producer took a liking to her and decided to make her a big star.

Richard Karajan had successfully produced some minor but well-respected artists and that was exactly the kind of niche market Bebe had been hoping to break into.

"The first thing we need to do is change your name – Barbara Bolton sounds so ordinary . . . too provincial . . . there's no theatricality, no sense of the exotic." He tugged at his lip and stared into the distance. "Barbara Bolton . . . Babs Bolton. No . . ."

He thought about it some more and then clicked his fingers.

"Yes! Of course! Barbara Bolton – BB, your initials. We'll call you Bebe." Then, his eyes fell on a bottle of champagne that nestled in an ice bucket on her dressing table. It was his present to her at the end of her gig. His eyes lit up when he read the label on the bottle, and so the name was born.

She liked it, and Bebe was eternally grateful ever since that the champagne in question had been Bollinger and not Piper-Heidsieck.

The other thing we need to do is to teach you how to walk on heels without your glasses on," Richard had said.

She looked at him with outrage, but his smile was warm and disarming.

"Darling you've got sex appeal. It's time you started showing off."

"My father always said I should know my place," she replied. "When it comes to my looks, I'm not going to be flattered."

"Nonsense," he replied and squeezed her buttocks. "I know better than your dad. And you know better than him, else you'd still be singing show tunes."

He didn't wait for her response and took her glasses off.

"Now walk. Take as long as you like. Walking slowly can add a lot of gravity to a singer's image," he said.

Under his adoring and encouraging comments she found confidence. The focused walk that resulted from Richard's training was a signature move of hers that made her instantly recognisable whenever she went on stage. It did give her an air of mystery and caught the audience's attention. Her unfocused stare added to that mystery and her young, curvy body appealed to the audience.

Bebe's first single entered the charts low but gradually moved up. Thanks to ever-increasing airplay, the song made it to the top twenty. Richard's drinking buddy was working for the BBC and he had successfully persuaded some of his friends to put Bebe's song on their playlist. It could pass for a jazz number if you were looking at it benevolently, and it was beautifully in sync with the moderate feminism that was emerging at the time.

Her follow-up hit *Losing My Mind* enjoyed a very positive reception. It was less catchy than its predecessor but the orchestration built up to a great big finale. BBC airplay ensured that she made it on to the *Top of the Pops* show. By then her husband, Richard decided it was time that Bebe record her first album. Her blend of soul and jazz was aimed at the more sophisticated niche of the music market and she preferred it that way. She rather fancied herself as a serious artist, and for such a precious image she happily would forfeit monetary gain. With Richard by her side it was easy to forget about money anyway.

The less appreciative members of the public, however, soon started to make fun of her signature stare. Stand-up comedians and TV comedy programmes were cruel and in that regard the title for her second single had been unfortunate. *Losing My Mind* gave the mocking audience a line to associate with her trademark facial expression, which became a stigma she carried around with her name for the rest of her career – and beyond, as was shown by the *Comic Relief* script.

Bebe's albums for the next several years, however, sold steadily. She did the odd musical – as 'a favour to Andrew and Tim' – and a few TV theme tunes to remind the broad public of her existence. She also went on tour every other year.

The surname Bollinger served her well until a certain Evelyn 'Champagne' King arrived on the music scene in 1977. Because of the correlation of their names the two singers were often mentioned in the same breath, a trend that Bebe found outrageous and insulting.

Bebe with the lesser success in the charts looked suddenly slightly ridiculous, despite all the hard work she had put into her career, and she resented the associations because of Evelyn's, in Bebe's eyes somewhat 'tacky' image.

In 1982 Bebe released another new album. Inspired by the success of Renee and Renato and a trend for pop-operatic style, it was cheesier than she would have liked it to be. Some of her core artistic audience finally turned their back on her and concert bookings were only sold out in gay or gay-friendly venues.

And then everything in her life fell apart. In 1983, Yazoo broke up and Alison Moyet went solo.

"She 'stole' my niche in the market," Bebe wailed to her manager at the time. "Releasing a jazz-inspired album is what I told you we should be doing."

"She took the entire industry by surprise," he admitted. "If she'd come to me with this pitch, I would have laughed at her. Turns out, the fame of Yazoo was enough for her to pull it off. We couldn't have done the same for you."

"It's not too late," Bebe said. "I'll give her a run for her money."

"Darling, don't be a copycat. There's hardly enough record buyers for one jazz artist in Britain, let alone for the two of you."

As Alison's solo career took off, Bebe's sales started to dwindle. Even 'her gays' started to shrink in number at her concerts: Alison easily took that market off Bebe's hands too.

When Bebe refused to comply with the studio's plans to tour the gay clubs with a Best-of-Album – the ultimate end of career gesture – her record label ditched her and shortly after that her husband Richard left her, too. "With your career gone, we have little in common anymore," he had said. "I need a working relationship, not some bourgeois living by numbers." Weeks later she found out that he was seeing a double-D model, who consequently did well in the Italo-Disco market and had a few big hits in Europe.

Just before the marriage was over, Bebe had fallen pregnant – after a rare and unexpected occurrence of make-up sex. But Richard decided to stay with the younger, aspiring and more energetic starlet and had no intention of reconciling or taking responsibility for the unwanted offspring, or Bebe for that matter.

The newspapers had a feast at Bebe's expense, or at least that was how she saw things. Humiliated, she divorced him and got herself a new life in the hamlet, away from the buzz of journalists and schadenfreude.

Her hopes, as well as her dignity, suffered a devastating blow in 1991 when Alison Moyet recorded two songs on her new jazzy album that Bebe once had covered, too. Bebe was furious but there was little she could do since unfortunately Richard had retained the rights to all of her songs. He had literally sold her out, probably to pay for another facelift on his little tartlet. Bebe knew that a major career revival on the basis of her old songs was now totally out of the question. In the mid-90s Annie Lennox recorded *Diva* and *Medusa*, two albums with the kind of music she would have had in mind for her own new direction, leaving Bebe with nothing but the memories of her fame and her own private music-making with Maurice.

She cursed those women who had stepped on her turf, but a small part of her believed that if the public was willing to buy Alison's and Annie's albums then there might be a chance for her to muscle her way back in to the market at some stage. Tina Turner had bounced back at a similar age; why shouldn't Bebe Bollinger do so, too? So she kept signing up with new agents and sent off demo tapes, year after year.

It still hurt her to think of those dreadful days. What wouldn't she do to pull off a comeback and show them all what she was made of?

The road conditions were far too demanding for her liking. Even on a good day, Bebe was not the best of drivers and she got distracted easily. She was lucky that the motorway into London had been cleared both ways and that she got back home safely – with all the things whirling round her head at the same time. As she turned off the main road in to the lane leading to Llangurrey she was relieved to see that driving conditions on this last stretch of her journey were still good enough for her to get home. Even better: all the lights in the hamlet were back on. The power cut must have come to an end. Thank god.

She would go straight down to the basement to work on her Donna Summer cover and try that Yvonne Fair song. Then she'd have a long session on the Wii Sport. After all, if she was going to be filmed this week she would have to look her best and do the little she could still do in the short time span. Bebe almost crashed into a Mini abandoned in a ditch by the side of the road. How bizarre, she thought, that someone would have left their car here in the snow. Whoever owned it would have to wait a long time before someone could tow them to a garage in this weather. She felt sorry for the poor devil, whoever it was.

Her charitable mood and musings came to an abrupt and immediate halt when she saw lights on in her cottage. She recognised her daughter's car on the lane and would have loved nothing more than to crash right into it. What cheek of Helena to show up like this. She didn't even have a key to the property anymore. Several years back she and her friends had raided Bebe's house for money and booze, an event that ended with the arrest of one of Helena's friends for drunk driving and with Bebe changing the locks to her cottage. How had that cheeky little minx got into the house this time, she wondered?

Helena had parked so awkwardly that Bebe had no option in this weather than to park her car across the yellow lines that Christine had painted on the tarmac. Bebe slammed the car door shut and stomped angrily towards her front door. She was still wearing her high heels – of course she would not have been found dead at the BBC headquarters in sensible winter clothes and be branded as the Babooshka from the country. She lost her balance and fell, fortunately without major hurt or broken limbs. Only her composure had suffered from the sudden trip and that didn't bode well when trying to exude authority and power over her rebellious and outrageous daughter.

The loud rap music that blasted from her living room was just as upsetting as the intrusion itself. Bebe hated rap. Before she would confront Helena that awful noise pollution had to be switched off. She silenced Dr Dre or whoever it was with such unseemly lyrics, but that very moment she wished she hadn't. Upstairs, Helena was screaming the house down in ecstasy and all Bebe could do was to let Dr Dre resume his shouting, that being the lesser of two evils.

Bebe checked the house for damage – as so often happened when her impulsive daughter came to stay. She was furious when she saw the broken glass by the back door. She picked up the slivers and then taped the gaping hole with cereal cardboard to stop at least the worst of the draft. Meanwhile, the show upstairs was still going on. Bebe toyed with the volume control to see if it was safe to switch the dreaded music off, but it wasn't. However, she found an old recording of herself on tape and played it instead. That should announce her arrival to the filthy beast that was her daughter.

Helena and her lover, however, did not respond and continued to rhythmically and vocally let the neighbourhood know about their pleasures. Then the doorbell rang and Bebe's face flushed with shame. How could she explain to the complaining neighbours that, when it came to her daughter the Diva had no control? The bell went again and again and then someone banged at the door.

Bebe took a deep breath before she opened it, braving herself for a lemon-faced speech from Christine about the parking in the lane. Instead, a red-haired woman simply pushed past her into the house and ran up the stairs in the direction of the offensive noises.

At first Bebe was upset about the intrusion but then she felt a little relieved. It looked as if this entire problem would take care of itself. Let those hot-blooded youngsters sort out their mess. Bebe would not have to say anything to her daughter – that red-haired hurricane of a cheated wife was probably going to do the job for her just nicely. Bebe went to the kitchen and made herself a cup of coffee. Upstairs, the sex noises had stopped and were being replaced by more banging on doors and shouting, threats and screams.

What Bebe could hear suggested that Helena and her lover had locked themselves in either the bedroom or bathroom. She couldn't hear what was being shouted, but emotions were clearly running high.

Bebe was starting to get worried. This was going on for too long. She feared the drama could not possibly be ignored by her neighbours. Someone might call the police, or – perish the thought – the press. This could turn into a major disaster, a scandal with potentially huge repercussions for her career before it had been revived from the dead. Thank God she lived in such a remote place. Somewhere else there would be reporters and paparazzi around already.

She frowned, listening as one woman, quite possibly her own daughter, was shouting loud obscenities. The man tried to calm everyone down, then one woman cried, then the other, more banging and throwing of things, screams, shouts and more crying.

"I love you."

"I'll kill you!"

"Bugger off!"

"Shut up!"

Then, to Bebe's big surprise, there was a moment of silence. When the voices resumed they were more subdued. At last the red-haired woman came running down the stairs, holding her face as if it just had been slapped, and stormed out of the door. A rather handsome young man rushed after her, putting on his clothes as he was doing so. Finally, Helena followed. While the first two had disappeared into the night on foot, she started the engine and went after them in her car.

Bebe shut the door and put on the safety chain. She went to the back door, locked it and removed the key. Then she went upstairs to the bedroom that her daughter had just so grossly defiled, took the sheets off and put them into the washing machine. Everything that did not belong to herself went into a black bin bag and that she left outside the front door. That was enough drama for one day, Bebe decided. If Helena came back she would see that she was not welcome.

Thank God the neighbours had turned a blind eye and a deaf ear to this episode. There were no lights on over at Ian and Christine's house and Dora seemed to be watching TV with the curtains drawn. That was lucky.

Bebe went down to the basement and started playing with her recording equipment again. She thought she could hear some banging at her front door but refused to get involved. If she kept quiet maybe it would all go away. No doubt it was her daughter back again with her lover. Helena would have to sort out her problems by herself for once.

When the banging stopped Bebe waited a little while, then she cautiously went upstairs and saw that there was no trace of Helena or her car. The black bags had also gone. Bebe closed the curtains and got on her Wii, feeling really motivated with the *Comic Relief* filming on the horizon.

Chapter 8: Trapped

Bebe

The next morning the snow had returned to its catastrophic levels. Bebe got on the phone to Bertie but his line was engaged. She left him a few messages for good measure and then waited for him to phone her back. She was in the bath when the call came.

"The casting director loved you!" he said before she could say anything more. "She thinks you could become a side character in Jennifer's next series, you know, like the way Lulu and Emma Bunton keep popping up."

"Really?" Bebe screamed, ecstatic. "That's how I'd hoped this would develop! I knew it. I felt it in my guts that there was something big in the offing."

"You're also going to be in a second sketch," he continued, by his mellow standards sounding very animated. "You'd be a bridge partner of June Whitfield and they'd make you look a little older. They think your famous stare would be a hilarious running gag. They have plenty of ideas, like that you cannot see the cards while playing etc, something along the lines, she hadn't finished the idea but something to go along with June's character's Alzheimers' Disease."

"Can't they think of something a little bit more sophisticated than just going on about my eyesight and my ageing?"

"Darling don't be so sensitive. Think of Joanna Lumley. She started out with Ruby Wax taking the Mickey and that was what got the ball rolling. Who cares now that she was ever in *The New Avengers* but we remember her for her Comedy Bafta Awards, all thanks to Jennifer. Joanna wasn't stuck-up about her image and just rolled with it. If Joanna had a back catalogue of music like yours, people would be buying it in bucket loads ever since the show took off. Trust me. I think it is fantastic that you can do that kind of comedy. You are a natural, the casting director said so herself!"

"Bertie, I'm calling because of the dates for the filming," Bebe started wobbly. "I'm snowed in again in that bloody hamlet of mine."

"Then get out of there now!" Bertie screamed. "Ski, snowboard or walk but get out of there. This is the best opportunity you've had in years. You have got to take it, come hell or high water.

I don't care how you do it but you have to be at the BBC tomorrow morning or they're going to rewrite the sketch again without you."

Bebe hung up and ran across the street to Ian – well swimming through the snow might have been a better description for it. Maybe he and his Rover could get her to the end of the lane or someplace where she could catch a train or a taxi.

Ian did better than that – he offered to drive her to London, but when they tried to get out of the lane they couldn't get through the mountains of snow. The road was completely blocked again.

"If you wanted we could try and walk down the lane to the main road," he suggested.

"It's worth a try," Bebe said bravely. Ian took her luggage and started walking ahead. Bebe's fragile sense of balance and the uncertainty where the road exactly was underneath the white malice made her slip several times. She suffered from progressive arthritis and her knees were killing her. The wind was howling and snow kept landing in her eyes. Her face was frozen and she was soaking wet in no time. This icy storm and the raising levels of snow on the road were too much. Freezing cold and already exhausted, she knew she couldn't do this for another few miles, even with Ian's support. She had visions of herself falling into a snowbank and never coming up again. With tears in her eyes she scanned the damned blanketed fields.

Before she could say: "I'm sorry Ian. I have to give up," Ian let out a big cry and fell on the floor.

"Ouch," he screamed and tried to get back up, but to no avail.

"What's the matter?" Bebe asked, wondering if this day could get any worse.

"I've sprained my ankle," he said, sitting in the snow and holding said body part.

Bebe fought her way through the snow over to him and offered him her hand.

"Try to get up," she encouraged him. He managed but he swore under his breath with every step he took forward.

"We'll have to abandon mission," he said. "I'm lucky if I make it back home.

Without waiting for a reply he turned and hopped awkwardly through the deep white menace, 'ouching' and 'hissing' all the way. Tears ran from Bebe's eyes as she grabbed the luggage he had so kindly carried up to this point and began her march back to her cottage. Ian apologised for letting her down and refused her offers to help him with his injury.

Back in her cottage Bebe spent the night hoping and praying that the snow ploughs would come again during the night so that she could drive to London, but she had no such luck. The next morning the snow had reached further heights. She was undoubtedly stuck and had missed her great chance with Comic Relief.

Determined to do something constructive for her career, she sat down on her sofa and wrote letters to Will Young and Michael Buble, explaining her proposed new musical style and her ideas for duets with them.

Road services didn't come to clear the road that day or the day after. Well, now that her career was back in the dumps it didn't matter. In fact, if Bebe couldn't get out, then at least nobody could come in, either and that meant she would not be drawn into her daughter's dramas any further. Helena had called a few times but Bebe had not answered the calls and just sent a quick text telling her daughter to sort out her life on her own. It was highly likely however that Helena would come the moment the snow had melted.

The entire nation was suffering from this latest heavy snowfall.

Dora had knocked on the door twice to invite her round for dinner.

"Thank you Dora," Bebe said. "I'm terribly busy. I'm sure Ian will be very happy to be mothered."

Dora shrugged and walked away.

The arctic weather had settled over Britain and would not move an inch to the left or to the right. An end to the current situation was not in sight. Bebe scolded herself for not having stayed in London.

Bertie had called to reassure her that all was not lost. Bebe had not been the only person in the industry stuck in the snow and he said it might still be possible to film some scenes for the show later. The producers were happy to keep the door for Bebe open. Bertie did have a habit of saying things just to keep her in a positive frame of mind, though, and she was trying not to cling to his words too much.

Two days after her attempt to walk through the snow with Ian, Bebe finally woke up to the sound of the snow plough. She was over the moon. She was free! She would not risk staying here until the road was snowed in again. She packed a bag with a few clothes and essentials, had a quick shower and breakfast and then ran to her car. She could not have been longer than an hour since winter services had freed her but to her astonishment there was a clamp on her front wheel.

How on earth had that happened? Was this a new council thing because of the snow plough? She searched for a notice on the clamp or the windscreen for a number to call to get her car released but there was nothing. She saw no light in Dora's cottage, so Bebe decided to speak to Ian to find out if he knew anything about it.

To her surprise, his wife Christine answered the door, with a face sporting small red patches and trembling cheeks.

"I've clamped your car, Bebe," her uptight neighbour said with a forced smile that barely concealed the raging emotions underneath.

"You did what?!" Bebe asked, her head spinning between rage and bewilderment.

"You know damn well that you are not supposed to park beyond the yellow dotted line," Christine said, her hands pushed fiercely into her hips. "I have mentioned that many times but you clearly think that the rules of polite conduct don't apply to you. Do you think that you're better than anyone else and don't have to consider others with your actions?"

Bebe was in no mood to argue, she didn't have the time for it.

"I'm sorry Christine," she apologised with the sweetest fake smile she could muster. "I didn't mean to park there but in the snow it wasn't even possible to see where the line was. You know that I always play by your rules. Can you please unlock the clamp, I'm in an awful hurry," Bebe said.

Christine still looked angry and took a long moment to reply.

"Well Bebe, you really should never make an exception. We don't have these rules for no reason. If you park where you did then it's impossible for a larger car to get past you, especially in this snow. You made it very awkward for me to turn into my own driveway."

Bebe was fuming but she needed the fastest solution to this problem, not the best. She would get back at Christine for this some other time. For now, she calculated that involving the police over this would take longer than sucking up to Christine and getting the clamp removed immediately.

"There was enough room on the road for the snow plough, Christine. Can we please discuss this some other time, I'm in a terrible rush." Bebe was amazed at her sudden acting talent. What she really wanted to do was grab the snow shovel by the door and lump this woman one.

"When we had the scaffolding, your car was in the same spot and you weren't answering your door. The poor guys had to carry every piece of metal and wood for an extra two yards because of your inconsiderate ways. It's time you learned about inconvenience yourself," Christine snapped and closed the door on her.

"You'll regret this!" Bebe shouted and banged on the door. When this didn't yield any results she ran to Dora for help.

Her neighbour had been fast asleep and was rather confused to find Bebe outside her front door. Once she had heard about Christine and the clamping she immediately got into her boots and winter coat and gave Bebe a lift to the train station in Carmarthen. For once Bebe was pleased with her neighbours' willingness to face the outside world in minimal attire. The trains were running on a limited schedule because of the weather and the platform was crammed with people. Bebe was lucky to get on the first train and even managed to find a seat. In moments like these politeness went out the window and elbows came into good use. She tried to call Bertie but, as always, he was on the other line and ignored her. Shortly after she had reached London, several hours later, he called her back.

"I'm in Paddington," Bebe informed him triumphantly. "Tell Jennifer that I'm available."

"Darling it's a bit late for that," Bertie replied abruptly.

"I know, but this was the first opportunity I got. We had metres of snow. Get on that phone to Jennifer and arrange for another meeting," she ordered him. "I'll find myself a nice hotel room and wait for your call."

"I can try but I doubt it will make a difference," Bertie said. "The last time I spoke to her assistant it sounded as if the entire scene had gone to editing."

"Then let's hope that some of it is sub-standard and that Jennifer needs a little re-shooting," Bebe said and hung up.

None of the great hotels had affordable rooms and so she ended up in one of the cheap no-frills chains, but at least she wasn't far from the BBC headquarters. She was ready.

To her surprise Bertie did get back to her with good news: Jennifer had some use for her on the show and would even be prepared to meet her that very evening.

Full of excitement, Bebe squeezed into the tiny bath tub and began an afternoon of pampering and preparation for the big show.

There were plenty of more calls from Helena, but they remained unanswered.

A little too early, Bebe arrived at Jennifer's office. Bertie was already waiting.

"Fantastic you are here," he sang. "Jennifer can't join us after all, but we have the assistant producer here with us and the script."

"What does she want me to do? Sing or act?" Bebe asked him impatiently. Was this going to turn into a better opportunity for her, or worse?

"Both, actually, but we need to get you to make-up first," Bertie said shyly. "Now don't get mad. They got Kathy Burke to play you in the sketch instead. They just want you to do a little voiceover for that part. Later in the sketch they are going to show a picture of you being overweight and blind in a wheel chair. The make-up girls are going to make you old and obese."

"You've got to be joking," Bebe said sounding indignant. "No wonder Jennifer didn't show her face tonight . . . That's an outrage!"

"The make-up will be way over the top," Bertie tried to calm her. "People will know that you're not that old or chunky. Have a sense of humour, Bebe. It will open a lot of publicity opportunities for us if we go along with it. Imagine, going on Richard and Judy or Lorraine Kelly, the One Show and showing off your real face and figure. It might ignite a lot of interest in you. You never know."

"I can't imagine Kathy Burke being particularly kind when playing me. She is too good a comedienne, no, Bertie, this isn't right."

"Bebe, the public love a makeover. Vanessa Feltz, Alison Moyet, Bonnie Tyler, they all got fat and then lost the weight again. The magazines went raving mad about it. That could be you!"

Bebe didn't know what to say to that. How could he have mentioned the "A- word": Alison Moyet? Did he know nothing about Bebe?

"Be grateful they want you for the voiceover," he added. "Your voice is your best tool. People will recognise it."

Bebe hesitated for a moment. This was not what she had hoped for and not what an agent should have negotiated for her. But it seemed for now it was that or nothing at all.

"Fine, I'll do it," Bebe gave in. "I'll do it."

She sat patiently for a few hours as a team of young professionals padded her out and prepared her for the shoot.

The singing was done in no time at all and by midnight Bebe fell in to her bed at the hotel.

Chapter 9: In The Meantime...

Dora

Dora in the meantime had made it back home. The snow already started to pile up again on the roads and made it difficult to navigate. Thank God the Mini had disappeared from the road.

Bebe's car was still clamped. It was inconceivable to think that Christine had the audacity to do such a thing. It had to be illegal, Dora was sure of it. Had this been happening to her, she would have called the police in no time. If it weren't for poor Ian and the repercussions for him, she would report this anyway, but Bebe, worried about any scandal, had implored Dora not to do anything. Neighbourly disputes could harm the reputation of celebrities, and Dora agreed.

It was odd, though, that Christine kept the clamp on. Now the car would be stuck in the wrong space even longer. That couldn't be in Christine's interest, either, could it? As Dora got out of her car, still wearing only a winter coat over her dressing gown and her boots, she could hear Christine arguing with Ian. That poor man . . .

Over breakfast Dora had an idea and started to get creative. She manufactured a large cardboard cut-out the size of Christine and painted a lollipop lady outfit on it. She managed to make the face look almost exactly like an irate Christine, particularly with those famous red fluster patches and hollow cheeks. Then she put the cardboard figure in her front garden. If someone should ask her she would simply say it was a scarecrow.

Sure enough, within twenty minutes of her erecting the figure, the doorbell rang and Christine stood outside, her face flustered and her cheeks trembling.

"Good morning," Dora said provocatively. She was still in her dressing gown and she could see her visitor's eyes running up and down her body with disapproving looks. "What can I do for you?"

"I have come to return the food you so kindly lent to my husband," Christine said, business-like. "I would hate for you to be out of pocket, given that you rely on your ex-husband's money to make ends meet."

"Don't you worry about me and money," Dora said. "I have all that I need and then some. There are better ways to repay a favour than to reimburse money."

"I did wonder," Christine said slyly. "I see you put up a scarecrow, that must mean you ran out of bird feed."

"Oh yes. That scarecrow looks terrifying, doesn't it?" Dora said with a broad grin directly into her visitor's face.

"I want to give you the money," Christine insisted, ignoring the insult. "I don't like owing anything to anyone."

"Money is no substitute for kindness, darling. Don't spend your savings paying me back. If you want to be in credit with your neighbours stop buying clamping devices and invest in a psychologist, or buy yourself some sedatives." With that Dora slammed the door.

Christine stood speechless for a few seconds, then began ringing the doorbell repeatedly and banging on the door. Dora went to the living room and put on one of Bebe's CD's and let *Losing My Mind* blast back at Christine in response.

Christine eventually gave up and returned back to her house. However, the peace did not last long. Dora had just started making herself some soup when the doorbell rang again. She went to answer it so she could have another shot at slamming the door in the nuisance neighbour's door but it was Helena standing outside, with tears streaming down her face.

"Do you know where my mother is?" she asked while she tried to dry her eyes.

"She went to London. I had to give her a lift because that trollop over there clamped her car," Dora told her.

"She's locked me out!" Helena said like a little naughty schoolgirl.

"Darling, that cute number is not going to wash with me," Dora said coldly. "I saw you breaking into the cottage by smashing the back door and I heard your loud music and your ecstatic screaming. If you came here to lull me into helping you, then let me stop you right here and now. It is not going to happen. You are a grown woman; sort out your problems alone."

"I have nowhere else to stay," Helena whimpered. "This is the only place I have left to go."

"You can come in here for a warm cup of soup to warm yourself up but then you'll have to leave and sort out the mess you've made," Dora offered.

Helena walked right in.

"Would you mind taking your shoes off?" Dora said abruptly. The girl had not even wiped the snow off her boots.

"Sorry," Helena said quietly but sounding impatient and annoyed. She got out of her boots and walked to the living room.

"Tell me about your troubles, then," Dora said once she joined her visitor, serving the promised bowl of soup on a tray.

"I only married Aidan for the security," Helena began, holding the cup with both hands instead of making attempts to eat it. She stared into the soup as if it were a crystal ball. "Before him were a string of bad guys who did me no good and got me into trouble time and time again. He was like my saviour, but there was never the kind of heat that consumes you. Do you know what I mean?"

She looked at her hostess. Dora nodded warmly. She knew all too well. She'd probably loved and desired her husband more than Helena had with her Aiden, but she remembered the electricity and sexual tension with her first boyfriend, something that no other relationship had ever quite matched, especially not her husband. At the age of fifty Dora still felt desires like everyone else, even though she didn't act on them.

"I guess so," she replied.

"Dominic and I have this amazing connection, I can't describe it but it is beyond my control," Helena explained.

"Darling, I was in a loveless marriage for almost a decade for the sake of my children. We all have our burdens to carry and our decisions to make. If you want to throw away your relationship for some fun that is your business. But why are you involving us in all of this?" Dora asked. "It is making me quite angry, you know. Go to a hotel and, most importantly, sort it out with the people you are hurting, like his wife and your husband."

"I can't go back to Aidan and this lifeless existence. He's such a boring man," Helena almost screamed like a toddler.

"Well, you can't stay here and I doubt your mother wants to have you either. Why don't you shack up with that Dominic if he is such a great man?" Dora asked.

"He'd be penniless if he left Ellie. All of their money comes from her parents," Helena explained.

"Money should not matter if he loves you."

"I wish it were that simple."

"It *is* that simple," Dora exclaimed. "Does he love you?"

"I think so. It's a bit early for saying it," Helena said, sounding evasive. "We've only just met."

"If I was you I would pay attention to the writing on the wall," Dora said. "Dominic looks like he is going to stay with his wife, if she will forgive him."

"Do you think?" Helena seemed surprised.

"Well, tell me — where is he now?" Dora asked.

"With her," Helena said abashed. "He can't support himself. I know that."

"If you ask me, she is very forgiving to have him back," Dora said, using all her willpower not to start swearing.

"*I* need him back!" Helena said sobbing.

"There are plenty of others where you found him," Dora interjected.

"Not like him. No one has ever done the things he did to me," Helena blurted out.

"Too much information, young lady!" Dora said with alarm. "I don't need to hear any more."

"I need him," Helena cried.

"You have a few options," Dora said, looking at the young woman purposefully. "Learn to stand on your own two feet and leave your husband, or go back to your husband and hope he will have you. That Dominic seems to have no backbone. Regardless of the things *he does to you!*"

"Didn't you stay with your rich husband for the money?" Helena tried to turn this round.

"I stayed with him for the children," Dora explained, taken aback by the implication. It was the same rude assumption that Ellie had made. These two young women were as bad as each other and, in Dora's view, they both deserved what they had coming. She touched her cheek to feel how the wound was doing. It was still swollen.

"You certainly didn't say no to the golden handshake and this cottage," Helena added, as if it were an agreed fact. "Don't get on that high horse with me!"

"Darling, the little I took is nothing compared to what I could have taken him for. When you are older you'll learn about real pride, not the ego games you are playing at the moment," Dora defended herself. She was getting angrier by the minute and began to entertain the idea of kicking Helena out. Who were these young women to speak so out of turn? "Think as you please about me but consider what you are doing to your own marriage," she said coldly. "Don't be a coward and just run away. Sort it out, one way or the other."

"It is easy for you to say that," Helena said. "You have money. My alimony won't support me and Dominic."

"Shocking!" Dora said drily. "You are already planning ahead and you don't even know if Dominic will have you? Look who's counting their chickens!"

"I have no choice, that's the problem."

"First of all, it is not fair that you should cheat on your husband, and taking his money to support his successor is just outrageous," Dora said dismissively. "And besides, how do you think you could prevent a loose man like Dominic from leaving you?"

"We have that connection, it's quite amazing," Helena repeated.

"So far that has not stopped him going back to his wife!" Dora pointed out.

"Only until we sort something out," Helena replied.

"Something involving your mother?" Dora asked.

"I don't know. Maybe. She has some cash stashed away . . . shares and stuff."

"I am sure she can't wait to bail you out," Dora said.

"She must," Helena said convinced.

"Good luck to you!" Dora said and turned away to the window. "I think it is time for you to go before it's too late and you get snowed in here."

Dora noticed with delight that Helena's car was also parked in a way that broke Christine's rules. She only hoped that it hadn't been clamped as well.

Unfortunately, Helena couldn't get through the heavy snow in her car either and came back minutes later.

Dora agreed to let her in for a coffee and while she called a taxi to get Helena to the train station. Dora left Helena in the living room to her own devices and busied herself in the kitchen. She had no inclination to talk to that cow any more. The slapping from Ellie had made her worried that Helena might behave in a similar way. An hour later the taxi company rang back and advised them that due to the conditions on the road to Llangurrey even the four-wheel drive that they had sent to get Helena could not make it through.

"Oh dear Lord," Dora sighed and put the receiver down. She joined Helena in the living room and switched on the television. Helena didn't seem to mind that she was stuck here. Dora observed the parallels in Ellie's and Helena's behaviour. Dominic seemed to have a certain type. They hadn't been watching for long when the doorbell rang again and again, followed by a violent banging at the door.

"Here we go," Dora said with a grin. "The lollipop lady Christine and her parking rules booklet, I expect."

"I'll tell her to go to hell if you let me," Helena offered. "I'm in the mood for a fight."

"Knock yourself out!" Dora said.

Helena ran to the door with a look of childish anticipation. Dora heard the door opening and she braced herself for a big drama. She was in for a big surprise.

"Dominic!" Dora heard Helena calling out. "Dominic, oh my God, you came for me."

"Yes, I did, Helena. Of course I did."

Dora couldn't believe her bad luck to be stuck with the two of them now.

"How did you get here?" Helena asked at last.

"The taxi couldn't get through, so I walked here from the main road," the young man replied. "I'm freezing. I couldn't get changed into something dry and warm, could I?"

"Of course," Helena said, "I'm sure Dora will find you something. Dora, guess who's here?"

"Hello," Dora said, making her way to the door. "I've heard so much about you."

She shook his hand.

"Nice to meet you, too," Dominic replied, seemingly unaware of the sarcasm in Dora's voice.

She had to admit that there was something devilishly attractive to this man. He was not only one of those muscle men that probably had the perfect abs and the perfect biceps underneath their shirt. He

75

had a raw sexual magnetism that ran deeper, coming from his eyes and his cocky demeanour.

"Just so that we are clear," Dora said. "If Dominic could walk here, then you both can walk back the same way he came. You can warm up but then you'll go. Both of you."

"Of course," Dominic said with a gentle wink. Dora doubted that he meant it.

"You can save your Casanova eyes for young and impressionable girls like Helena here," Dora said harshly. "I'm old enough to be your mother and I'm not falling for that."

"How did you know where to find me?" Helena asked, staring at him with adoring eyes.

"I saw your car and then the bloke in the other house said that you were here. I couldn't believe my luck," Dominic said, smiling broadly at Helena.

Dora rolled her eyes.

"You probably will have to start thinking of walking back soon before it gets too dark, don't you think? Bebe's hotel is closed for business and you two cannot stay here," Dora said abruptly.

"Can't we get in through the back door?" Dominic asked Helena with a little grin.

"Mother has locked the door and taken the key away."

"I wonder what she meant to tell you with that," Dora said. "Now get yourself warm before your journey."

Dora served the couple hot drinks and lent Dominic a sweater and a pair of old sweat pants that just about fitted him. However, another heavy snowstorm blew over Llangurrey, which made an exit for the love birds impossible. By the time it had calmed down it was too dark outside to make the long trip. One could hardly see where the road was supposed to be even in daylight. Dora had to accept that she was stuck with two uninvited guests.

"Whatever you guys are doing, keep the noise down tonight," Dora ordered them, "or you'll find yourselves outside."

Helena giggled whereas Dominic nodded obediently. "I promise."

They both went upstairs to 'freshen up' while Dora turned up the volume on the radio and made dinner. At least the lovers made true their promise and kept the noise down, even though the swaying chandelier in the living room told a tale on its own.

After dinner the three of them settled on the sofa in front of the TV. Helena wanted to watch a programme on haunted houses but when it came on she talked all the way through it about a ghost exorcism that she had participated in.

Dora buried her head in a crossword magazine. She could not bear to listen and judging from his expression, Dominic seemed not that keen on her talking either.

"I could totally feel the cold energy," Helena said, like an expert on the supernatural, "totally freaky, you know, I knew there was a ghost there. We didn't have those fancy instruments as they have in this show here but we didn't need them. My friend told the spirit to go into the light and it did, all of a sudden the room was so much warmer. Really spooky."

Fortunately for Dora, when the programme was finished, her visitors made their excuses and went to bed.

Chapter 10: Dream Big

Bebe

The next morning Bebe woke up in her hotel room, full of self-doubt. When she switched on the TV there was a news item about Engelbert Humperdinck singing at Eurovision. She couldn't believe it. Her close friend Engelbert was going on that show? The huge star? If she had known that he was considering the show as a platform then she would have given the offer more consideration when it had come her way. She had told Bertie to get lost when he had mentioned this to her. What did Engelbert know that Bebe didn't? If he was interested there had to be something to it. She had to call him and ask for specifics. If he did well, maybe next year it could be her turn?

Then she realised that this meant that it was his role she had taken at the *Comic Relief* sketch and that made her already a lot better. So she was replacing someone of quite a substantial reputation. She could only dream of selling as many records as Engelbert had. His performances still filled concert halls worldwide. That thought cheered her up a little. She was ranked amongst his league! Bebe had left the set yesterday feeling utterly humiliated, ugly and exactly what she had tried to portray as a joke: her being a has-been. Now it seemed not such a bad idea after all.

She learned that the song for Engelbert had been written by reputable people, the names associated with Adele and James Blunt. The BBC sounded rather optimistic that Engelbert would do very well. The song would be announced soon.

She took out her mobile and left a message for Engelbert, who of course was busy answering questions and promoting Eurovision.

His publicity woman from his team called Bebe while she had her shower but she jumped out and caught it in time to have a little chat.

"You must have read my mind," a smooth voice purred into the phone. "We were about to call you."

Bebe was confused what the woman was trying to say.

"How come?" Bebe asked bewildered.

"We're trying to get a few big names as backing vocals," the woman replied. "You know, not some young girl who gets nerves and fucks it all up for us by singing out of tune, we want class and experience. This has to be foolproof for once. Britain has done so badly at the contest, with some vocal performances dreadfully off key, we need to gather our best resources and come back with a bang!"

"That's a very nice way of calling me an old battle-axe," Bebe replied, joking.

"That's not how we see it," the woman assured her, as her kind always did to the artists, as if they were stupid. "He still sells millions of records, yet he is prepared to help to get the national pride back and win the show for the UK. He'd be pleased to work with a professional like you."

"I'll think about it," Bebe promised, swayed in a little by the flattery. "I'll have to run it past my agent anyway."

"Oh it was Bertie who suggested you in the first place," the woman informed her. "We know he's on board."

Bebe was flabbergasted. Bertie had pretended not even to know who was doing Eurovision, neither had he mentioned talking to the team behind Engelbert. Then another thought occurred to her.

"Are there any more 'professional and experienced' backing singers apart from myself?" she asked, suddenly many more questions flooding her mind. Why hadn't Bertie told her about this?

"Yes, there are a few," the assistant said nonchalantly, "but it's too soon to tell. You were the first we had contact with."

"I'll sleep on it," Bebe said and hung up. Backing vocals in Eurovision? Laughing stock in *Comic Relief*? Her comeback was not quite how she had envisaged it.

First she had a bone or two to pick with that agent of hers. Bertie was very defensive when she got hold of him.

"I knew you wouldn't like being a background singer. I told them they had to call you if they were interested and hope that you were open to the idea."

"They said it was *your idea*," she cut him short. "It is humiliating Bertie, that's what it is. Open to the idea? And it sounds as if they aren't even sure they wanted me. I'm the first they got hold of, yet it was me who called them. It doesn't sound promising. After the career I've had, I can't do that!" she said indignantly. "I can't audition for a gig this low?"

"European superstars do not share your attitude, Bebe," Bertie replied. "Al Bano, one of Italy's superstars lent his support to a young aspiring Swiss girl. His sportsmanship was well perceived. Gary Lux from Austria did the same for some talented newcomers. We will market the entire affair as a 'Best of British' campaign. The audience is an estimated billion. If only a fragment of them buys your albums you can get a new sports car from it!"

"Come on, Bertie. The press is going to ridicule us as a bunch of geriatrics! They'll have a right laugh."

"Let them, but we can create some other publicity around this. It will be great!" Bertie assured her. "Sixty is the new forty!" he added.

She gasped for air. It was a bit soon for the 's' word. She had two more years before turning sixty.

"Are you still there?" he asked.

"Yes," she said, fuming, but swallowing her pride once more. "When would we be recording the song?"

"Next week, darling. They are still making the final changes to the arrangements. From what I hear it's a great song."

"You would say that. You try to sell me anything as the best thing since sliced bread. Bertie, I want my old career back and not half-hearted, second-rate stuff. Can't you get me something more sophisticated . . . some new material? A TV show? Cilla Black had her own show for crying out loud."

"Yes, but Cilla didn't sing on the show. She pursued an entirely new career as presenter. If you are chasing after ghosts past and a life that has gone, then we have very few prospects, darling. Things might develop but not necessarily as you would like them to. Times have moved on. We need to find a new niche where we can try and squeeze you in and then see whether it works."

"I'm not doing a gardening programme like Kim Wilde or anything like that. I'm a musician!" Bebe insisted.

"Of course you are," Bertie said comforting.

"I want to sing with the likes of Will Young or Olly Murs," Bebe said defiantly.

"Just make sure you are in London on Monday for the recording," he said and rang off.

Bebe contemplated to stay in the hotel longer to be available at short notice, but she had not brought enough clothes, make-up or entertainment, and she was desperate to practise her singing.

She dolled herself up in her Russian winter outfit and hit the shops. Once again, she was astonished how easy it was for her to remain anonymous. Tourism had taken a hit in the cold and there weren't many shoppers around in this weather. Bebe was almost alone in Bulgari. She didn't really mean to spend that kind of money just to impress Engelbert and his crew but then the woman in the store recognised her and all of a sudden Bebe found it impossible to walk out without at least buying something.

"I remember that song of yours, '*I surround myself with sorrow*'," the shop assistant said as she wrapped the handbag for Bebe and hummed the tune.

"Darling that was Cilla. I didn't record music until at least seven years after that," Bebe said, indignant. Could she storm out now and leave or would the assistant tip off the press about it? Well, better not risk anything, she decided, and so she bought the handbag and left in a huff.

When she returned to the hotel to extend her stay she was told that it was already booked out over the weekend.

"Of course with the snow disruption it would be possible for you to stand by and wait if a room becomes available again sometime later this afternoon, Mrs Bollinger. We could keep your luggage if you so wished," the receptionist told her.

"How come the hotel can be booked up when the normal transport has only just resumed?" Bebe said suspiciously. "There are bound to be cancellations left right and centre."

The receptionist, a woman in her twenties, was polite but unmoving. "We have a bar mitzvah party and a national conference block-booking, and neither of them has released any of the rooms. We have had a lot of stays extended because of the transport situation and now there is going to be a backlog with the flights getting people out of the country. I do apologise but there is a lot of uncertainty in our hotel overall. As of now, though, I cannot offer you a room."

At least the girl had the decency to look forlorn about the news she was imparting.

Bebe went to her room and called a few other hotels but when that didn't result in a red carpet treatment she checked out and took the train back home. The weather was still poor everywhere in the country. The snow kept coming down and there was little chance of her getting a taxi back home. So she bit the bullet and took a bus and then walked what seemed a hideously long way in the deep snow to her house. She was soaking wet and absolutely exhausted when she got to her home. The exercise on the Wii had paid off, but her arthritic joints were killing her. Thank God things weren't as bad as it had been a few days previous when she tried the same adventure with Ian. At least there was no snowstorm, and in the daylight it was easier to spot icy patches. How she wished she hadn't bought all those clothes and accessories.

Bebe froze in shock when she saw Helena's car outside her cottage. Her own car had been un-clamped. Christine was lucky that Bebe was so tired, or else she would have been right over there and giving her a piece of her mind. She sighed with relief when she got into her house and noticed that Helena hadn't broken in. A message on the answer phone revealed that her daughter was next door with Dora. Bebe decided to lay low. Once she had locked the front door she ran a hot bath to warm herself up. After that she went to the basement and did some voice exercises.

Dora

Next door, on the morning of the same day, Helena and Dominic had slept late and seemed in no hurry to get out of Dora's house but they had not reckoned with the forcefulness that was their host.

"Enough," Dora shouted as she walked up the stairs at noon and knocked at their door. There was no lock to the guest room and she had to announce herself briefly before she entered.

"Up you get and out of the house," Dora said with a broad grin. "Weather conditions are perfect right now; we are not going to waste that window of opportunity. Get your stuff and get going. Pronto!"

She was met with the sound of moans of complaint from the snuggled-up lovebirds.

Dora raced to the windows and opened them wide.

"Time for you to get used to the fresh air," she said and with that she left them alone, only to come back with two mugs of coffee.

"Excellent, I need that," Helena said, reaching out from the duvet and trying to grab a mug, but Dora was faster and pulled away.

"The coffee will be waiting for you downstairs," she said, "and when you are dressed and ready to go you can have a slurp to warm you. Up and out!"

She wasn't going to let any delaying techniques work.

Ten minutes later, the pair was down in the kitchen drinking lukewarm coffee. Dominic peered out the window to study the road.

"We're not going to make it by car," he said, shaking his head. "It's too dangerous."

"If you drive carefully, I'm sure you'll be fine," Dora assured him, handing him his coat. "It's only until you're on the main road," she added.

"I used to work as mechanic," Dominic said. "I know about these things. Driving in these conditions is trickier than people assume."

Helena nodded vigorously in a bid to back him up, but Dora wasn't having any of it.

"Bon voyage," she said opening the front door, ignoring their protests and ushering them out. Helena and Dominic left the hamlet on foot, missing the returning Bebe by only a half hour at the train station.

Chapter 11: The Body

Dora

The next morning Dora was ecstatic to find that the snow had stopped and the sun had stuck out its shy head behind the clouds. She was also pleased to have the house to herself, as she looked from her bedroom window over the hamlet for a long time and basked in the peace and quiet.

She saw that the curtains were drawn in Bebe's bedroom, which meant the singer was back. Ian was shovelling snow from his doorstep and the driveway. He moved with a bad limp and waved awkwardly at her. She waved back. Christine had to be still in bed with one of her migraines or else he'd never have risked the friendly gesture. Dora made her way downstairs for her first cup of coffee of the day.

Suddenly she heard Ian scream hysterically. "Help! Christine, call an ambulance. Help!"

She dashed towards the window. Ian was bent over on his driveway. She pulled her boots and coat on and ran over.

He was digging with his hands. Dora got closer and saw that Ian was trying to uncover a body from underneath the snow; a woman with red hair. It was Dominic's wife, Ellie.

"Is she dead?" Dora asked.

"I don't know," he said, his face flushed. "She must be, after being buried in the snow. I can't feel a pulse. Call an ambulance, quick. And get Christine."

Dora got her phone out.

"Revive her," she urged Ian while fiddling with the phone. "Give her mouth-to-mouth."

He tried and then shook his head and got up.

"She's ice cold. She must have been dead for some time."

"Nonsense," Dora said. "Keep trying!"

"She was buried under the snow, of course she's dead," he said but squatting back down.

"Do you know anything about resuscitation?" Dora asked, still not calling for an ambulance.

"I do," Ian said. "She's cold and there's no pulse. That's all we need to know."

"You need to find the right spot on her chest for resuscitation," Dora insisted and moved him aside. "Don't waste time, any second counts."

She handed him her phone, opened the woman's jacket and once she was satisfied about the correct position she interlocked her fingers and started to push down hard on the woman's chest while Ian left her to it and instead called the ambulance from Dora's phone.

"We should really give her mouth-to-mouth," Dora said to him when he had finished the call. "But I can't face kissing a stranger. Let's hope the heart gets pumping!"

Ian bent down by the body's head and continued to dig at the snow. Suddenly he stopped.

"Look at all the blood here," he said and pointed at it. "It's definitely too late for mouth to mouth."

"Keep going!" Dora shouted while she continued with the chest compressions.

"Give up, she's long dead," Ian insisted.

Dora continued for a few more minutes, before finally giving up.

"Who is she?" Ian asked Dora.

"I think her name is Ellie. She's the cheated wife of Helena's current lover," she said, her eyes welling with tears.

"Really!" Ian asked, looking confused. "That's her? Never."

"And I don't think we have to wonder who killed her," Dora added dryly and looked over to Bebe's house.

Half an hour later a snow plough came through the village, followed close behind by an ambulance and a police car. The paramedics confirmed that Ellie was dead. Suddenly the place was heaving with police. Yellow tape cordoned the Morris residence while a forensic team went on the hunt for clues. Detectives questioned Dora, Bebe, Ian and Christine and took preliminary statements while photographers filmed every inch of the crime scene. After the police had done their work, the body was removed from Ian's driveway.

Chapter 12: Detective Sergeant Beth Cooper

Detective Sergeant Beth Cooper was in a foul mood. Working weekends didn't agree with her, and things weren't helped when she spilled a water bottle on herself as she tried to switch off her iPhone alarm. The sound of Bob Geldof singing *I Don't Like Mondays* filled the room. Lately, every day felt like Monday morning for Beth. Today she was hungover and damn tired.

The bottle of water next to her bed had been to help detox her but she had forgotten to put the lid back on. Probably too tipsy to bother with it last night . . . She dried herself with the sheet and looked at her Buddha statue. There'd be no chanting this morning. Loving kindness and forgiveness were not coming naturally to her right now. Since she had been dumped a few weeks' back she had been in a bad state and spiritual ambitions had given way to bottled spirits and nights out in town. Why had she allowed herself to be led astray yet again? she lamented. Her body craved a greasy breakfast, not Bircher muesli, and she longed for a cigarette, a habit she only recently had beaten for good.

The first one of the day was the one she missed the most. No other cigarette ever gave her quite the same rush. Unlike the straight-A students in her school, from an early age onwards, Beth saw herself more like as a society's misunderstood and stigmatised outsider and smoking befitted that image. Her decision to join the police force raised a few eyebrows.

Poacher turned gamekeeper was how her friends described it.

She ended up a Detective Sergeant for the murder squad in Cardiff.

Now at the wrong side of thirty – or teetering on the abyss of forty to be more precise – the rebel in her was still alive, albeit less active and noticeable. Going to the local Buddhist centre and living healthily wasn't the panacea she had hoped it would be.

She slipped out of bed and grimaced as she stepped barefoot on her jumper, also wet from the water spillage. She ignored her pressing bladder and put the kettle on to be one step closer to that much-needed caffeine fix. As she entered the kitchen she saw that there were several mugs on the table. Fred (nee Fredericka) her ex-lover and now 'friend and flat mate', must have had another book group meeting yesterday. Surprise, surprise: There was no coffee left.

Her only choice was herbal tea. Ill-tempered, she assembled the progress report on her current case files that she'd have to present later in the day. Her latest case had been stagnating for a long time and she knew a scheduled early morning meeting with her boss, Detective Chief Inspector Peter Warwick, would be a rough telling off.

She had a quick shower. Once she had dried herself she glanced in the mirror. Her dark short curly hair was just on the verge of turning into something longer and more difficult to manage. A quick dab of gel took care of that though. Who needed expensive trips to the hairdresser? She preferred to just slick it back and be done with the issue for the rest of the day, but it was exactly this lack of vanity that got her under constant fire from her friends and family – let alone her boss.

"Why are you going out of your way to make yourself ugly?" was her mother's favourite line. "You've got a beautiful figure, curvy and all, you should be showing it off, not hiding it behind baggy jumpers and tucking it away in those horrible jeans. You'll end up an old spinster!"

Beth rolled her eyes just thinking of those words. She, too, wanted to be sexy and admired but not in the same way and certainly not by the type of men that her mother regularly tried to set her up with. The fact was Beth was gay and, for the entire 16 years that had passed since she had come out, her stubborn mother had insisted on trying to find the 'right one to put an end to that adolescence phase'.

Beth made herself put on a dress, tights and high heels. She was going to be scrutinised for her incompetence by her choleric boss and hoped this would lessen his anger. Her dressing up was in a sense an admission of guilt if ever there was one.

She liked what she saw in the mirror. Maybe her skin was a little worse for wear and her complexion paler than could be thought of as healthy. Some make-up covered the paleness, but a critical eye could still detect the signs of nicotine and vodka abuse. She sighed.

"All right!" she said to herself in the mirror. "Let's see if we can pull this off." She put on extra lipstick, grabbed the large leather handbag her mother had given her on her last birthday and wobbled on her heels towards the door. Beth could do sexy very well but she had to be in the mood for it. Today just wasn't one of those days, and she would have preferred to shout at the people on the pavement who would not get out of her way rather than smiling seductively and obediently at men who had no clue how little she was interested in them. Still, she tried hard to get herself into an agreeable and inoffensive frame of mind.

On the bus she sat opposite a 'briefcase', the name she had given to the middle-aged men she guessed were accountants or advertising executives of the lower ranks who were either on the phone to Terry in the office to talk about the email they had definitely sent yesterday or who were reading tabloids and dirty magazines. Today's specimen was shuffling some documents on top of his briefcase but spent a considerable amount of time staring at Beth's cleavage. "Well, you put them on display!" he'd probably tell her if she complained about his obvious drooling.

She got her phone out and pretended to be talking to a friend

"Oh yes, thanks, the interview went very well," she said loud enough to make sure the pervert opposite would hear every word of her fake conversation. ". . . The filthy swine was staring at my breasts the whole time . . . of course not. He was wearing a wedding ring naturally but you know the type. Greasy hair, growing belly and a moustache, thinks he's god's gift to women and that I dressed specifically to cater for his sexual appetite . . . probably not getting any at home . . ."

She was very pleased to see that her words hit the mark. 'Briefcase' was no longer paying any obvious attention to her but was sorting his documents head down. As she was basking in her little victory over chauvinism on the underground, her phone rang while she was still pretending to talk to her imaginary friend. 'Briefcase' was looking at her with a mixture of contempt and hostility. Unable to think of a face-saving way to recover, she answered the call. It was her boss, Warwick, to enquire why she was late.

"So sorry," she said in her sweetest voice. "I'm on the bus and won't be long."

She hated giving 'Briefcase' the satisfaction of witnessing this transformation – if he was still listening.

"Listen *Coopette*," her boss DCI Warwick shouted into the phone, as he always did. She hated when he called her that name. "Don't bother coming in today. I've given your current cases to someone more reliable. I have statistics to run and need to show that the department can solve at least some cases. I know that you've got nothing on the Schreiber case, and nothing to report on the Miller murder. I want you over in Carmarthenshire. They're struggling after the snowfall. Yesterday, a 28 year-old woman turned up in the snow with her head bashed in, near a hamlet – Llangurrey. I've emailed you all the details. Go home, read the file and head over to Carmarthen police station. You'll be in charge of the investigation."

"But . . ," she began to protest, but her boss had already rung off.

Darn it! This was the worst possible punishment: *A Midsomer Murder* setting, a ninety minutes' drive into the motorway-less Welsh countryside. God, how she hated Warwick . . . He had done that on purpose.

Back in her flat Beth changed into more sensible clothes. And she finally had a settled stomach and the time now to have breakfast. She helped herself to one of Fred's cherished fruit salads while reading the memo from her boss.

In the hamlet of Llangurrey, graphic designer Ian Morris had discovered the dead body of a 28-year-old woman from London, Ellie Seaborne, hidden under the snow on his driveway. The victim had presumably been struck on the head but the coroner had not finished his report.

Beth had a headache from this brief already.

Well, she might as well hurry and get there soon so that this nightmare could begin and hopefully be over quickly. Warwick had said he believed this to be a simple case, that's why he had given her this job in the first place. She would not be able to mess this up. She was angry at the insult, although the break-up from Fred had made her commit some very unprofessional howlers. Still. It wouldn't have hurt for Warwick to tell her a little more instead of instructing her to get to Carmarthen police station to find the full briefing. She had a long drive ahead of her that she could have used to let the facts of the case sink in. What an idiot.

It took a while to get out of Cardiff and then all the way on the M4 past Port Talbot with its smoke-shrouded steelworks and the nuisance average speed-check. Only then did she find herself surrounded by countryside – wide fields, small mountains and fewer and fewer buildings. She had expected more sheep, as the stereotype about Wales went, but in this cold many had been taken in by the farmers, she expected.

She got to Carmarthen at lunchtime and spoke to DCI Sion Jones, a round-faced, middle-aged man more use to shuffling papers than in examining dead bodies, by the sound of things. He'd been the first officer on the scene. As Beth listened to his briefing, she soon realised that it was not as simple a case as Warwick had made out. A cheated-upon wife had been killed, possibly with a snow shovel, in the same hamlet as her philandering husband's current lover's mother. An oddity was that this had happened not in front of said woman's house but a few yards away on a different property.

"Seems like she could have been struck while walking away from the Morris residence, either that or she was dumped there, but that's hardly likely," said Jones over a cup of coffee from the station vending machine.

"Murder weapon and time of death have yet to be confirmed by the coroner. The husband and his lover have an alibi in London, so motive and suspects aren't obvious so far. We really appreciate the support. We'd handle this one ourselves, but all resources are being used in trying to deal with this weather. We're run ragged dealing with call-outs – crashes, elderly people stuck in their homes, even some enterprising local scumbags taking the opportunity to stage break-ins. Our response time is pretty terrible in these conditions, so they're making hay while the snow falls, so to speak."

He gave her a heads-up on the set-up in the station – shift times, desk sergeants, coroner's number – and then finished their coffees. Beth thanked him and they went their separate ways, Jones to get stuck into the latest list of snow-related setbacks, while she got settled in.

Beth was allocated a small room on the first floor with a single desk and a computer. When she started reading the preliminary statements in more depth, she didn't like the sound of the people she would have to interrogate: a precious has-been singer, a flamboyant woman from Portugal, an uptight businesswoman and her long-suffering husband.

The notes from the coroner, when they did arrive, didn't add much to what her colleague had said: time of death was difficult to determine because of the cold but guessing by the contents of the victim's digestive system it had occurred approximately four hours after her last meal, which, according to credit card receipts, had been bought at a fast-food chain in Carmarthen at 7pm. A blood stained shovel, found on the Morris driveway had been taken to forensics and looked a perfect match for the victim's wound. Analysis of the blood type and search for fingerprints might yield further information later. Linking any other suspect than the residents to the crime scene would be difficult since the snowstorm had covered all tracks overnight. Why Warwick had called this an easy case was beyond her. She went downstairs to the vending machine and got herself another coffee. She resisted the urge to join the smokers outside. She was a Buddhist now, her body was her temple. She shouldn't even have the coffee, let alone the drinks she had consumed last night.

Back in her office she turned to the suspects: Ian Morris, who had found the body, and his wife, Christine Morris, should be the obvious suspects but they had no apparent connection with the victim and seemed genuinely upset about the murder on their doorstep. Mrs Morris was described as defensive and reluctant to cooperate. Ian Morris had an ankle injury from a slip in the snow a few days previously, when he had tried to escort his neighbour to the main road. Due to the severity of his limp, the Carmarthen team judged him incapable of yielding the murder weapon and were working on establishing a motive for the murder that involved the Morris household.

Dominic Seaborne, the husband of the deceased, and his mistress Helena Quinn, the obvious prime suspects, had an alibi. They were miles away when the murder had happened, having left the hamlet in the afternoon that day to stay with friends in London; they had witnesses and stamped train tickets to prove it. At least the couple were now on their way from the Seaborne residence in London to Carmarthen to give further statements. Warwick had sent her an email stating that the widower had not been overly upset about the passing of his wife but the alibi had been verified by Warwick that morning. They had both suffered from food poisoning and had time stamped receipts from the pharmacy to prove it. Beth wouldn't have minded some help from the local constables in this investigation but she hated to have Warwick breathing down her neck.

Reading between the lines, the local residents seemed not to think highly of Helena Quinn, nee Bolton, who was having an affair with the victim's husband. Too bad her alibi checked out, and that of the husband.

Dora Jenkins, nee Rodriguez, a Portuguese divorcee, had mentioned that Christine Morris had an obsession with parking and other rules for the hamlet, which could easily have led to all kind of clashes between this Christine Morris and the victim. It wasn't much as motives go, though . . . hardly one that would lead to murder.

Dora Jenkins was the only person who vaguely knew the victim. She had spoken to Ellie Seaborne on a previous visit to the hamlet and discouraged her to continue her search for the philandering husband. She had invited the victim into her home briefly during the snow but the two women had an argument and parted ways. Mrs Jenkins was playing the argument down, but Ian Morris had reported that Mrs Jenkins had been hit and had sported a scratched cheek and cut lip that day. It wasn't the most convincing motive for murder, but, given that the main suspects had alibis, Mrs Jenkins had to be considered a strong suspect. The woman had given Jones a lot of inside information on the relations between the residents of the hamlet, which made her sound like a gossip monger and someone who might be keen to put the blame on someone else's door. Beth cringed when she read the transcript.

Last but certainly not least there was Barbara Bolton, or Bebe Bollinger, a once mildly famous singer. She stated that she had briefly witnessed a violent exchange between the cheating couple and the victim but swore that she had never spoken directly to the dead woman. Mrs Bolton/ Bollinger was clearly disinterested in the case and in her daughter's affairs, and was described as most unhelpful in the questioning, quoting career obligations as reason to cut the interview short. She was the prime suspect in Warwick's eyes, who was convinced the 'deluded wannabe star' had killed the love rival of her daughter in a fit of megalomania. Dora Jenkins, however, had emphasised how poorly mother and daughter got on, so Jones had thought this scenario much less likely.

Beth picked up the notes and went to her car. It was time to make up her own mind about the people of Llangurrey. Maybe statements would change and the discrepancies would point her into the right direction.

At the Morris residence an abrupt and tense-looking woman answered the door wearing marigolds and an industrial looking apron.

"I'm Detective Sergeant Beth Cooper from the Metropolitan Police in London. I'm here to go over the initial statements and ask a few more questions. I apologise if you feel like you have answered them already. I have to do my own investigation."

"I apologise for my appearance," Christine Morris said," but I have been away for almost a fortnight and my husband has left the house in a terrible mess. Have you not found the culprit yet?" she asked with a condescending head tilt.

"No," Beth replied. "Can I come in?"

Mrs Morris's nose wrinkled but she nodded silently and waved Beth through.

"Ian!" she screamed into the back of the house. "Ian! Come down, the police is here – again."

"No need to call him just yet," Beth said. "We can begin with you and I can question your husband later."

"Oh, separate interviews. Are we suspects?" Mrs Morris snapped.

"Not at all," Beth said cheerfully, although she began to warm to the idea of arresting this woman.

Mrs Morris took off her marigolds. Once the Detective had taken her shoes off, Mrs Morris ushered her into the living room: a white-walled, sterile-looking place with glass table tops and leather furniture, some of it covered with neatly stitched linen throws. Beth sat down and opened her notebook.

"Did you know the victim?" she asked.

"I knew *of* her," Mrs Morris said. "My husband told me there was some sort of scene when she arrived at Dora Jenkins' doorstep."

She averted her eyes as if the mere thought of her neighbours was painful to her.

"Could you quickly run me through your movements of Thursday night and Friday morning?" Beth asked.

"I already said that to the uniformed officers when they took my statement after they were called to the scene: I haven't left my house for days. I once went over to Mrs Jenkins to reimburse her for some expenses but apart from that I only caught up with my paperwork and, of course, the order in the house. I spent a lot of time Thursday night cooking since my husband depleted our emergency rations from the freezer while I was gone. I would have seen anything going on outside since the body was found right by my kitchen window. I went to bed around 10pm on Thursday night, too tired to watch the late news. I suffer from anxiety and use sleeping tablets and industrial earplugs. I heard nothing all night. The murder would have had to happen after 10pm and before 10:27am, which was when Ian says he found the body."

"Are you quite sure of that?" Beth asked.

"As you can see the windows aren't double glazed. I can hear everything from my kitchen. I wish I didn't. Mrs Jenkins frequently speaks to the birds in her garden or in the summer when she sunbathes in her skimpy bikinis, she sings along to her music. It is very annoying. If the buildings weren't all listed it would be easy to install double glazing and shut out all the noise. I presume you know that Mrs Bolton is a singer, and also often *entertains* us with her talent. Thursday night was very quiet while I was awake. You could have heard a penny drop in the snow."

"The storm hadn't hit the village by 10pm?" Beth asked and made a note of it.

"Occasionally the wind made a noise but apart from that I didn't hear a thing. As I said, I took a sleeping tablet and didn't wake up until the police arrived."

"Oh well, do you have any thoughts as to why Mrs Seaborne was murdered or how all of this has happened on your doorstep?"

"Mrs Bolton's daughter Helena is a very common little thing," Mrs Morris said, her lip curling to add to the disdain in her voice. "When she used to live here she was a real handful."

"Mrs Quinn has an alibi," Beth replied.

"The kind of people she mixes with, I'm not surprised there's murder and unruly conduct," Mrs Morris said suggestively. "Whatever it is, it has something to do with her. Maybe Mrs Seaborne dealt in drugs. Blackmail? If it wasn't Helena herself, someone in her dubious circles did it. The answer lies certainly not in Llangurrey, that's for sure."

"You don't think that Mrs Jenkins or Mrs Bolton could have anything to do with this?"

"Ha-ha, of course not," Mrs Morris laughed loudly. "Mrs Bolton couldn't lift a shovel with all that body fat and her arthritis to hit someone hard enough to kill them. Mrs Jenkins would be able to, but she is far too emotional to kill someone quietly or in cold blood. She would shout and scream at her victim first. As common as my neighbours are, I don't think they'd be capable of murder."

"Thank you, Mrs Morris," Beth said and scribbled away in her notebook. "So if it were to be one of the two it would have to be Mrs Jenkins?"

"I didn't say that," Mrs Morris said.

"I know," Beth replied. "May I speak to Mr Morris now?"

"Of course, I shall get him."

With that she stormed off. Beth could hear her stomping up the staircase, some not-so-muffled scolding words being exchanged and then the perfect image of a broken man slowly limped into the room and sat down awkwardly opposite Beth.

"I'm sorry to disturb you," she said. "I just wanted to speak to you in case you had remembered anything new or had any more thoughts about the tragic event."

"No problems," Mr Morris said quietly.

"I understand that you never met the deceased?"

"Never in my life," he said, head hanging. "This is so sad."

Beth nodded.

"Well?" she asked when he remained silent. "Have you got any idea why this could have happened?"

"Not a clue," he replied. "I'd left the shovel by the gate. Christine made me buy a few of them in case one of us ever got home during the snow and needed to clear it from the driveway to reach the front door. We have a shovel by the front door as well. Anyone could have taken the one by the gate. I know for a fact that Mrs Bolton used the shovel to free her car a few days earlier. I bought a shovel for Mrs Jenkins during last week. It's hard to imagine though who here would have a bone to pick with the dead woman. I can't imagine anything else than the murderer being from outside the hamlet."

"What about Mrs Jenkins? Didn't she have an argument with the deceased? She played it down to our officers, whereas you mentioned a small injury to Mrs Jenkins' face. Isn't that so?"

"Yes, she did have a small scratch, but if Dora didn't kill the woman when she was hit, why would she do that days later on my property?" he asked. "This is preposterous."

"I assume you know about the love triangle?" Beth asked.

Ian nodded.

"Helena is a wild child but she's no murderer, either," he said. "I wouldn't want to point fingers, but the husband seems the obvious suspect."

"He appears to have an alibi, though," Beth said. "As has Mrs Quinn. Can you remember any more details about Thursday night or Friday morning?"

"None at all."

"Your wife said she would have heard a fight outside from the kitchen. Do you think that statement is realistic?" Beth asked carefully. "That would be important to establish the time of death and any alibis."

"While she was awake, absolutely," Ian said without a moment of hesitation. "My wife suffers from terrible anxiety and nervousness. Every sound outside gets her to run for the window and take a look. She always hears our neighbours leaving their houses. She has an excellent sense of hearing."

The door opened and Mrs Morris, wearing a cotton wool kitchen apron this time, brought in a selection of homemade cakes and drinks.

"I'm so sorry for being somewhat abrupt earlier," she said with the sweetest of smiles. "You caught me off guard. I've made a pot of coffee and a pot of tea since I forgot to ask which you would prefer."

Without waiting for a reply she turned away and quickly added: "Don't let me disturb you. Enjoy!" and then she closed the door.

"My wife gets a lot of bad press for her manners," her husband said. "But she has a giving side to her if you stick around long enough. She just has a terrible mistrust of people."

"That much is obvious," Beth blurted out before digging into a Victoria Sponge cake. The hangover still made her crave sugar. "Oh my God, but your wife can bake! This is delicious!!

Beth could understand the marriage a little better now.

"What time did you go to bed on Thursday night, Mr Morris?" Beth asked.

"After my wife went to bed I watched the News at Ten and then I looked at websites for our summer holiday. It must have been 1 or 2am when I turned in."

"Did you hear or see anything outside, maybe?"

"Nothing until the snow storm hit us around 11pm. I'm afraid I saw nothing of interest to you. My office faces the other way. The bedroom windows overlook the crime scene but the curtains were drawn, so I never looked outside once I went to bed."

He cleared his throat.

"What do you think of Mrs Jenkins and Mrs Bolton?" Beth asked.

"Mrs Bolton is a bit big-headed, but benign. Mrs Jenkins is very European and very kind. Both women are eccentric and certainly not murderers."

"I see," Beth said.

"I'm sorry I can't think of anything more helpful to add."

"Thank you all the same."

Beth retreated to the privacy of her car and re-read her notes. It was frustrating; the Morris's had told her little she didn't already know. The body was found on their doorstep, so they were prime suspects – either of them could have done it, or both together. Yet, if they had done it, they should be eager to divert attention away from themselves and point the finger at other possible suspects. Neither of them had taken the opportunities to do so. She made a note to check if there was any way of linking the couple to Ellie Seaborne, and then headed out to the cold to see what Dora Jenkins could tell her.

Her heart seemed to skip a beat when the door was opened by a very attractive woman in her late forties. She was tall, with swept back brown hair and eyes that seemed to float over Beth as though they were preoccupied, or maybe they were just dreamy.

"Oh no, you have more questions about the poor woman?'

Beth had to jolt herself out of the reverie she suddenly found herself in.

'I'm afraid so, yes,' she said, hauling herself back into professional mode. The woman was talking again . . .

"Honestly, this whole affair makes me so sad," Dora said, holding her face with both hands. "Well come on in, I'm just having lunch. Would you like Greek salad?"

"Thank you," Beth declined, smiling. "I'm stuffed from the cake at the Morris residence."

Dora led her into the living room. It was cosy, Beth decided, with a beautiful fireplace, even if the fire itself was fake. The house was toasty and Beth had to take off her jacket to adjust to it. She wore a thin cashmere jumper that showed off her curves, something she wasn't comfortable in while in the presence of such a beautiful woman. The environmentally conscious Fred continuously dialled down the heating in their shared flat and since Beth spent far too much of her pay packet on meals out and concerts she had to be grateful for the money that her efforts at energy conservation saved. But it was nice to be somewhere this warm for a change. Even compared to the Morris residence, the room was boiling.

"I don't think I can tell you anything new," Dora said after they had settled down on the soft sofas. "Ian found the body and screamed for help. I tried to revive her, then the police came and that was it. That time I spoke to the woman when she was alive, she was distraught, but who wouldn't be if you found out your husband was cheating on you. She looked a bit like a hippie, but not a convincing one. Her outfit and the henna hair didn't fool me. Her Mini was brand new."

Beth nodded and made lots of notes. She'd heard about that Mini being in a local garage somewhere, waiting to be repaired.

"As far as I know the wife's money is not in her name," Dora continued. "That's what Helena implied. The husband gains nothing from her death. He needed her alive as his meal ticket and that's probably why he hadn't left her. The finger points clearly to Helena here, only she's not tough enough if you ask me. She's all mouth but no action, nothing but a lazy, self-centred immature girl who would steal and lie to get her way but who would never go this far."

"You seem quite certain about this," Beth observed, trying not to stare at the beautiful smile of the woman opposite. Dora was clearly hetero, but she seemed very flirtatious and situations like these had got the police officer in trouble before.

"Well, that is my opinion anyway," said Dora and smiled broadly. "I don't know Helena that well."

"But you said in your previous statement that Mrs Quinn and Mr Seaborne stayed with you one night during the snowfall?"

"Yes they did, but she and her beau spoke little at all while they were here. Helena seemed hung up about the guy; she is very needy, but that's not her fault. The mother also needs a lot of attention: that's where the girl has got it from."

"The lovers have a water-tight alibi. Who would you think did it then?" Beth asked.

"Maybe Dominic has a different lover?" Dora ventured a guess. "Men like him are pigs and I doubt that Helena was the only one he had on the side. Helena is not that good-looking or special that anyone would kill his wife only to be with her. It has to be someone else who wanted to harm him indirectly or even try and frame them.

"There were no signs of a struggle or a fight associated with the killing," Beth said. "How do you explain that in connection with a crime of passion?"

"Ah, you make a valid point," Dora admitted. "Well, I don't know then. You've got to find out for yourself, detective." The beautiful woman winked at her, which made Beth blush. "Snoop into Ellie's life and find out what skeletons she's got in her closet. Maybe it's just a coincidence that she was murdered here. Maybe someone was following her and took advantage of the shovel?"

"We are looking into that as we speak," Beth admitted, trying to keep her cool. "We wish we knew how she got here in the first place. Her car has been for repair in a garage for several days and she had no courtesy car. The London team are tracing her steps over the last few days."

"It is possible to walk in the snow," Dora said. "Helena and her beau did it."

"Interesting," Beth said and noted this down. "I didn't think of that."

"Well, if I can be of any assistance to you, let me know," Dora offered as Beth stood to leave.

"Thank you," she replied, coyly. "I do have one more question about you and the argument you had with the deceased."

Dora smiled. "Oh that," she said and shrugged. "I tried to make her see sense and leave the bastard alone. It was so obvious to me. Unfortunately, I didn't get my message through to her and she just tried to insult me and eventually she hit me. So I naturally kicked her out but I didn't bear her a grudge. The poor girl was madly in love and hurt in her feelings. I didn't take it personally. I felt sorry for her all the time."

"That's mighty forgiving of you," Beth said, hoping her professional obligation to provoke wouldn't upset the woman too much.

"I was fuming," Dora admitted. "I am not going to deny that. I've learned to control my temper, though, and took the high road."

Beth made more notes and then took her leave. Could this lovely cougar of a woman have controlled her temper enough to delay the act of revenge for a few days? Could she have let the victim go the first time but when she spotted her assailant on the Morris property, she cold-heartedly took the shovel and killer her – was that thinkable?

Once outside, she had to capture her breath. Warwick was right: Beth was unprofessional. She had found it so hard to stay on the topic of the murder. She had wanted to ask Mrs Jenkins more personal questions but hadn't dared for fear it would appear she was flirting. Her attraction to one of the suspects had all the signs of a rebound crush and if she wasn't careful it would deliver Warwick the final excuse to get rid of her. Still, she found it hard to see Dora Jenkins as the murderer, even though that was a distinct possibility.

Next door at the Bolton/Bollinger residence nobody answered.

"She often works in the basement with her headphones one," Dora shouted across the fence while Beth was at the door. "If she is, she can't hear you and won't answer the door."

Beth nodded and after there was no reply several minutes later, she drove back to the police station.

Chapter 13: Carmarthen Police Station

Beth

Once back in Carmarthen police station in her tiny first-floor office she called Warwick

"Do you have any leads about Ellie Seaborne's life in London?" she asked. "Any connections to Mr and Mrs Morris or Mrs Jenkins? Any suspects or leads?"

"I take it you haven't found out anything yourself then?" the boss replied, evading her question.

"No," she said sheepishly. How she hated his superiority.

"No news about Ellie Seaborne at all," he said. "She worked for a publishing company. No known enemies at work or in her private life as far as we can establish. Everyone close to her blames the husband but, although he's in love with another woman, he would lose his financial security, so in my opinion, he has no motive. Mrs Seaborne has no money to her name at all. The residence is owned by the parents and they top-up her salary every month, which enables the couple to live as glamorously as they do. And, of course, let's not forget his alibi."

"Does he have a job?" Beth asked.

"Now, don't laugh, Cooper. He used to be a mechanic and then became an underwear model, but he hasn't landed a good gig for some time. Apparently he's lost his competitive drive at the gym, lately, and has become the lead singer in a pop band. When everything comes so easy to you, why bother with work, right? You'd know all about that."

She could hear his chuckles down the phone.

"Very funny."

"Anyway, his agent dropped him after he put on a few pounds and since then he's stopped trying to find new work so he can concentrate on his music career. He's in a band and the rest of the time he's a full-time house husband now. So it's not in his interest to have his wife topped. She had a life insurance policy but that only covers her wages, not the money she gets from her parents. He'd be much better off with her still alive. Now he'll have to find work. It's his worst case scenario."

"Then could it be an indirect revenge thing against him?" Beth asked. "If his life is ruined by her death, maybe someone did it to hurt him?"

"Far-fetched, but possible," Warwick said. "He has enemies galore, of course. Everyone hates a lazy pretty boy who cheats and doesn't pay his way. Whether any of them hated him enough to kill his golden goose is another matter that we're looking into. But you'll get the opportunity to interview him shortly and find out for yourself. He might have an idea who is behind this."

"Where has he spent his time since the murder?" Beth asked.

"He's moving. Mrs Seaborne's parents own the marital home and on learning the circumstances they demanded that he move out of their property within twenty-four hours. I've searched the flat and let him put some of his stuff that isn't needed as evidence in storage. He intends to move in with Helena Quinn, I suspect at her mother's. He said he'd make himself available for questioning today at the Carmarthen police station."

"You allowed him to do this?"

"He has a tight alibi with friends in London, miles away from the murder with food poisoning. Then he was seen in a restaurant in the morning. Right now, with that many confirmed sightings away from the scene, he isn't a suspect. We in London are re-focusing our resources on the more complex and prolific cases, like Miller and Schreiber. Remember? Your country murder is hardly a top priority for us. There are a few open leads to check out. That's your responsibility, Cooper."

"I got it," she sighed and hung up.

Beth sat down in her small office in the local police station. Downstairs was frantically busy. Additional accidents, break-ins and traffic control took their toll on the man force and there were long queues on the corridors. Upstairs was much calmer. The walls in her room were bleak and in dire need of a repaint. The floor was made of ugly PVC tiles and the room smelled of old paper. She started typing up her notes while waiting for Dominic Seaborne and Helena Quinn to make an appearance. Warwick was right. There were a few avenues to explore and one of them could point to the murderer soon.

Two hours, a lot of coffee from the vending machine and some failed chanting later, the widower and his lover arrived at her desk. Dominic Seaborne wore leather trousers and a hair band like

Beckham. He was just the type Beth hated: always looking in the mirror and adjusting his hair, tall, so she had to look up to him, conventionally handsome – and he knew it – with cheek dimples and toned muscles. Seaborne was all smiles and appeared to be flirting by frequently raising his eyebrows and winking at her. 'Boy, is he barking up the wrong tree,' she thought, but she winked back, humouring him to see if he was just routinely buttering up every woman around him or if it was a ploy because he had something to hide.

Helena Quinn seemed oblivious to the flirting and looked around the room nervously. Her lack of confidence surprised Beth.

"If it's okay with you I will speak to Mr Seaborne first," Beth said and had the anxious mistress put into a waiting area. The longer she could make that fidgety woman wait, the better for the investigation.

Beth set up the microphone.

"Are you happy with us recording this?"

He nodded confidently.

"Are you sure you don't want a lawyer present?" she asked.

"Positive," he said. "I have nothing to hide."

"That's not always the main reason to have a lawyer," Beth pointed out.

"I don't care." He shrugged and leaned back, his hands stretching above head, not unlike one of Warwick's favourite poses.

"That must have been a tough few days for you," Beth said with puppy eyes. "Your wife is murdered and you're being evicted from your home."

"Oh yes, well, yes, it's sad," Seaborne stammered, no longer playing the Casanova. To her, he seemed actually confused more than anything else. "I mean, you know I'm with Helena now, well . . . but it's kind of weird."

"How is it weird?" Beth asked sympathetically.

"I loved Ellie, you know. I'm pretty sad but then I again I'm also really happy that I'm with Helena now. I don't know what to feel."

"Oh," Beth said and nodded. "Do you have any idea who murdered your wife?" she asked. She knew this was why she recently had not achieved anything as a detective. Since her breakup she had no patience to trap the bad guys. She tended to get her suspects via evidence and good instincts, rarely by getting them to confess. She found it hard to keep faking sympathy.

"I can't think of anybody," Dominic said. "Ellie got on with everyone."

"How about some of your former mistresses? Is there anybody who would want to hurt you and decided to do so indirectly?" Beth asked.

A smug grin briefly flashed across his face.

"This can't be your first extra-marital affair," Beth added coldly. "Your reputation suggests otherwise. Maybe one of your exes had a hand in the murder? Any names spring to mind?"

"I can write you a list," he said and ran his hand through his hair.

Beth handed him a pen and paper, glad he seemed to be losing his innocent act.

"Excellent. Names, addresses and numbers please. Can I wait or are you going to be a while doing this?"

"Won't take *very* long," he said and began writing down a list of his exes. The rest of the interview went by smoothly. He still didn't seem to be too broken over his wife's death and spoke animatedly into the microphone as if he was giving an interview for a fashion or music magazine. He held firm and consistently to his story. She judged him a poor liar but there was also something vaguely rehearsed about his statements.

"We went to the train station, caught the 14:05 train to London, took the Tube to my friends' flat in Camden and stayed there. My friend has already vouched for us and here are the tickets and receipts," he said assuredly. "In the morning we had breakfast in London. Maybe the people there will remember us, too."

"I see from the reports that you went to bed at 8pm. That's extremely early. You could have snuck out, made it to Llangurrey and killed your wife."

"Well we didn't go to sleep immediately," he said with a grin.

"Of course," she said. "But I guess there aren't any witnesses for that, so we have to take your word that you didn't leave the premises."

"Yeah right," he laughed. "Sneaking out after 8pm, making my way through the snow storm on the off-chance that my ex-wife hangs out in a stranger's driveway and then kill her, return to London in the snow and have breakfast at eight in the Brasserie Filou?"

"We've checked the train times. It would have been just possible for you to do so," Beth said. "You love Mrs Quinn and want to be with her."

"Well, I didn't sneak out or kill my wife and you won't find anyone who saw me doing any of those things."

"Thank you."

Helena's statement confirmed everything he had said. Apparently her current anxiety had nothing to do with the murder case. She was more concerned about securing Dominic's love now that he was free and penniless.

"I can't bear to lose him," she admitted in the interview. "I'm scared Dominic might look for another rich woman to replace Ellie and might lose interest in me. And then there is the major headache of avoiding my husband and finding a place to live," Helena said under tears. "I had assumed my mother would let us stay for a few weeks to give us time to re-establish ourselves but she has dodged my calls."

"What do you think about the murder?" Beth asked. "Who would have had a motive to do it?"

"What can I tell you?" Helena countered abrupt. "I don't know the woman from Adam. I only saw her when she came to my mother's house and slapped me."

"So you had reason to be angry at her?"

"Naturally," Helena said. "She was making things unnecessarily hard for me and Dominic."

"So you wanted her out of the way?"

"Absolutely," Helena said. ". . . out of the way, but not dead."

Beth nodded. That sounded interesting.

"I don't understand why you even need to talk to us when we have alibis."

"Standard procedure. Be sure to let us know where you stay," Beth said before releasing the young woman.

All that interviewing had not yielded much concrete results, but at least Beth had a few leads to follow up now. Someone in London would have to call all of Dominic's exes and see if any of them had no alibi and was still bearing a grudge. Someone else would have to find Helena's husband and she would like to speak to Ellie's parents herself. The police also had to find Bebe Bollinger, who currently was not answering her phone.

Chapter 14: A Meeting of Minds

Bebe

Bebe was oblivious to the world outside. The death of the cheated wife had shocked her at first but then it had carried her away artistically and inspired her to take on some James Bond themes for her repertoire. Wasn't it time someone gave *Goldfinger* a jazz-over, or *All Time High* and *Nobody Does it Better*? She couldn't believe that a murder had really taken place in her hamlet, and the tragedy was best worked through with music. Locked in her recording studio since lunchtime she was so entranced in the 'new musical arrangements' for these songs that she forgot about the time and her promise to remain available for further questioning. It was quite late into the afternoon when her mind returned to the police investigation outside. She found a note in her letterbox asking her to contact the police. Bebe put it aside. The body had been taken away and the crime scene unit had left the hamlet, too. In some way Llangurrey had nothing to do with the murder any longer, and Bebe wondered what else she could possibly contribute to the investigation.

The insinuation that her daughter was involved in the death was preposterous. Helena wouldn't have the guts to do such a thing. The police had to see this. Luckily, the girl had an alibi and was spared being treated like a prime suspect. Bebe was of course a suspect, too. Everyone was theoretically: all residents and all involved in the love triangle; but in practise, to Bebe, none of them could seriously be considered to have done it. Who could have murdered that woman? As morbid and inappropriate as it was, Bebe was getting plenty of inspiration from the drama and had the idea of adding a murder mystery theme to her future new album. *Bang Bang*, by Cher, was a song that she always thought had not got the attention it deserved from the record-buying public. Bebe would try to revive it in honour of the star.

When she checked her phone she found several messages from a female police officer asking her for another interview. She wanted to help and clear her daughter's name, if possible, but did these people think she had unlimited time to spare? She had told them everything she knew already the morning the body had been found.

When she spoke to Bertie on the phone about it, however, her agent was most insistent that she return the call and arrange a meeting.

"Just think of the bad press it might bring if it became known that you didn't do everything in your power to assist the police in a murder investigation. You also want to stay close to the action to find out where the police are looking. You wouldn't want to be involved in a scandal."

"I remember distinctly when we discussed me going into the Big Brother house that you said that there was no such thing as bad press or publicity?" she said.

"Honey, if the body had nothing to do with you then we could surely capitalise on the oddity that someone dead was found outside your house," Bertie explained. There was a nervous breathlessness to his voice. "What we do not want is anything to do with your darling daughter Helena to reach the press. You know that wild child is a loose cannon on a good day. You don't want to jeopardise your comeback prospects with her love scandal!"

"What do you want me to do?" she asked, helplessly.

"Speak to the police again," Bertie urged. "Butter the officers up and try and find out what they are thinking about the incident. Who are they suspecting? Is the investigation going to impact on you and Helena? Get on that phone and call the police, and do it now!"

Bebe dreaded the idea of going through yet another lengthy interview with the police while her mind was working overtime on album fillers and key changes, but Bertie was right: Keep your friends close and your enemies closer.

She hung up and immediately rang the police officer.

"This is Bebe Bollinger, returning your phone calls from earlier about a second statement," she sang into the receiver.

"Mrs … Bolton, thank you so much for calling," Beth said. "As I explained I'm from Cardiff and would appreciate it if you could meet me today. Any chance you could see me let's say in an hour?"

Bebe cringed at the use of her 'civilian' name.

"Of course you can, darling," she replied, overly sweet. "I apologise for calling back so late. You know how we artists are; we get carried away in the moment. When I'm in my recording studio I completely forget about the world." She threw in a helpless titter for effect.

"No problems. Can I see you in about 45 minutes at your house? Would that be convenient and at all possible Mrs . . . Bollinger?"

"My pleasure," Bebe replied.

Well, thought Bebe, this artist approach seemed to have worked. She would have to lay on some more of that. She went upstairs and changed into one of her flamboyant dresses, a purple gown that reached to her ankles and a lilac throw, topped with a boa. Just the kind of image a star from the past would be 'surprised' in by impromptu visitors, she suspected.

Bebe thought she could detect a suppressed grin on the detective's face when the diva opened her front door and invited her in with a flourish. Police staff always looked so grim and unfriendly. This would be hard work.

"Mrs . . . Bollinger, I will try to make this quick, so you can go back to your rehearsals," Beth said politely. "I know you spoke to my colleagues yesterday but I would be grateful if you could just tell me one more time in your own words what you did Thursday night and Friday morning, and what you know about Ellie Seaborne."

"Quite simple," Bebe said magnanimously. "I was indoors Thursday night and all day Friday. It was nothing short of a miracle that I noticed the police outside. The officer had already given up knocking on the door, I'm told. I saw nothing at all. I went to bed after midnight and returned to my recording studio at seven the next morning. I never set foot outside my house, didn't call anyone or see anything. Your colleague checked the log times on my computer."

"Of course, I know all that. But you knew the deceased?" Beth asked.

"*Knowing* her is stretching it," Bebe replied, wondering how she could get the officer to tell *her* things instead of the other way round. "I'm being so rude. Would you care for a hot beverage or maybe even something a little stronger? It's the weekend after all and late afternoon. You shouldn't be working at all, should you?"

Beth was tempted. Fraternizing with suspects was a controversial strategy and drinking on duty was particularly bad. On the other hand, she still felt a little hangover, a small headache was annoying her and no amount of water and coffee had taken care of that. It was time to fight fire with fire. One drink couldn't kill her and nobody would have to know about it, either. After this interview she would be going home to her house in Cardiff.

"What the hell," she said. "Yeah, one won't hurt me."

"What do you usually have?" Bebe asked. "Are you a Cosmopolitan girl, a champagne sipper or would you like a Bloody Mary? Or what's your pleasure?"

That got a smile. "I do fancy a Bloody Mary," Beth said. "You have to make it a weak one, I still need to drive home later," she added sheepishly.

"I love it," Bebe chortled. "My kind of drink. I used to prefer the bubbles but with a name like mine you get oversaturated, you know. And then there was that rival of mine, Evelyn 'Champagne' King. She and her cheap tunes got me right off the stuff."

"Evelyn, who…?" Beth asked.

"Exactly," Bebe said and beamed a big smile.

"Now, who do *you* think killed that poor girl outside the Morris house?" Bebe asked after she had served the drinks. "You must have a suspect by now."

"I was going to ask you the very same question," Beth said with a grin. "We're following up a few leads but nothing serious yet. What do you make of all this, Mrs Bollinger?"

"Please, call me Bebe, darling," the star insisted. "Everyone does."

"Alright Bebe," Beth said hesitantly. "What do you make of it? You've met the victim, you must have an impression of what could have happened?"

"Could it not have been an accident?" Bebe suggested. "Maybe a snow plough came through and hit her? There really isn't enough money involved to make a murder worth anyone's while. From what I saw the girl was pretty and sweet, a bit upset at the time but not a complete trollop or psycho. She would have been able to find someone better than that gigolo in no time. Have you seen that peacock of a man? Quite ridiculous to think anyone is running after him. All facade, no brain."

"I couldn't possibly comment," Beth grinned. "But we are getting off the subject."

"Of course, we are. Well, the girl came to my door to see her husband, who's unfortunately involved with my daughter at this moment in time, and they had a noisy argument, but then Mr

110

Seaborne left together with Mrs Seaborne and my daughter followed them. That's all I know."

"Tell me what your theory is. You must have wondered and an intelligent woman like yourself must be able to come to some conclusion?" Beth probed.

"My guess is an accident," Bebe replied. "Something odd, something you have not thought about like a chain reaction. I cannot imagine anyone hating such a sweet girl enough to kill her. Nobody would have even known she was here."

"You raise a few interesting points, Bebe, but that accident story is a bit far-fetched," Beth pointed out.

"Maybe it is, but you hear about these things. Don't you watch TV?"

"Maybe I watch too little and you watch too much," Beth said, seemingly enjoying herself more after the Bloody Mary.

"What about Mr and Mrs Morris as suspects?" Beth asked.

"Like I said to your colleague, they're not the murdering type," Bebe said. "Another drink?"

"I'd better be going now," Beth said, "before it gets too dark and icy on the road. Here's my card. If you can think of anything else worth mentioning let me know. Anytime!"

"Is Helena a suspect?" Bebe asked, worried.

"I can't comment on the investigation," Beth said, "Her alibi seems to hold, but we can't rule out anyone just yet," she added with a wink. "It looks like Helena's biggest problem is her addiction to Dominic."

"Tell me about it," Bebe agreed. "I must say though that if it weren't Dominic it would be someone else. My daughter has a notoriously bad taste in men. It never really bothered me, it's her own life and not for me to judge. However – and I must swear you to secrecy about this – I'm on the brink of a potential comeback and a scandal breaking about this incident could damage my chances of pulling it off."

"Say no more," Beth said and squeezed Bebe's hand gently. She wanted to lull Bebe into a false sense of security to relax her and maybe share secrets she would otherwise conceal. "I'll do my best to keep it low profile. My boss wouldn't have given me the case unless he thought it unimportant, if that's any consolation to you. He doesn't generally like me much."

"But why on earth not?" Bebe said surprised. "You're the first officer I spoke to that had any manners and kindness."

"That's probably it," Beth said. "I'm not professional enough. I shouldn't be drinking and telling you things, should I?"

"Oh men," Bebe said. "They and their ideas of professionalism . . . Sod it. Now tell me, what kind of music do you usually listen to? Do you like jazz or soul at all?"

Beth looked apologetic. "Sorry to disappoint you, Bebe, but I'm more of a techno chick."

Bebe sighed. That would have been too good to be true to have a guest she could ask for their opinion on the song she was working on.

"Never mind. Now drive home carefully!"

After Beth left, Bebe called Bertie who for once picked up the phone straight away.

"What do they say? Do they have the killer yet? Are you OK?" he asked.

"God you seem very interested in this affair. The policewoman from Cardiff is a total darling, a bit naïve and easily led. It looks like I'm not a suspect, though," Bebe said confidently.

"Well you say that now," Bertie said nervously. "These investigations tend to have a nasty habit of taking new turns. So they have no clue as to who did it?"

"Bertie, if I didn't know better I'd say you did it yourself. Why are you so concerned about this?" Bebe wondered.

"*Comic Relief*'s a big deal, Bebe. Don't mess it up, OK?" Bertie said with put-on gravity. "That can open doors for me as well as for you. We don't need it to be jeopardised by some stupid scandal outside your front door."

"Nothing is going to come of any of this," Bebe assured him, then she hung up and went for a long soak in the bath where she listened to her latest recordings and pampered her skin with her large selection of lotions.

Chapter 15: Viva La Diva

Bebe

The weather gods shone kindly on Bebe and her career ambitions and although it still snowed considerably the roads were clear enough for her to make it easily to the recording studio the next morning.

She was slightly taken aback when she realised that her good friend Engelbert was not there himself for the recording.

"Darling, his part has been long done," his producer said in a condescending tone. "Do you think he's got a minute to spare this week? The presentation of the song is at the end of the week, so we'd better hurry."

"Let's get to it then," Bebe said, keen to prove her professionalism.

The song was beautiful and the recording itself went very well, she thought. The production team was polite but professional. Between the various takes Bebe tried hard to find out who else would be doing the vocals.

"We don't get the actual names until they march in here," one of mixers said abruptly. "Sweetheart we need to get on. The next artist will be here soon. We have a lot of possible angles to consider for the song."

"What do you mean by a lot of possible angles?" Bebe asked alarmed.

Right then the producer tapped the mixer on the arm and then said to Bebe: "Just sing your heart out, darling, that's what you're here for. Let us worry about the rest. If things work out you'll be included in the promotional campaign and be on the road with Engelbert from the weekend on."

"I didn't know this was an audition!" Bebe protested.

"It isn't an audition as such," he tried to pacify her. "You're a big star, that's why you were invited to do this, but we're keeping all our options open. When we hear the different versions we decide which one to go with," the producer said. "None of us want to do a Eurovision gig at all, but apparently it's a matter of national pride and some people are prepared to put the cash up for it. How on earth are we going to figure what will make Europe vote for us? We'll have to

113

come up with a few ideas and then take a gamble, ok? Now time is money, you know that darling, you're a professional. So keep calm and let's go. From the top…"

After that Bebe found it hard to disguise the upset in her voice and was sure she'd blown the audition. She would give Bertie a piece of her mind about this. He must have known and yet he'd sold her out. It was she who'd contacted Engelbert's people, all he had to do was pan out a great contract with them, and even that he had failed to achieve. If it were not for the *Comic Relief* gig she would have fired him there and then, but it was best to wait a little to see if maybe he could deliver her a career revival.

Bebe left the recording studio in a very fragile mood. It didn't surprise her that Bertie dodged her calls. She needed to do something to make herself feel better. First she tried to call her son-in-law to find out how he was doing, but Aidan's phone was switched off. The poor man had probably broken down somewhere. Helena had texted several times, begging her mother to take her and her lover in until they had sorted their affairs. Bebe wasn't having any of it.

She needed to take her mind off her troubles and decided to have a drink in the trendy bar next door. It was full of recording hopefuls and producers talking about contracts and demos, with more names being dropped than you'd find in a copy of Rolling Stone. It was enough to set Bebe's teeth on edge. She knocked back a Bloody Mary but the presence of so many young starlets with their 'sponsors' – usually twice their age – only made her feel worse, so she soon left and headed instead, to a piano bar not far from the studio. Maurice occasionally worked here. The lighting was low, so nobody would recognise her and she could take a moment to get over her worries and anger. There seemed to be a kind of tea dance or cabaret act in progress. Someone sang a very bad rendition of *That Ole Devil Called Love* – another Alison Moyet hit. Bebe had enough and turned round, ready to go back to her car and be done with London, when she heard a shrill voice screaming her name.

"Bebe Bollinger? Oh my God, it's her!"

Instantly flattered and in a better mood she turned around and saw two middle-aged gay men with moustaches and jeans and leather attire fall over themselves to run after her. She couldn't suppress a smile.

"We're such big fans," the two men gushed in unison and grabbed her hands "You must come inside and sing for us," one of them insisted. "Please, please, please!"

Her face flushed with happiness.

"Darlings, my manager won't let me sing without his cut," she said evasively. "You need to book me properly sometime. I'd love to sing for you."

She blew them an air kiss with her free hand and tried to free the other one, but her admirers didn't loosen their grip.

"Just the one," they insisted. "*Losing My Mind*. Please!"

Bebe turned her head left and right. The road was deserted, nobody had seen her; she could do this. This spontaneous gig was exactly what the doctor had ordered.

"Fine," she said.

They led her into the piano bar where a crowd of drag queens were holding a karaoke event. Some of them had impeccable make-up on, Bebe noticed. It put her to shame. Glitter, feathers, disco-lights and size 11 heels – this place had it all.

"You look fabulous darling," one of the drag queens reassured her.

"You think?" she asked. "People keep telling me I'm too old."

"Nonsense," her admirer said and waved his hand dismissively to the side. "Jealousy, that's all it is."

Here, she was a star and treated like royalty. Drinks were ordered for her, she was begged for autographs and people were reminiscing about their favourite moment in her career.

"Remember that time you were on *Top of the Pops*?" a guy asked her. He had a grey woollen vest on and wore thick glasses, like her. He looked like a librarian.

"Which time?" she said. "I managed a few gigs there, thank God."

"The show with Renee and Renato," he said. "You sang right after them and they stayed and brought you flowers afterwards, remember? *Cabanero* was your song. I remember it well." She looked at him with astonishment. Even she had forgotten about the flowers from Renato. Renee had been nowhere to be seen.

"Aren't you a darling," she said and kissed him on the cheek. The man shrunk shyly and played nervously with his glasses.

"Bebe Bollinger to the stage," the DJ called out, "Or we'll all loose our minds." Her heart pounded with joy.

She sang four of her songs – pleased to see that almost her entire repertoire was in that karaoke machine. She made a note to get one of these things herself. It seemed a lot easier than her recording in the basement.

"So what is new with you?" another drag queen asked after the show. "Are you going on tour again sometime? I'll be at every show."

"She's not joking," added a stunning-looking woman, half Bebe's age. "She really is your number one fan."

"Well then I'm very pleased to meet you," Bebe said. "And thank you for sticking by me." She found it very difficult not to spill the beans about her Engelbert gig or ask these fans about their opinion on her further career plans. As loyal as these guys were, they were only a fraction of the music market and she needed to think bigger.

"Come back soon," the DJ said when she made her goodbyes.

Bebe left London on a high. In the car home she thought of the appreciation she had enjoyed. It made her wonder: where was Bertie's enthusiasm? Why was her manager not her biggest cheerleader? By the time she arrived home, late that night, she was very annoyed with him and had to vent her anger at something and someone. So she parked deliberately right across the yellow line on the lane. Christine would not dare do anything stupid, and if she did, Bebe would make a call to her new best friend Beth Cooper of the City of Cardiff police force and let the arm of the law clamp down on Christine's illegal policing. Given the current interest of the police and the outside world in the hamlet it was unlikely Christine would risk it.

Inside her home a flood of messages awaited her on her answerphone:

Most were desperate pleas from Helena for money or, alternatively, to let her and Dominic stay. Her daughter was naming hundreds of reasons why there was no other solution: His father had refused to help, a deposit cheque for rented accommodation had bounced, Dominic's stuff was all in storage but that would have to be paid for at some stage or they'd never see that back either. Whatever

116

Helena touched at the moment turned into a disaster and surely Bebe would find it in her heart to help her out, just this once.

Bebe and her ex-husband Richard had bailed their nuisance daughter out too many times in the past. In Bebe's experience, Helena would spend the money on booze and luxuries and then she would come crawling back for more, now that the purse strings had been loosened once. Money given was always wasted on other things, so it was hard to believe a single word Bebe heard. She would not give in, nor reward this kind of behaviour by supporting her daughter until the girl deserved it.

Bebe was delighted to find a charming phone call from Beth Cooper thanking her for the chat and telling her that Beth's flatmate Fred had been overly excited when she heard who the policewoman was dealing with. Fred was in show business, too, and she had played a CD of Bebe's music for Beth, who was impressed. All their friends present in the flat at the time had been most excited about the chances of a revival of the singer's career. For a moment Bebe feared that her secret had been let out and her prospects were now jinxed. Timing was so important in everything.

Oh never mind, she tried to calm herself. Any rumours could only help. How sweet of that detective to call her, though. That woman had much better manners than it appeared at first sight.

The most important call came from Bertie, who told her with barely contained excitement that the record label had gone with Bebe's vocals and the arrangement that she had sung on.

"Now sit down, Bebe, because I have also some bad news about that."

She did as he had asked and listened.

"They are not going to do a promotion on the basis of 'Best of British' right now," Bertie said.

"What do you mean?" she asked.

"You will not be credited for the time being. The producers would want to find out how the public responded to the song and then be flexible in their campaign."

"I haven't signed a contract saying that. They will have to credit me or take my vocals out of it," Bebe said angrily.

"Don't do anything hasty, darling. You and Engelbert are close friends, you can't let him down. You know that. Just wait and see. This is all early planning stages and there are his agents, producers,

117

the BBC and the European Broadcasting Union all interfering with the project. It's total chaos and every five minutes the song changes direction."

"But you are saying that my performance at Eurovision is not guaranteed?" Bib screamed. "You said I'd be seen by a billion viewers if I went on stage in Germany with him."

"It's Azerbaijan this year, and yes, the producers have not confirmed you'd be performing. This is a silent stepping stone for your career, darling. Come on, you must wish Engelbert well and do as they think is best for his chances. He's your friend. See it as a patriotic duty, a good deed."

Bebe sighed.

"Bertie that gig at *Comic Relief* had better be good when it's finished!"

Dora

As she went to bed, Dora saw with delight that Bebe had parked across the yellow dotted line. She could see Christine busy in her kitchen, so Christine must have noticed the violation of her 'rules'. On a hunch Dora switched off her lights and waited in the dark. As she had expected, a few minutes later Christine sneaked out of her front door with a torch of industrial strength to examine the parking situation.

Dora slipped downstairs, opened her front door and ran towards Christine.

"What are you doing there?" Dora challenged her. "Are you out clamping again?"

Christine looked perplexed and started a hasty retreat, stumbling over her own clumsy feet.

"Let's hear it, Christine, what on earth are you doing out here? I'm sure the police would like to know if strolling around in the snow is a pastime of yours. You wouldn't have a shovel on you?"

Christine could not find her composure fast enough. She just turned around and ran back towards her house.

"I am watching you!" Dora shouted after her.

Ian

"I don't think you need to worry about your reputation," Ian said impatiently when his wife woke him up to tell him about the incident. "Ever since you bought that clamp and locked the first wheel you've lost their goodwill. You're making too much of this. You and I are excellent drivers. We'll always get into our driveway, wherever they park. Try and let it go."

"But what if she tells the police that she saw me near that car?" Christine said nervously. "What shall I say then?"

"You can say that you thought Bebe had left her radio on or something like that. Nobody is going to pay any attention to it. Dora is just winding you up. Don't let her, and I mean that for your own sake," and with that he turned over.

"We're murder suspects, Ian. Of course that's going to matter and come back to haunt us. Oh I wish I'd never gone outside tonight."

He remained silent.

"This murder business is really scaring me," Christine confessed. "If the police have no suspect from outside the hamlet, then this little incident tonight could have disastrous consequences for me. I have a string of events coming up where I'm needed. I won't have time to sit at police stations answering more of their tedious questions, just because Dora is bad-mouthing me."

"Snooping around Bebe's car won't make you any more of a suspect, darling," Ian assured her. "You're being paranoid. You were sound asleep when the poor girl was murdered. They'll catch the real killer in no time. You have nothing to fear."

"What about you?" she asked, not letting this go.

"I don't know," he answered and shrugged. "I thought I'd be a prime suspect but I guess my strained ankle makes me too slow a mover to be considered a likely candidate. I could never have caught up with the girl like this, could I?"

"You and I know that, but the police might not buy into that as much as you hope."

He sighed and turned over.

"Try and get some sleep. You've got a long drive to Manchester tomorrow morning."

"Did you buy a new shovel?" she asked him.

"I forgot," he admitted.

"We need to replace the one the police took as evidence," she insisted.

"I know, Christine. I'll do it tomorrow. I promise."

"I wish I wouldn't have to go away and leave the hamlet until all of this has been sorted out."

"I know."

Chapter 16: Partners in Crime

Beth

At the police station in Carmarthen, Beth learned that the shovel had been officially identified as the murder weapon. The location of the wound and the angle of the impact on the head suggested a right-handed person taller than Ellie's 5 foot 4, probably 5 foot 6 – 9 inches height, although that was only a rough guideline. It was unlikely that someone hit her from a pedestal. Given the force used, Bebe with her dreadful arthritis would not have been able to kill the victim.

Colleagues from the City of London police had confirmed that Ellie's close friends and relatives had tight alibis, and all in locations far from the murder.

Forensics had not come up with any new leads from the crime scene itself. Because of the snowfall the culprit could not have come by car. DCI Warwick sent her a memo, suggesting that she hone the focus of the investigation on the hamlet and its residents. Obviously her boss didn't trust her at all, making her nervous that her days in the unit were numbered. She was getting desperate to solve this case. Stuck for ideas she decided to pay her 'new friend' Bebe a visit to discuss the matter. Who better to ask then the person who had just been eliminated from the suspect list, someone who had all the insider knowledge and also such a charming personality. It would give Beth the opportunity to examine Dora and Christine a bit closer.

"Oh darling, come on in," Bebe sang as she opened the door. "Now this time you will have to stay a bit longer and listen to my music. I need a fresh ear, and who better to judge than a techno chick, as you called yourself? Who knows, there could be a dance mix album of my songs, couldn't there?"

Beth smiled and walked past her hostess into the living room.

"Do you have any more clues or leads, yet?" Bebe asked excited as she ushered her guest on to the sofa and before she got an answer she went to the cupboard where she stored the drinks.

"Secret of the ongoing investigation, sorry. I'm not at liberty to divulge that information."

"I wish my daughter were a little more like you," Bebe said to Beth. "You seem so together for a young woman. Are you single?"

"I shouldn't be discussing my private life with you, either," Beth said, remembering many reprimands from Warwick about this. She smiled. Maybe she was being played, but she liked the attention. Her plan had been to use the growing familiarity to her advantage but she started to genuinely like Bebe and lost her professional reserve far too quickly. Warwick was right: she behaved like an amateur, not like a Detective Sergeant.

"Yeah, I'm afraid I am single," Beth confessed, brushing her doubts aside. "I saw a pilot for a while, but that didn't work out at all. Complete nightmare."

"I guess that pilot wanted a right bimbo by his side and not an intelligent, strong-willed woman with a mind of her own like you," Bebe said with a wink. "I never met the guy but I'm already pleased you are no longer with him."

"Oh, I thought you worked in show business, and you didn't figure I like women? You disappoint me, Bebe!"

"Oh my God, you're right. I should have seen it," Bebe said laughing. "In my defence, you are the campest lesbian I have ever seen. You could pass as a gay man trapped in that body. That's probably why we get on so well."

Beth smirked at the compliment.

"Can I push you to another Bloody Mary, or is it too soon for one?"

"I haven't had lunch, so I better not," Beth said. "Besides, I'm trying to become healthier. My Buddhist teacher says that alcohol consumption interferes with our quest to understand and develop the mind. The Buddha encouraged his followers to refrain from consuming any kind of intoxicant."

"I see," Bebe said. "Well, I find that the odd drink helps my inspiration."

She mixed two Bloody Marys regardless and handed one to Beth, who reluctantly took it.

"The drink helps my detecting, too," Beth admitted. "It relaxes me and sometimes I suddenly see connections that I missed when I was sober. It defies belief. It is highly inappropriate though."

"Professionalism can be overrated," Bebe said. "Results are what count."

"Anyway," Beth said, "tell me about Helena's husband."

"Aidan? A good topic. Do you think he could have done it?" Bebe asked.

"No," Beth replied. "I can't see why he would kill Ellie. Helena maybe, or Dominic, but Ellie hadn't done anything."

"I've tried to get hold of him but he doesn't answer his phone," Bebe reported.

"He's in Greece with his sister and has been there since before the time of the murder," Beth said. "He knew about the affair, which is why he left the country. I'm only asking you because I want to understand more about the scenario."

"Oh Helena's husband is a lovely guy, but a complete pushover," Bebe said. "I never thought he would be, at first he seemed to have such a positive and stabilising influence on her, but then he lost the reins and she went off and did whatever she liked. And she's done so ever since. I'm pretty sure she's cheated on him before – mind you, they'd only been together for two months before they got married; that says it all."

"Will he take her back once Dominic has found someone more affluent?"

"Possibly. I doubt that Helena will go back to him, though. She clearly needs more excitement. She must get that from her father," Bebe sighed.

"You don't have any contact with your ex-husband?" Beth asked.

"None at all, I'm afraid. I would like to see him at celebrations, if Helena had any of those, but he takes too little interest in his daughter. I think his new girlfriend is even younger than Helena. Some days I just despise the music industry and the sleazy characters in it. Could you frame him for me?" Bebe asked jokingly.

"He'd probably deserve it," Beth said, "but no. We checked him out, of course, and you cannot beat being in Thailand at the time of the murder as an alibi, can you. He would have had a tough time doing that. It's hard to imagine he'd kill the love rival of his daughter if he takes so little interest in her, as you say."

"You're right," Bebe agreed. "Although a scandal around his abandoned daughter would be a thrill in his circles, I guess. For him that publicity would add to his wild image."

"Which brings us back to the residents here and their possible motives to kill Ellie Seaborne," Beth said in a sudden moment of focus and clarity. That Bebe had a way of lulling one in.

"Darling, I can't think of any motives," Bebe said. "I'm not in a serious mood."

"Go on, tell me whatever springs to your mind," Beth said. "Start with Mr Morris."

"If it was Ian he must have done it to protect his wife," Bebe said. "I think it's safe to assume that he and the victim didn't have an affair with each other, if she can pull a Dominic. Ian is a charming man. Very strong. He can definitely swing a shovel and the body was found on his doorstep. But again: he's got that injury, and why would he do such a thing?"

"Maybe it has something to do with his business. We've found no connections yet but their paths could have crossed on a professional level," Beth pondered aloud. "Someone in Cardiff is checking out those possibilities."

"Ian lives with a dragon but is still nothing but polite; to his wife and to everyone else," Bebe said. "I would think he'd kill his wife first before anyone else."

Beth had to laugh.

"So we've got Ian down as a maybe," Beth said. "If it wasn't Ian, how about Christine?"

Bebe took a long sip of her Bloody Mary. "There's got to be a thousand and one scenarios imaginable. The woman has so many pet hates and odd ideas in her head. For example, Ellie could have parked in the wrong place or her car leaked oil, she might have destroyed one of the plants or she was using her mobile phone outside Christine's window. Anyone could offend Christine without ever knowing it. Character-wise Christine is a great suspect, but let's face it, she'd probably hate to leave a mess and would have disposed of the body right away. She couldn't just let the body lie there."

Beth laughed.

"Good points," Beth said. "Is she strong enough to swing the shovel?"

"Definitely," Bebe said. "She's clamped my car because it was parked the wrong way. That says it all."

Beth made a note of this on her pad.

"So what about Dora?" she asked.

124

Her host's brow creased in thought. "I'm afraid I know very little concrete about her. She's a bit common, always wearing next to nothing, but she seems so self-contained and restrained. She shouts and barks but she doesn't bite, that's what I think. She would defend herself against Ellie, but unless there is some secret side to her, I cannot see her attacking someone in cold blood. And what would Dora be doing outside of Ian's house? It would have to be one of the Morris's for sure."

"Self-contained and restrained would fit the profile of a killer so quick and effective," Beth said. "If only the snow had not erased all evidence we might know more, so far we are lacking proof and, most of all, a motive." She sighed. "This is going to be a long headache of a case and I'll be demoted at the end of it."

"Now, now, don't be so negative," Bebe said. "There must be more background checking you can do. The right pointers will come up, for sure."

If only, Beth thought.

"We have tried everything obvious," she admitted, "but we cannot find anything else connecting the victim to the hamlet but your daughter. Several teams spent days going over documents, calling people to confirm alibis. My boss is still doing half of my work because he doesn't trust me and we've got nothing."

"It is an odd case," Bebe said and mixed another Blood Mary.

Beth tried hard to find a detail she hadn't thought about.

"The blood in the snow shows clearly Ellie was attacked near the Morris entrance," the detective said. "Unless a stranger has waited for her there, who else could it be if not Mr or Mrs Morris? No money was taken, no signs of sexual abuse. It's a total mystery."

"Well the simplest explanation is often the most plausible one. If Ellie had no enemies than it has to be Christine who thought it was an intruder and defended herself," Bebe said.

"If that were the case then Ellie's body shouldn't have been facing the road. It would appear she was already leaving the premises and not really trespassing," Beth pointed out.

"That would have been no difference to Christine. She's a psychopath! Maybe she thought Ellie was Dora, strolling around her property to provoke her? That's the kind of thing Dora might do, and Christine hates that woman," Bebe said.

"Well, thanks for sharing your speculations with me, that certainly helped me a bit to become clearer in my head," Beth said.

"Another Bloody Mary to wash away the clear?" Bebe suggested.

"Would be rude not to."

Beth

A few hours later Beth was slurring her words and unable to drive home. Bebe had long started to play on the piano and sing her repertoire. To her surprise, Beth had encouraged her and sung along.

"You connect me to a different type of audience," Bebe had said enthusiastically during her performance. "The young dance and techno crowd. If I can get you excited about my music then there's still hope."

The two had exhausted themselves soon enough, though, and Beth fell into the bed in one of Bebe's many guest bedrooms.

She had a rude awakening when her boss called her the next morning asking why she was not in the Cardiff office for a scheduled briefing. It was 11am and Beth had slept for over 12 hours. Her alarm either had not gone off or she had managed to switch it off. She rushed downstairs but couldn't find her hostess anywhere. Bebe probably had locked herself into the basement, as she had said she often did. Beth had a long drive ahead of her and no time for long farewells, although she could have murdered for a coffee.

DCI Warwick was furious with her on the phone and Beth realised she was in big trouble. Not only was she late for her meeting with the London crew of the investigation – who had come all the way for this - she would have nothing to tell apart from the fact that she had slept in Bebe's house. Warwick wouldn't be surprised to learn that Beth had improper relations with one of the subjects of the investigation. He'd already implied as much to her on numerous previous occasions. If only she had some leads to show him.

Ian

As Beth jumped into her car and sped off to London, Ian watched from his window and he didn't like what he saw one bit. The detective and Bebe getting along so well could not be good news. Christine had told him that the detective's car had been outside overnight. That had to mean that Bebe, Helena and her beau were no longer suspects in the murder case, which would bring the suspicion and the investigation back to the other three residents of the hamlet for sure. Since the body had been on his grounds, the police would be digging deep into his and Christine's past. What skeletons would they find? He could think of a few unpleasant surprises if the police knew where to look for them.

He was not so concerned about himself but for his wife. Christine had a bad name in the neighbourhood and had to be the prime suspect now. She would not be able to handle all the stress that an intense investigation into their private life might bring with it. Christine suffered so much already, if police officers were now to start coming to their door on a regular basis it would clearly tip her over the edge.

He could only hope that there were other leads, or that the lack of witnesses and concrete evidence would end the investigation. His task of keeping Christine balanced and this side of sanity was really hard some days. If it was not the neighbours' garden or the parking, it was something on the road, the inconsideration of others, their noise, their breath, their sheer existence – something always bothered Christine. He appreciated that her job was demanding, but instead of winding down and relaxing when she was at home she was just as tense and controlling here. When he had first met her he'd admired her organisational skills and her strength to see things through. Since then he had come to see the complete picture of a compulsive woman. He still loved his wife, but didn't always love his life with her.

The farm next door had been a source of great distress for Christine. After they had moved to Llangurrey the noise from the cow sheds soon became a worry and caused her to miss out on her precious sleep. Working full time in a high-powered position, preparing for her conferences at home and running a tight ship in her house, totally exhausted her. How she could find energy to even notice, let alone focus, on anything outside her immediate surroundings was beyond him.

They had been lucky, though. Rationalisation processes at the farm shut down the cow shed soon after he and his wife had arrived in the hamlet.

Then there were grave concerns for Christine over some building work going on at the farm. It only lasted a few days and turned out to be nothing more dramatic than taking out equipment for sale or presumably to transfer to the new cow shed on a different site. However, it made Christine fear that maybe the farmer was flipping the property and might develop it into apartment blocks, thereby increasing traffic and noise in the hamlet. The relief when the work stopped and nothing else ever came of it was enormous.

Since the cows no longer grazed there, suddenly there was an increase in the number of ramblers passing by the end of their garden, shamelessly crossing the gated field next door. This invasion of her privacy was a thorn in Christine's side. She posted several signs at the farm gate to advise hikers that they were not allowed on the field, but few seemed to take notice. On sunny weekends that was a major headache for her. Now this business with the corpse and the police and press attention might be just a little too much. He worried for her sanity. What could he do to distract her and to divert their suspicions? If only he could think of something . . .

Dora

Dora also saw the detective leaving Llangurrey. She could see Bebe's driveway from her bathroom window, only she had not noticed the officer's car outside Bebe's house the night before. Dora assumed that Bebe had been interviewed by the police yet again and that there was new information and leads on the case that involved the singer. Bebe would hate the scandal.

Dora regretted that it was not Christine who was targeted. She would deserve the harassment more, given how happily she dished it out to her and Bebe. Then again, maybe pushing the fragile bundle of nerves over the edge might backfire, regardless of how much *schadenfreude* there would have been.

Still, there were other reasons to be happy: her daughters were due to pay a visit. It was their grandmother's birthday this week and they had a habit of just showing up when they had access to the Jenkins family chauffeur to take them across the beautiful Brecon Beacons.

She hoped they would, but then again she knew that being young and having divorced parents meant extra time spent with grown-ups and that simply wasn't as much fun as being with your peers. If her daughters would show that would be great, but if they didn't, she knew it to be a sign that they were popular and busy with their own lives. A mother could not hope for more.

By lunchtime her daughter Julia called to let her know that she would not be coming today after all.

"I'm not supposed to tell you but Daddy got back from his holidays this morning, engaged to his secretary. Grandmother has threatened to disinherit him and leave everything to us instead," Julia said.

Dora almost fell over laughing. "He's getting married again? How old do we think his secretary is? Tell me it's not the one with the spider tattoo and the green glasses?"

"No, that was Theresa. She left a few months ago. This is Vera, her replacement. Despite being named Vera, I think she's in her late twenties, but I'm not entirely sure. "

"Oh my poor darling children," Dora said, suppressing her laughter. "I hope you don't mind his new liaison."

"I can't say I care one way or another," her daughter said. "We hardly see Daddy anyway these days. It makes no difference if Vera stays the night as well as the days."

"How is Isabella taking it?" Dora asked.

"She couldn't care less," Julia replied. "She's got a boyfriend in the village near our boarding school now. She didn't even show up for grandmother's birthday, and got away with it. Grandmother is fuming over that as well. I doubt you'll see Isabella anytime soon. I'll try and keep away from all the drama, too."

"I don't blame you, darling. You can always come and stay here if you need a little peace and quiet."

"Thanks, Mom. How is the murder case going?"

"Nothing much going on there," Dora replied. "I don't have even the remotest idea who the police suspect. The way I see it, nobody who has a motive could have done it, and everyone who could have done it has no motive."

"Are you a suspect, too?" Julia asked.

"I guess I am," Dora said. "I was in the vicinity, although fast asleep at the time. No witnesses for that, though. I certainly could have done it."

"And did you?" Julia asked.

"What a question to ask your own mother," Dora said and laughed.

"Mom, I wouldn't want to be on the wrong side of you," her daughter replied.

"True," Dora said.

"I'm glad you're taking Daddy's news so well," Julia said.

"It doesn't concern me, really," Dora said. "I hope this girl will make him happy. He's not for me, but your father is a good man."

"That's very noble of you, Mom."

"I know," Dora sighed and rang off.

Since her daughters were not visiting, Dora had plenty of time on her hands. She decided to take advantage of the favourable weather and re-stock her art supplies. If she should be snowed in once again, she'd need to keep herself occupied. Dora got into her car and headed towards Carmarthen. She was still on the tree-lined lane towards the main road, driving past hardened banks of snow piled there by the ploughs. The pristine whiteness now turned black and grey from dirt thrown up by the traffic. Dora wondered when the snow would finally be gone. It had lost its appeal a long time ago. She noticed the blur of an animal – a squirrel perhaps – dashing in front of the car, Dora hit the brake, but to no avail. The car didn't respond. Dora swung the wheel to avoid hitting the animal, but the road was far too icy for such a risky manoeuvre. The car swerved off course, spinning on some black ice and Dora could only watch helplessly as it smashed head-on into a tree.

Chapter 17: The Hair Do

Bebe

Bebe spent the morning in the basement, fully motivated from the evening before. The admiration from such an unlikely source had truly inspired her. She hardly slept a wink all night as new ideas kept flooding into her mind and she kept switching the light on to write them down. At seven o'clock she gave up on sleep and went downstairs to make a few recordings before breakfast. One thing led to another and before long it was lunchtime and when Bebe went upstairs to wake her guest, Beth had long gone. There was a considerate 'Thank You' posted on the mirror by the door. How sweet.

Bebe decided to call her friend Bryn to ask him round to do her hair. She was in the mood for a makeover but, unfortunately, he wasn't in. She left him a message and then rang Bertie instead.

"I forgot to tell you," she bubbled excitedly, "Will Young has named me as one of his idols on that TV show. You should try and contact his agent, so that he and I can get together and maybe discuss some ideas. I can't believe I forgot to mention that to you earlier. Suddenly there's so much going on."

"You did mention it, Bebe," Bertie said. "I'm already on the case."

"Good," she said. "And while you're at it, think about approaching Michael Buble, too. He and I share a lot of common ground."

"Of course you do," Bertie said.

She was just about to launch into a list of other suitable singing partners when the doorbell rang.

"I've got to go Bertie," she said and hung up. She could tell he wasn't listening anyway. She wondered who it could be. Maybe Bryn?"

Outside, however, stood Helena with Dominic.

Bebe shut the door immediately and shouted: "Go away!"

"I need you, mother," Helena begged and continued to knock. "Daddy is in Thailand. When he's back he promised to sort us out. We only need to stay a few nights until then. Please don't make us sleep rough."

Bebe frowned. She could suddenly see the headline: *Comic Relief singer abandons daughter, lets her sleep in the cold*. No, she couldn't risk that now. In a moment of weakness and against her better judgement, she opened the door again and let Helena and her boyfriend inside.

"Only a few nights," she said sternly. "And no loud music, trashing the place or rude behaviour. Is that understood?"

"Yes," Dominic and Helena said in unison. Helena tried to hug her mother but Bebe stepped back to keep her assumed air of authority.

"Fine, then let me show you to your room," she said instead and marched up the stairs.

The couple followed and then stayed put when Bebe went back downstairs to train on her Wii Sport. She put on loud music just in case her visitors were going to be noisy. She was in a happy mood and didn't want it spoilt.

Half an hour later Bryn arrived to do her hair. She had a fantastic time bringing him up to scratch with all the new developments.

"Am I making a fool of myself?" she asked him. "Do you think *Comic Relief* is going to be big enough to re-launch my career?"

Bryn stroked through her hair with his brush, a sensation that always soothed her.

"Of course it is big enough to bring you back into the limelight, sweetie" he said. "It's long overdue your return. Don't worry, lovely, you'll show them all how it's done."

The silence from Helena's room was even more encouraging. Maybe her daughter for once was desperate and humble enough to behave and follow her mother's instructions. Bebe was in a daring mood and asked Bryn to put in a few more highlights in her hair than usual. After all the talk about looking old and losing her eyesight for the *Comic Relief* gag she was eager to look younger, if for no other reason than for her own sense of youth. On the sketch she would appear old and awful. She hoped that there would be follow-up interviews and chat show appearances, when her rejuvenated look might come in handy.

Bryn was sceptical at first but he had never been able to deny her a wish and went ahead as she asked. During his work he told her all about his mother's health problems and his other clients' gossip, interspersed with compliments for her. Time flew by in his hands.

When Bebe saw the finished product in her bathroom mirror, however, she cringed. It looked a little tarty and desperate. She should have listened to him.

"Don't worry," Bryn reassured her. "You always look fabulous, darling. Truth be told: next to Engelbert you'll always be a spring chicken anyway."

"You mustn't tell a soul about this," she asked him. "Everything is still hush-hush, you know."

"Of course," he said. "I'm the soul of discretion."

After they had gone over Bebe's news a few more times Bryn had to go. She was on a high, though, thanks to his encouragement and the pleasant time with Beth the night before. She saw Bryn to the door and then went to her living room where two scantily dressed lovers had lit a fire, and sat watching horror films on her TV and rapidly depleting her stock of gin.

"You look awful, Mother," Helena said and giggled. "Bryn is getting old. You need a new stylist."

"Charming," was all Bebe could say and left the room. She stomped down to the basement, but now she was in no mood for singing. She texted her ex-husband to find out when he would be back in the UK, but to no avail. He rarely replied and she got a feeling that he was unaware of his daughter's distress and, even if he did know about it, he had no intention of rescuing her. Helena probably had made up the part about his promise and Bebe had been stupid enough to fall for it.

Chapter 18: A Trip North

Beth

Back in Cardiff in the DCI's office, Warwick brought Beth up to scratch with the investigation. There had been a few new leads — at last!

"Mrs Seaborne and Mrs Morris actually crossed paths in a very unpleasant way," he said as soon as Beth had sat down by his desk. "One witness, a friend of the deceased, has remembered the name Christine Morris very well. Their first business internship was with Christine's event management firm. Although that was some ten years back, it had gone horribly wrong for our victim, according to the company files, and resulted in her changing direction in her career."

"That's interesting," Beth said, making notes like an obedient secretary. She was delighted that they had something concrete, but wished it hadn't come from her smug boss.

"We have to bring Mrs Morris in for questioning," Warwick said. He had his hands crossed behind his head and was leaning into his chair and rocking back and forth like an impatient teenager. "She said she never knew the victim."

"In her defence," Beth intervened, "the victim has changed her name and hair colour, is ten years older and was dead when Mrs Morris saw her. If Mrs Morris isn't the murderer, then it's quite possible she really didn't know."

"True," Warwick said unconvinced, and continued with his swivel chair acrobatics, "but such 'coincidences' usually add up to something in my experience."

"So what is the scenario you're picturing?" Beth asked, fascinated more by his ability not to fall off the chair than by his case assumptions. "It was Ellie who should have killed Mrs Morris, not the other way round, if their past is anything to go by," she pointed out.

Warwick huffed.

"Mrs Morris seems highly strung, according to all reports. She might have felt threatened when she saw Mrs Seaborne come to the house and so she killed her in self-defence. It is a scenario well worth looking into."

"It's obvious that Ellie was in the hamlet to look for her husband," Beth replied. "You keep saying that the simplest explanation is usually the right one."

"And that's true," Warwick said. "Ellie was there because of her husband, then runs into the psycho boss from hell who wrote a damaging report on her and ended her first career choice in the middle of the night. Maybe she decided to take out her anger on Mrs Morris, was caught trespassing and then killed. Stranger things have happened."

Beth looked at her boss with bewilderment.

"You're not really buying into this, are you?" she asked.

"I'm telling you to use your own imagination and dig around a little," Warwick said. "What happened to my star DS with the high success rate? Bring her in, apply some pressure and show me some results."

"I had hoped for evidence linking the two of them in a more recent and relevant fashion," Beth said.

"It's a lot better than what we had yesterday," he said. The rocking of his chair became more intense.

"Do you have any other leads?" Beth asked. "What about the list of Dominic's former lovers? Have you spoken to any of them?"

Warwick grinned.

"Of course I have," he said and abruptly stopped his acrobatics. He picked up a small orange file, leaned forward and handed it to her.

"I checked all of them out. There were some real beauties that have dated our underwear model. Sadly, for our purpose, they all have an alibi. All but one, and she's happily married and seems to have moved on to better things. She's coming in later today to speak with us, just in case," he said. "Her name's Lorraine Laffey," he added with a dreamy look in his eyes.

"Thanks," Beth said.

"Don't mention it."

"Mrs Morris is at a conference in Manchester, as far as I'm aware," Beth said. "She won't be pleased to be called in and frankly, with a weak case like this, I'm not sure it's even fair to force her into the station."

"Then go after her there, Cooper," he said. "If a suspect's convenience is so important to you, put in the leg work. My God, you behave as if this is your first case. There's a lot of evidence pointing at this woman. If this was my investigation she'd be sitting here with a lawyer. I'm tempted to take this case off your hands the way things are going."

Beth obediently got into her car and drove to the conference centre near Manchester. The scenery wasn't as pretty as it was on her trips to Carmarthen. Instead of the hilly white and green and a peek of the Brecon Beacons she saw nothing but cars, concrete and rush-hour frenzy.

She had to admit that Warwick had a point. Although she believed Christine to be innocent and the evidence was far from conclusive, there was plenty of reason to be suspicious. On the drive she listened to Fred's Bebe Bollinger CD. It was a long car journey through poor weather conditions but the music cheered her up. Bebe did have a fine voice, and underneath the diva behaviour there seemed to live a fine lady. She scolded herself for being so biased and unprofessional, but she couldn't help it. She didn't blame Warwick for wanting her off this case.

At the conference centre Beth had a hard time locating Christine Morris. First, the woman didn't answer her mobile phone and someone had to page her. Then, when she arrived at the reception desk, she was clearly not amused to see the detective waiting for her. Christine looked very different with make-up on, heels and a tight-fitting grey skirt and blazer.

"I'm in the middle of work," she hissed, looking nervously around her before putting her professional smile back on.

"I'm sorry, but I do need to speak to you urgently," Beth said. "We can do this here and now somewhere private or I'll have to take you to a police station."

Christine froze.

"I've done nothing wrong," she insisted. Her voice was shrill and she started to play nervously with her delegation badge. Her right eye twitched every so often.

"Then it won't take long, Mrs Morris," Beth said. "I do need to ask a few questions and I came a long way to ask them, out of courtesy to your professional life. My superiors thought I was being too lenient. I'd appreciate a little cooperation."

"Alright then," Christine sighed. "Follow me."

She stomped down a corridor and used her key card to open the door to a tiny office with just enough space for a single table and two chairs. Christine cleared a section of the table for Beth and then sat down on a chair opposite, her legs and arms crossed and her foot tapping on the floor.

"Do start," she said, glaring across at her interrogator. "Let's get this over with."

"Alright then," Beth said and opened her notebook.

"It's come to our attention that you and the deceased did know each other after all," she said. "A fact that you denied . . ."

Christine looked genuinely puzzled.

Beth took a photo from a folder and laid it on the table.

"Have another good look at Ellie Seaborne."

Christine picked up the picture and stared long and hard at it.

"No," she said. "She looks vaguely familiar but I'm afraid I cannot place her. I will say that the picture is quite different from the image I had after seeing her dead body on my driveway."

"What if I told you that her maiden name was Ellie Winterbottom?"

Christine hesitated for a while, then she shook her head.

"Still rings no bells," she said, building herself up in her chair and leaning forward. "How do you suppose I know her?" she asked.

"Wind back the clock a few years," Beth said, "and remember an innocent intern at your firm who you wrote a devastating assessment for. Following her time with you, Ellie Winterbottom had a dreadful reference to her name, had to abandon her career plans for event management and changed course towards publishing."

Christine suddenly nodded and smiled as if she was more relieved she had figured out what the police meant than worried about the implications of it.

"Of course, I remember now," she said. "I would never have recognised her with her red hair. She aged well."

"So tell us a little more about it," Beth demanded. She was gobsmacked how cool Christine suddenly was, for someone who suffered from anxiety and had just been told there was a murder motive linking them to a dead body on their doorstep.

"If you know about Mrs Winterbottom's time in my company then you will probably have read my full assessment. You know the story," Christine said. "What else can I tell you? Ellie was dreadfully disorganised and unprofessional. I had nothing against the girl, in fact, I felt very sorry for her. She had such great aspirations but simply no talent to make them true. Nothing I asked her to do was ever done properly. She lost memos, forgot to take important details down and spoke to clients out of tone. She wasn't in the least suited for a career in events management and I spared her and us a lot of grief by stopping her in her tracks before she wasted any more time on a path that would never lead to success. As far as I remember now, she took it remarkably well and seemed even relieved when I told her."

Beth let that sink in.

"So you claim that there were no hard feelings between the two of you?" she asked after a long pause, which was intended to make the other woman uncomfortable.

"On the contrary," Christine said, most animated. "My secretary knew that Ellie was a bookworm and we found her the placement with a publisher, so the poor thing wouldn't be stranded. She lost one career path because of me but she got onto the other one thanks to my support. You know how important PR is in my business. I can't afford to have disgruntled staff harm my reputation. I went out of my way to part on good terms with her and she was extremely grateful for my help."

"And yet, the woman shows up in the middle of the night outside your house and is found dead in the morning on your driveway," Beth said, suggestively. "That seems an odd coincidence," she pointed out. "How do you think any jury will see this?"

Christine's face flustered and her cheeks trembled.

"This is preposterous," she said. "It's obvious that the woman was in Llangurrey to look for her philandering husband."

"Yes," Beth said. "Then you spotted her on your driveway that night from your bedroom window. You didn't know about the love triangle next door. You thought she had come to seek revenge. You're a nervous person, driven by anxiety and prone to exaggeration, according to witness statements. And why wouldn't you be concerned, even if it wasn't someone from a dark moment of your past? Any person loitering on your property must be suspect to you, more so when it's dark and the roads are blocked. The police won't help you: they can't get through the snow. You feel threatened, you aren't going to wait for her to make the first move. Your husband can't kill a fly and doesn't take you seriously. Here's an intruder, someone you can legitimately defend yourself against. She's trespassing . . . a woman who's out to get you . . . maybe planning to burgle you or kill you. You have to act while she's still unsuspecting. It's understandable, frightened people get carried away..."

"I did no such thing," Christine screeched and stood up. Tears glistened in her eyes. "How dare you suggest I did?"

"The body was on your driveway, Mrs Morris," Beth said. "You said yourself you are suffering from anxiety. Forgive me for taking that possibility into account. Your resentful attitude towards the investigation isn't working in your favour either."

"If I had hit her with the shovel I would have called the police that instant or disposed of the body right away, wouldn't I?" Christine said. "Why leave her there?"

"That's a good question," Beth said. "We call it an alibi. By leaving her there you gave us a reason to believe that it couldn't be you, exactly because it wouldn't make sense. If you can pull it off, it is a clever move!"

Christine's hands trembled. She sat back down and put them firmly on her shaky legs. Beth knew it wasn't ethical to push a fragile woman so hard, but she felt it necessary to get nearer the truth. Christine Morris was hiding something.

"Picture this" Beth said. "After the event, you call your husband for help; he knows about the love triangle, recognises Ellie and realises that suspicion will fall on the more obvious connection to the hamlet, so you cover your tracks and go to bed as if nothing ever happened, putting the blame at someone else's door."

"That's a nice little yarn you've spun," Christine said. She suddenly had her composure back, but her eyes were full of hate. "I wish I had time for your far-fetched theories. Unfortunately, I'm in the middle of a busy conference. I can assure you I didn't kill Ellie Winterbottom on my driveway that night. I went to sleep as I told you and didn't find out about her until the next morning. I didn't recognise her as the intern and if I had, I would have spoken to her and asked her what she was doing here in the middle of the night. She was useless as an intern but she was a lovely girl and wouldn't have frightened me in the least."

Beth jotted down some notes, but she could tell that even this was not bothering Mrs Morris now. The moment of weakness had passed and Beth was no longer sure that the woman had anything to hide in the first place.

"Can I please return to my work now?" Christine asked.

"Yes." Beth nodded. "For now."

It was past midnight when Beth got back to her flat in Cardiff. She didn't look forward to meeting Warwick the next day. She knew he wouldn't be pleased with the way the interview with Christine had gone. Then again – what had he expected? Beth had never bought into his theory that Christine was connected to the murder, so it had been inevitable that she hadn't produced any concrete results. In her assessment, Christine had repudiated all suspicions. Mrs Seaborne had enjoyed a decent career in the publishing industry, so an old, professional grudge didn't seem likely. The intruder-theory also didn't hold beyond reasonable doubt. The DCI was scraping the bottom of the barrel with his quest to make a motive stick. He probably knew it, too. His obsession with quick results for the crime statistics often clouded his judgement. Warwick should have gone to Manchester himself and left Beth to question Dominic's ex, Lorraine Laffey, but it seemed on this occasion her boss had chosen eye candy over statistics. Beth could imagine how that interview had gone.

Chapter 19: New Leads

Things did turn out differently, though. When Beth got to work the next morning her boss had big news. She noticed it the moment she got into his office and saw him standing up, pacing the room instead of playing with his swivel chair.

"Dora Jenkins was involved in a car accident yesterday and has been admitted to a private hospital in Carmarthen," he told her full of excitement.

"Is she alright?" Beth asked, genuinely concerned for the beautiful woman.

"Yes," he said, raising his eyebrows to clock his surprise at her response, "she's fine. Whiplash, a few scratches and a broken rib. She'll be out soon."

"Thank God."

"What interests us about this is that her brakes didn't work," Warwick said and looked intently at her as though Beth herself had somehow been involved. "Mrs Jenkins was lucky. She was attempting to stop for a squirrel on an empty road. Had she tried to slow her vehicle down closer to the junction with the main road or for another vehicle in the narrow lane this could have had fatal consequences for her. The mechanics say that her car might have been tampered with. We have a team looking into that right now."

Beth cringed.

"Do you think there is more than one killer on the loose in Llangurrey?" she asked.

"Things don't look good for Mrs Morris now," he said, rubbing his hands together. "She's obsessed with the parking in the lane and that makes her the prime suspect for tampering with cars. After all, she recently clamped Mrs Bolton's car. Mrs Jenkins stated also that she had seen Mrs Morris on the lane by Mrs Bolton's car late the night before the accident. That and her psychological profile together make for a fascinating case study."

"Are you going to arrest her?"

"I'm thinking about it but we need to have the full report about the car before we can go ahead with that. There is a remote possibility that all Mrs Morris did was cut the brakes. There is another strong suspect for the murder of Mrs Seaborne right now."

"There is?" Beth asked.

"Yes," Warwick said, seemingly spreading the smugness that bit thicker. "Remember Lorraine Laffey, Dominic Seaborne's ex? She came in yesterday and made a statement that she was at home all Thursday."

"I remember," Beth said, watching her boss parading around the room like a proud little boy.

"To back up her alibi she allowed us to access her mobile phone records so we could verify that she never left her house on Thursday. That was very foolish of her. Although the records confirmed that she had not been to Llangurrey that day, they showed that she has been to the Carmarthen area several times in the past week. Digging a bit deeper we found that she separated from her husband last year, a fact that she failed to mention to me during the initial interview. And while her phone was at home on Thursday, according to a location stamp on a Facebook post of hers she was in Carmarthen round about the time of Ellie's death. When people use social media for their alibis they really should know better how they work and eliminate such obvious traces."

"Blimey," Beth said.

"Exactly," Warwick said. "She broke down immediately and admitted to lying. She said she was in the area stalking Dominic and Helena, but denies any knowledge of the killing."

"Do you believe her?" Beth asked. She understood a little better why nobody had been arrested yet. In the presence of several suspects it was hard to judge which the most likely one was. It was still nothing a jury would be able to make stick, beyond reasonable doubt.

"Of course I don't believe her," Peter said abruptly. "We know now that she stayed at the Lodger's Inn in Carmarthen on Thursday night. According to the room key log she entered her room and didn't leave until the morning. We've requested access to the footage from the security camera to double check. Someone from the Carmarthen station is looking into it. At the moment we have to give her the benefit of the doubt. But her story stinks."

"Yes," Beth agreed, "it does. I've got a team meeting set for tomorrow morning. I hope we'll have the result by then. Lorraine could have easily left the door on a latch and sneaked out, couldn't she?" Beth suggested. "If she was cunning enough to leave her phone at home, she would have found it easy to play more tricks. The question is, whether she was clever enough to pull it off. Judging by her Facebook posting, it doesn't look like she thought it all the way through."

"Exactly Cooper," Warwick said. "Now you're starting to think like a detective."

Beth let that insult pass.

"Just as well," she said instead. "I can't imagine Mrs Morris being a double murderer, however much I dislike that woman."

"I can imagine that very easily," he said, "but, unlike you, I really don't care one way or another as long as we close the case pronto and move on to the next one. So I suggest you use the time constructively until we have more on Mrs Laffey and grill Mr Morris about his wife's connection to the victim. If it was her, he's likely to be her accomplice. See if you can squeeze him a little. He might deviate from their previous statements."

"Fine, boss."

Beth got up and made for the door.

"And *Cooper*, go and see Mrs Jenkins in hospital."

"OK," she said obediently and marched off, cursing to herself.

When Beth reached Llangurrey a few hours later, Ian Morris wasn't home. While she waited for someone to answer the door she looked around the building to get another feel for the location of the crime. She recalled the layout of the cottage inside. If Christine had left her bedroom to kill Ellie Seaborne, would it have been possible for her husband not to notice? The stairs were very noisy, as was the creaking of the front door. There was a snow storm that night, would one hear the door creak? His office was next to the bedroom upstairs. Then Beth suddenly remembered that Christine had mentioned something about her husband using headphones. Maybe the woman had killed Ellie in cold blood and was even fooling her own husband. Her success as a businesswoman suggested Christine Morris could be a lot more calculating and cunning than Beth gave her credit for. Her instincts were, however, decisively against Christine as a suspect. If she *was* the murderer, then Ian Morris might have been her accomplice. She still thought a scenario involving Dominic Seaborne more probable, but she hated to admit it: Warwick had solved more crimes than she had, and Christine Morris as the murderer was the simplest solution.

Beth turned around and studied the Bolton residence. Maybe she could pay Bebe a brief visit and stay for a friendly beverage. There was a good chance that by the afternoon Warwick had linked Lorraine Laffey to the murder scene and the whole case was closed anyway. Beth sensed that she was probably wasting her time.

What she hadn't foreseen though was Dominic Seaborne opening Bebe's door in a fluffy morning gown that hardly covered his underpants. She was grateful that at least he was wearing some. God, that man was tall.

"Can I help you, officer?" Dominic said, again winking at her as if it was an innate reflex for him to flirt.

"Yes," Beth said, "by confessing to the murder, so I can take the rest of the week off."

Dominic looked baffled.

"Only joking, I am," Beth said, glad to have found a way to shut him up. "May I speak to Bebe? Is she at home?"

"She's in the basement, recording stuff," he said and pointed at the door behind him. "Down this way . . ."

He turned around and walked towards the living room, the robe revealing two bare butt cheeks as he did so. Beth grinned. It had been years since she had known someone wearing a jockstrap. These had to stem from his time as an underwear model.

Bemused she closed the front door and headed for the basement.

Bebe was wearing a wide purple robe and a pink feather boa. Beth chuckled. You couldn't make this stuff up.

"I know I look silly, dear," Bebe said and pointed at her outfit. "Some days I need to get into these costumes to make myself feel like a star. My daughter and her new boyfriend have no style whatsoever and are bringing me down. It starts to affect my creativity, so I need to lay on some extra glamour to compensate."

"Whatever helps," Beth said and air-kissed her host on the cheeks.

"Exactly," Bebe said while returning the gesture. Then she turned to the mini bar and began mixing a Bloody Mary.

"Make it a weak one," Beth said. "I've got to drive later."

"Shame," Bebe said, clearly not being stingy with the vodka as she was preparing the drink. "I could do with your moral support in this madhouse. I can cope with my daughter on her own, but having

144

her common boyfriend here as well, it's ludicrous. They behave like spoilt teenagers: reckless, rude and without boundaries."

"Speaking of ludicrous," Beth said. "I had a long conversation about you with my flatmate Fred. She's in the music biz and she said that you should stay clear of that Eurovision thing at any cost."

"Really?" Bebe said.

"Yes," Beth said. "Fred claims it's the kiss of death – for years it has done nobody any good who has represented Britain. Fred also made a really good point: it's been a while since k.d. lang has had a decent hit. There's a niche market aimed at the sophisticated audience that you could try to exploit. That would be much classier than Eurovision. If you wanted to reinvent yourself, why not do it at the upper end of your spectrum?"

Bebe paused for a moment. "That makes a lot of sense," she said. "I wish I could get my agent to make suggestions like that."

"Fred knows a few people in the industry and would love to meet you," Beth said. "I never knew this about her but she's a big fan of yours."

"That would be lovely," Bebe said. "I have long suspected that I was working with the wrong type of management. Bertie has no real ambition. I don't think he sees me as one of his bigger assets. I would love to work with someone who is an actual fan. Why don't you bring her with you next time you are in the area?"

"Certainly. Or, why don't you come to Cardiff with me?"

"I dread to think what would happen to my home if I left Helena and her beau alone."

"I can understand that," Beth said. "I'll see what I can do."

"So, what is happening in the murder case? Any new twists?" Bebe asked.

Beth knew it was unprofessional of her to discuss matters with Bebe was a useful sounding board for her. Breaking the rules had helped her a few times to crack insolvable cases. And when she got results, Warwick was happy to turn a blind eye. So she told her about Ellie's link to Mrs Morris's event management company.

"I so want to put that clamp-happy mad woman behind bars," Bebe said. "However, it's one thing to clamp cars in the middle of the night and write nasty letters. Physically attacking someone is something else and I don't think she's capable of doing that. I'd sooner believe that her husband did it for her."

"Even with his handicap?" Beth asked.

"I wouldn't be surprised if he was laying that on now for effect," Bebe said. "I'm not a medical expert but I would have thought that if his ankle was still so bad, it would be too swollen for him to walk in his winter boots and shovel snow."

"So you think he did it and is trying to cover it up?"

"No," Bebe said. "I don't think that at all. If they thought it was an intruder, Ian wouldn't have been afraid of her, and if they knew it was her, a dispute and drama at their door step wouldn't warrant killing her. I think Ian just wants to make sure he doesn't become a suspect. Probably for Christine's sake."

"It's looking bad for her," Beth confirmed. "He should take the heat of her by playing his injury down. However, even with this new information about her connection to the victim, I don't think we don't have enough to make a murder charge stick to her beyond reasonable doubt."

"Oh dear," Bebe said. "If it's that hard, then I really don't envy you the job."

An hour later, Beth left the singer and headed for the hospital to visit Dora Jenkins.

"How sweet of you to visit," Dora said when the detective entered her private room. She had one arm in a sling and had stitches over her right eyebrow. Apart from that, she looked healthy and as gorgeous as ever. "How is the investigation going?"

"So, so," Beth said. "We have many promising leads, but no concrete results."

"You poor thing," Dora said. "It must be dreadful having to dig around for clues here in the countryside. A girl like you belongs to the city, I can tell."

Beth nodded.

"I do have a few questions for you, though, if you feel up for it," Beth asked.

Dora smiled gently. "Always," she said. "It's not as if I have anything else to do right now."

"Thanks," Beth said and sat on a chair by the bed. It was a very intimate setting and the sensation of being next to this attractive woman made her flush. She cleared her voice and hoped her crush wasn't obvious to the patient.

"You mentioned to my colleagues that the brakes on your car didn't work," she said, opening her notebook and trying to look as professional and focused as she could.

"Yes," Dora said. "That was really weird."

"Was that the first time you noticed a problem with the brakes?"

"Yes," Dora said. "I'm very careful with cars. If I had known that there was the slightest problem I would have had the garage pick it up right away and would never have driven."

"When was the last time you used your car?" Beth asked.

"Good question," Dora said and pondered. "Quite a few days ago, I think. I gave Helena a lift to the train station. The brakes were working well then. Maybe it was the cold, or a fox bit the cable or something."

"Maybe," Beth said. "We're having your car checked out to be sure."

"Murder, sabotage . . . who would have thought a small hamlet like Llangurrey could produce so much drama?" Dora said and laughed. "And my ex-husband is getting married to a child bride. At this rate I don't need to watch soap operas; it is all happening at my doorstep."

Beth laughed, too. She was glad the woman had kept her sense of humour. If she had been involved in an accident, she would have been more shaken, she reckoned.

"Wait until you get home," she said. "Helena and Dominic have moved in with Mrs Bolton. I fear this will end in tears."

"Lovely," Dora said.

"Seriously, though," Beth said. "If someone had sabotaged your car, who would you suspect?"

Dora laughed. "Nobody," she said with feeling. "It has to be a mechanical failure, or the doing of a fox."

"What about Mrs Morris?"

"Christine?" Dora laughed hysterically. "I know I said that she was on the road that night and that woman isn't right in the head, but she wouldn't go this far. She would have clamped my car like Bebe's."

"Whoever did this might have meant it as a warning shot? In snow conditions they wouldn't expect you to drive particularly fast."

"Nonsense," Dora said. "I'd sooner believe that my ex-husband was doing it to stop paying my alimony."

"Now that's a thought," Beth said and made a note of it.

"Darling, the Jenkins family is loaded. If they wanted me gone they would find a surer way than cutting my brakes. That wouldn't guarantee my death. And they wouldn't do that to the girls, killing their mother. The amount that they pay me, it wouldn't be worth the risk. Don't be so melodramatic."

"It's an avenue worthy pursuing all the same," Beth said. Had the ex-husband fallen on hard times and wanted to cut some of his expenses? Was that 'child bride' a gold digger who wanted her predecessor dead? Beth would have to get someone to check those avenues. Given that the murder victim had slapped Dora and now the woman was involved in a dubious car accident – Beth decided to have someone sniff out the Jenkins family and find out more about Dora.

"Thanks for the visit," Dora said and yawned. "If you have nothing else to ask me, I think I would like to rest now. I feel very tired all of a sudden."

"I'm not surprised," Beth said. "You must still be in shock."

Dora closed her eyes and nodded.

"Well, get better soon," Beth said and left the patient.

Back at her car she checked her phone for messages and found one from Warwick.

"We've arrested Christine Morris," the message said. "We found new evidence that suggests she was going after Ellie."

Beth drove to the Carmarthen police station as fast as she could.

"Mrs Seaborne had the negative evaluation of her internship, written by Mrs Morris, by her bed stand in the hotel room. It was decorated with some very graphic drawings," he explained to her when she called him from the station.

"I don't understand," Beth said. "Why didn't we hear about this before? That would have saved us a lot of time and trouble."

"I know," Warwick said. "Our colleagues in Carmarthen will hear from me about this, for sure. How could they have missed this important piece of evidence, collected and labelled from the hotel room? For now I'm just glad we're closer to a motive than we were before. It's obvious that there were a lot of hard feelings between the two women. I've spoken to the victim's mother, who now remembers that Ellie considered launching a harassment case at the time but was persuaded otherwise."

"Is that enough evidence to convict her?" Beth asked. "Without fingerprints and witnesses we're still on dodgy territory."

"We got a warrant to search the Morris residence and found a pair of brand new pliers in the garage. The size fits the damage to Mrs Jenkins's cut brake. The technicians found remnants of a plastic sheet on the brake cable, the type used as seal. The pair of pliers we found in the Morris residence had the same plastic seal. With the hamlet having been snowed-in at the time of the murder, any jury would be stretched to the limit of credibility to assume someone else came into Llangurrey, borrowed the pliers to damage a random car and then killed Mrs Morris's enemy on her doorstep."

"Brilliant," Beth said. "Has she caved yet?"

"Mrs Morris isn't answering any of our questions," Warwick said. "A further sign of her guilt if you ask me."

"Well I never..." Beth said.

"Exactly," he said with emphasis. "You never."

She didn't like that tone.

"How many cases have you solved in the last few months?" Warwick asked. "None. It never occurred to you to examine all the evidence from the hotel room again. *You* missed that letter, too, Cooper, not just the Carmarthen team. I hate to smash your dream of becoming the next Miss Marple but I've decided it's time I let you go from the team. You had a great success rate when you started but you're slacking. I think you just haven't got what it takes to be a detective. You're highly unprofessional, disorganised and act on hunches that, lately, never turn into anything other than embarrassment. Take a few days off and think where you see yourself within the police force. I'm not a prick. I'll do what I can to help you find something more suitable than this . . . within reason, of course."

Beth was still gasping for air when he hung up.

149

Chapter 20: Her Saviour

Bebe

Bebe was torn. Bertie had called her as a matter of urgency and asked her to come to London for another meeting with the *Comic Relief* team. Will Young had responded to her suggestion and asked that he and Bebe do a comedy sketch together on the night. She would feature twice in one night. It was almost too much to think. She wanted to go right away but she was very concerned about leaving the house. Helena and Dominic behaved like wild teenagers, drinking and smoking weed all day – she was sure she could smell marijuana on them. Two very expensive vases had been broken already, there were stains on the soft furnishings and on the carpet and Bebe dreaded to think what would be damaged next. She needed help to get the unwanted pair out of her home before she was able to leave. She still had a few hours to spare before she had to start her journey. And Bebe knew just who to ask . . .

"You're in luck," Beth said when she heard of Bebe's dilemma over the phone. "I'm free indeed. I've just been sacked from the investigation. I'm coming over to sort out your mess."

"Oh darling, are you alright?" Bebe asked. "I don't like the sound of that. You aren't joking, are you?"

"I'm not joking," Beth said. "But I'll be alright. You go and tell your daughter to pack her bags or I'll pack them for her when I get there."

"With pleasure," Bebe said and hung up.

Beth

Beth ran to her car. She would show those two wastrels what an angry lesbian policewoman could do. She was delighted to have an outlet for her anger and looked forward to the confrontation.

When Beth arrived in Llangurrey there was nothing she could do. Helena and Dominic, forewarned by her mother's announcement of an upcoming eviction, had barricaded themselves in one of the bedrooms and refused to leave.

"We've got nowhere to go," Helena pleaded under fits of giggles, which reinforced the suspicion that Bebe's daughter was stoned.

"You ungrateful child," Bebe called through the door. "No wonder your father won't help you if you never grow up and behave like an adult. I should never have taken you in, either."

There was only laughter on the other side and a big plonking sound as if someone had fallen. Nobody seemed to be injured, though. All Beth could hear was more giggling from her daughter and that awful man of hers. The lovers wouldn't leave voluntarily and remained safe behind the closed door.

"I could break that door in for you, if you wanted," Beth offered, "but it would be a shame to damage this beautiful oak."

"If that is our only option, go ahead," Bebe said, but her voice lacked certainty and determination.

Beth banged loudly against the door.

"Come out," she shouted. "You can't hide in there forever."

Again, the only reply was giggling and laughter.

Beth kicked against the door. Then she let herself sink against the wall and slid down on the floor.

"What happened to your job?" Bebe asked. She sat down and put her arm around Beth.

"A long story. I'll tell you some other time. I'm too angry right now."

Bebe gently stroked Beth's cheek and said: "I've still got time if you want to get this off your chest."

"No, don't worry," Beth said. "You don't want to run into traffic and be late for Will Young. I'll stay here," she offered. "At some point the two of them will get hungry or need the loo. That's when I'll get them. By the time you get back to Llangurrey, your house will be free of parasites."

Bebe hugged Beth and got up.

"Thank you so much. Oh, and be gentle with them," she said. "We don't want a scandal."

"Of course we don't."

Bebe

Bebe rushed into her bedroom to grab a few essentials, more clothes and her make-up bag. She couldn't be late, Beth was right, and there could be traffic. *Comic Relief* was going live this weekend and the producers wanted all pre-recorded material in the can as soon as possible.

All the way to London she couldn't wipe the smile of her face. Bless that darling Will Young. She wondered what the idea for their sketch was. It had to be better for her than the Jennifer Saunders thing. It would be her long awaited break. Then she'd tell Bertie to stuff the Eurovision gig and then she'd find a new agent. After her appearances on *Comic Relief* the public would have to notice her. Two national gigs; that had to translate into a career revival, a recording or some other fame.

At the BBC headquarters Bertie was waiting for her in the lobby.

"Great news," he said. "You and Will are doing an Abba song together. You'll record it tonight and then you'll be doing a live act on Friday night. You're going to be a huge part of the main show. Isn't that fantastic?"

Bebe had tears in her eyes.

"It is, Bertie, it is."

Will Young proved a delight to work with: professional and utterly charming. Oh, how she loved her gays, always so appreciative and attentive. And what a great voice that man had. It fitted with hers perfectly, just as she had thought it would. The song was done in a simple arrangement; it was most undemanding for professionals like herself and Will. The time in the recording studio flew and Bebe was sad when it was over so quickly. It had been a long time since she had worked with other professionals and she had missed this.

The stars were rushed out of the studio and dolled up for the photo shoots. Everything had been immaculately prepared. The producer explained that there was going to be a collage of Abba-esque images of the two singers in a video. She wasn't surprised that it involved a lot of wigs, prescription glasses and heavy make-up. She had a great time, though, knowing she was with such a big name. How she wished there had been more time to chat and exchange stories with Will, but he had his own dressing room, while Bebe was stuck in hers. Unfortunately, Will also had a tight schedule and had to leave as soon as possible. Bebe usually had a great time with the make-up artists and costume makers. They were normally all fans of hers. Today, unfortunately, the young women who dealt with her seemed hugely disinterested, which made the moments spent with charming Will stand out even more. Wasn't life great all of a sudden?

It was long after midnight when she left the BBC. Bertie had organised a hotel room for her in the city. He had his uses, she had to admit it.

Exhausted, Bebe sank in her bed the happiest she had been in a long time.

Beth

Meanwhile in Llangurrey, Beth was making progress with the eviction. After Bebe had left her house, Beth positioned herself on a chair outside the bedroom and bided her time. Every minute she waited she grew angrier at Warwick for sacking her, and angrier at herself for having messed up the case. Helena was still giggling now and then and the lovers could be heard whispering. This wouldn't take long, Beth realised. She tiptoed down the stairs and opened and closed the front door noisily. Then she walked back up again, as quietly as she could and waited. The squatters didn't need much encouragement to come out of their hiding, convinced that Beth had given up.

Dominic was first out and as soon as Beth saw him she put him into a headlock and dragged him down the stairs. He was surprisingly weak and compliant. She managed to handcuff him to the banister, and then she ran back upstairs. Helena hadn't even bothered locking herself in again. She lay on the floor, doubled over and laughing hysterically. Beth packed everything she deemed a possession of the two lovebirds in a black bin bag, then she pulled Helena off the floor and bundled her down the stairs.

"That's not fair," Dominic said, half-heartedly. "Bebe can't just kick us out like that. She promised us she would look after us until Helena's dad is back from Thailand."

"Yeah, guess what," Beth said. "Bebe changed her mind."

"We've got nowhere to go," Helena said with put-on sadness. She seemed to be sobering up a little, but her puppy face was unconvincing.

"You should have thought about that before you got stoned and drunk," Beth said. "Bebe warned you to behave."

"We *were* behaving," Helena insisted, still trying to convey innocence. "It's not our fault my mother is so overly sensitive and bourgeois."

153

"Here's fifty quid," Beth said, handing over a few bank notes. "You can stay in a hotel in Carmarthen with that until you're sober."

Helena took the money and began to put her clothes on.

"Come on Dominic," she said. "We'll think of something."

"I'll call you a taxi," Beth said and took his handcuffs off. He put on the rest of his clothes and then held Helena's hand.

As Beth stepped outside she saw Ian Morris coming out of his house. When he spotted Beth he humped across the lane as fast as he could with his limp.

"Have you lost your senses?" he shouted as he came towards her. "My wife's no killer and you know it."

Dominic turned round to the detective.

"You think his wife killed my Ellie?" he asked. Beth noted how surprised he sounded.

She was about to explain to Mr Morris that this entire investigation had nothing to do with her anymore but she never got a chance.

"You've got no idea what you're doing to my wife," Ian continued, angrier than she had ever imagined him to be. Spittle flecked his lips and his face was bright red. "She suffers from extreme anxiety. You can't just arrest her without proof. I know my rights. I'll sue you all!"

He stood about a metre from Beth but his stance was so tense, she expected him to jump at her any moment. She put one of her hands on the handcuffs to see if they were ready to use, if needed.

"The body was found on your doorstep," Helena said, goading him. "What more proof do we need that your wife killed Ellie? It's a miracle the police took so long to arrest her."

"You shut your face, you tramp. It was probably you," Ian spat.

"It couldn't have been me. I was in London," Helena said, triumphant.

"Yeah, we have proof for that," Dominic said, nodding several times for emphasis. "The police have nothing on us!"

Beth turned on her heels and walked back inside. This mess had nothing to do with her and she was glad of it. If she was to be fired, at least right now she could benefit from it.

"I loved my wife," she heard Dominic shout.

154

What a joke. She noted that neither of the couple had said that they were innocent. Maybe it was because they were stoned, or maybe it was just poor phrasing. If she was still on the case she'd check the lovers' alibi one more time. All of a sudden she was no longer sure about them. Who had dug into their background story? Warwick, the Carmarthen team or her colleagues in London? She suspected that whoever it was, hadn't really bothered with them because of their alibi.

She leaned against the closed door from the inside and took a deep breath.

"It's not my business anymore," she told herself, while outside the screaming and shouting continued.

That Dominic really was something else. The nerve to say he loved his wife. While he seemed too stupid to commit a successful murder, Beth couldn't shake off the feeling that he had something to do with it. Or could it really have been Christine Morris?

Outside the quarrelling stopped when the taxi arrived, taking the couple away. Beth saw the car recede into the opposite direction of Carmarthen and the train station. That also seemed odd. Did Helena have friends left in the vicinity? Why had nobody on her team checked that possibility out? Did the lovers have a local accomplice? She was certain that she was onto something here, her sixth sense came through loud and clear but she wasn't sure if it was worth the effort. On one hand she wanted to redeem herself and solve the case for real, on the other, it was unlikely that Warwick would even listen to her. He'd just go bonkers if he found out that she continued to investigate a case from which she had been removed.

Beth spent a few hours half-watching TV as she mulled things over. When she was sure that Helena and Dominic were not coming back, she locked up the house and drove back to her flat in Cardiff. Fred had gone to see a band in London. It was the perfect opportunity to combine business with pleasure. She left a message for Bebe and suggested that they meet for breakfast with Fred in the Brasserie Filou next morning in Soho. It was one of the places that had helped confirm Dominic and Helena's alibi and was not far from the friend who had put the lovers up on the night of the murder. It couldn't hurt to sound that place and the alibis out; if for nothing else than her own peace of mind. Maybe Peter hadn't been as thorough as he had implied. Maybe her failure was also his doing, at least in parts.

Chapter 21: On The Radio

Bebe

Hearing that her nuisance daughter had left Llangurrey and that she would have breakfast with a fan who worked in the industry was music to Bebe's ears. These trips to London were so good for her. While she didn't miss the problems of living in such a metropolis with the vast distances between places, the busy roads and the dreadful pollution, this was the place where everything happened.

She got dolled up for the day – a dark blue woollen dress with a white Mexican-style throw made of cashmere, and a black hat. She liked what she saw in the mirror. She still wasn't sure about her hair, though, and preferred to cover it. She had apologised to Will about it –actually fishing for a compliment if truth be told – and he had kindly dismissed her worries. The make-up artist at the BBC on the other hand had not responded when Bebe tried the same tack. She'd just shrugged her shoulders and said nothing.

Bebe put on her sunglasses and headed down to the lobby. The concierge ordered her a taxi. She stood outside the hotel, enjoying the milder temperatures and feeling positive and optimistic. Spring was around the corner and with it endless opportunities. She hummed an old Diana Ross song and bounded out onto the pavement and into the taxi, full of anticipation.

The driver paid little attention to her and was listening to the radio, which suited her fine. She remembered how, at the height of her popularity, it had become exhausting having to make chit-chat with every person she happened to meet, especially taxi drivers, at the end of a long night of singing and performing.

The big news on the radio today was Engelbert's song presentation. Then the song was played.

"Would you mind turning it up a little?" she asked the driver. He gave a grunt, but obliged.

"What a load of rubbish," the driver said after the first chorus. "It stinks."

Bebe didn't like his rude tone. She thought the song was beautiful. What was it with London taxi drivers? Couldn't they be a little bit kinder? What she liked even less was that she couldn't hear any backing vocals while the song was playing. Was that her imagination or was it the inferior sound system in the cab? As the song built up to a big finale she could hear a backing vocal, but she was sure that it wasn't her voice. The producers had cut her part out. She was furious. There she had been persuaded to stay in a project she had mind to pull out of and now she found out that she wasn't even in it anyway. Did Bertie know about this? He probably did and had agreed to it. She would have to pick a serious bone with him when she saw him. Well, she could get satisfaction out of the fact that she'd been snubbed by Cliff Richard and he had lost at Eurovision. Engelbert would probably not win, either, that much was clear. If a simpleton like this taxi driver didn't get the song, what chance had Engelbert to woo the rest of Europe? She should be relieved that her name wasn't attached to this sinking ship. Besides, she had bigger fish to fry now. Still, it hurt to be snubbed, whether by Engelbert, his managers, the BBC or whoever else had had the final say and had cut her out.

If the food at Brasserie Filou made as much of an impression as the building itself, then Bebe was in for a treat. The restaurant that Beth had suggested for breakfast was full of atmosphere — a converted warehouse, it had large windows and a central island where customers could watch the chef cook. There was a touch of a New York loft apartment, and the jazz playing softly in the background added to the ambience. Why it had the French name was beyond her. Beth sat on a table alone, fiddling with her phone.

"My saviour," Bebe said, hugging her warmly. The Detective Sergeant seemed very subdued today, which reminded Bebe that she still hadn't heard the full story about the dismissal.

"So what happened with your job?" Bebe asked. "I must say, I'm surprised they'd let a woman like you go."

Beth explained the situation.

"Christine a murderer and saboteur? Well I never," Bebe said. "That can't be right."

"She had opportunity, motive and the means, as they say. It's hard to argue with that."

"How have they determined that it was her and not her husband? Theoretically he could have done it to protect her. And he is a lot stronger than her."

"I'm sure they are looking into this as we speak," Beth said. "It's no longer anything to do with me, or you."

"It doesn't sound like you're ready to let it go, though," Bebe observed. "You've got that look on your face of a dog with its chew toy. Reminds me of my Richard when he was about to compose a song. I could see it coming long before he did."

Beth grinned, picking up a bread roll from the basket on the table and proceeding to pick at it.

"I have my suspicions about that Dominic," she said as she chewed. "He could be a tad more shocked and upset about his wife's death."

"Yes, I give you that," Bebe said.

"This morning I checked out his alibi," Beth said. "I'm no longer so sure it's as tight as DCI Warwick made it out to be."

"What makes you say that?" Bebe asked. She was starving, but this was too important.

"Let's order our food first," Beth said and browsed through the extensive and exquisite menu.

"How odd that Helena and her beau should have come to such a fine place," Bebe said. "It doesn't seem the right place for them. No wonder the waiters remembered him."

"Exactly," Beth agreed. "That could have been planned. And it did strike me as suspicious that Dominic had kept the train and underground tickets, and yesterday he seemed very smug about his alibi," she added.

"His friend's flat – the one he and Helena stayed in – is close by, and when I spoke to his mate earlier, I had a look around the flat. According to the statements the lovers went to bed early and weren't seen again until after their breakfast here the next morning. They had contracted food poisoning and went to a pharmacy to get a remedy for it. The floor in the flat is carpeted and the door shuts quietly. They had ample opportunity to sneak out and make their way to Llangurrey."

"You really think my daughter killed the woman?" Bebe asked.

"I don't know what to think," Beth said. "I checked the train times and they could have made it to you in time for the murder and taken the first train back to get here for breakfast. I did the maths, it could have worked."

"Where would they have stayed overnight?" Bebe asked, her face ashen. "Have you checked the hotels in the area?"

"The Carmarthen team and the colleagues from the City of London did the early stages of the investigation," Beth said, "which is why I failed to question the alibi. But they overlooked important evidence. As did I. If I were still in charge of the investigation, I'd have them check out the camera footage around Carmarthen train station for sightings of Dominic or Helena."

Bebe took a breadstick and began to crumble it between her fingers.

"When Seaborne and your daughter left your house in the taxi yesterday they asked the driver to take them in the other direction, away from the main road. Where do you think they went?"

"I have no idea," Bebe said. "The road is only of agricultural interest as far as I'm aware. Eventually, you get to an abandoned farm building and then the road loops back to the main road. The winter services didn't even clear that part of the road during the snow, that's how off the beaten track it is."

"Are there any B&B's that way?" Beth asked.

"I don't think so," Bebe said. "You can't be serious about this. My daughter is no murderer."

"I would like to think so, but the whole thing is strange," Beth said. "I think they are hiding something from us. You find in investigations that things just don't add up. Often the reason for this is that someone didn't tell the whole truth, usually, to avoid becoming a suspect. When you discover the lies you can find the missing piece and figure out who did it. Rarely the person who lied, but someone they were unknowingly protecting."

Bebe was worried by the insinuation about Helena and wanted to find a way to get the detective off that line of inquiry. Suddenly she felt pleased that Beth had been sacked from the investigation. Bebe could only hope that this dangerous speculation would go no further. It hurt to think that her new friend Beth would even pursue this. Didn't she know how damaging that could be for Bebe's career? These thoughts were quickly dispersed when Fred walked into the room. She recognised the singer immediately and waved enthusiastically.

Fred was a beautiful lipstick lesbian with a curvy figure and huge cleavage. She wore a tight red velvet dress, heels and had the most disarming smile.

"Wow," Fred said and air-kissed Bebe. "I'm losing my mind!"

Bebe couldn't' suppress a smile at the reference to her big hit.

"So nice to meet you," Fred continued and grabbed hold of Bebe's hand. "Oh, you were my big celebrity crush when I was still in the closet," she said. "I faked to have bad eyesight so I would get glasses like yours. My mother was so relieved when you stopped wearing them and I gave up cheating at the eye doctor."

"It's lovely to meet a fan," Bebe said. "It's been a while since someone had a crush on me."

"I think you're wrong there," Fred said and kissed her hand.

Bebe coyly took her hand away. She didn't want to be a tease, regardless of how much she enjoyed attention. Beth didn't seem to like the admiration Bebe was getting from her former lover and stuck her head into her phone instead of participating in the chat. It had been a long time since someone had been this charming and gallant with Bebe. She almost regretted not being a lesbian. In her experience, straight men were rarely this kind and flirtatious with her and really meant it. This adoration from Fred was genuine.

"I think you'll be pleased to hear that I'm not going to do Eurovision," Bebe said and told her of the shocking moment when she had heard the song on the radio this morning without her vocals.

"Totally their loss," Fred said and waved her arm dismissively in the air. "Look at the dreadful track record for the participants. It's been a dead end road for most. Last year, Blue tried to revive their career. They had a great song but got slaughtered by the juries, and the record-buying audience did not reward them. The song got next to no airplay, so not even the BBC tried to help them out. Jessica Garlick, with her third place in 2002, didn't make it big after the show, either. It's best to stay clear of it if you can."

"You know a lot about this," Bebe remarked.

"Looks like I know at least more than your manager," Fred said and opened her purse. "This is my business card. I work for a small talent agency in Soho. I may not be as well connected as your manager but I've worked with TV and several musical production companies. Nobody can be as ignorant as your current agent. He must be suicidal to suggest such a move."

Fred then launched into a long rendition of her favourite Bebe songs, where she had heard them and how they made her feel.

"*Beach Fever* was such a great holiday song," Fred said. "I still get goose bumps when I hear *Is it Over?*"

"Thank you," Bebe said all the way through the talk. Fred bombarded her with compliments and questions. Bebe hadn't felt this adored for years. Thoughts of her daughter and the murder drifted towards the back of her mind and all concerns about Beth's line of inquiry and her loyalty to the star were slowly becoming insignificant. Introducing her to this well-connected and informed gem had completely redeemed the detective in Bebe's eyes.

Chapter 22: The Satchel

Dora

Dora was released from hospital with her left arm in a sling. The broken rib hurt like hell every time she moved the arm. Her luxurious private insurance provided her with home care, since Dora insisted on leaving the hospital as soon as possible. Her daughter Julia promised to check in on her regularly and stay with her on the weekends. Her ex-husband's engagement to the young woman was still poisoning the atmosphere at the Jenkins residence, she learned, and the girls were eager to get away.

Dora found herself frustrated before long. She was surprised how much the pain handicapped her. All she could do was watch TV. Even minor manoeuvres with her hand hurt. She'd always thought of herself as rather resourceful but she was astonished at how little she could do with just one hand.

She still laughed at the thought that someone had sabotaged her car: that policewoman really was useless. Accidents did happen, cars had faults and not everything in the world had an evil cause. The murder had inspired people to think the worst and lose all connection with reality. To Dora, the incident was nothing more than a reminder of how fragile life was and how much one had to enjoy it to the full while one still could.

Unfortunately, now that she was told to rest by the doctors, she felt more energetic than usual. She was in the mood to tidy her house and do chores she had been neglecting. Restless and defiant she started to hoover the living room and to tidy up, as much as her handicap allowed. She numbed the pain generously with the prescription drugs.

A delivery man brought her two plastic bags with the contents of her car. Dora was delighted. That had to mean that the police had finished examining her vehicle and that it was being sent to a garage for repair as her daughter had arranged with the authorities. Not that she would be driving it any time too soon, but it was a step in the right direction. She looked forward to the end of all the drama in the hamlet. It was sad enough that the woman was dead. To assume foul play and conspiracies in everything unusual because of it could only do harm. Dora and her neighbours were already divided enough.

Paranoia would turn them more against each other. The police were clearly tapping in the dark if they had to go to such lengths to connect her accident with the dead woman.

Amongst her shopping bags and CD's Dora found a small leather satchel that wasn't hers. How had that been muddled up with her things? She wondered to whom it belonged. There had to have been a mix-up at the garage. She had a look inside: a notebook, a diary, the pill... She didn't want to go through someone else's stuff but she hoped to find a phone number or a name that would make it easy to reunite the owner with their bag. The notebook featured some amateurish pencil drawings of people, which didn't really give much away. The diary was empty and only had some credit card receipts. The owner of the satchel had eaten at a fast-food restaurant in Carmarthen several times and had stayed at the Lodgers Inn. They also had shopped in a hardware store, which meant they could have purchased a pair of pliers. All well before Thursday, the day of the murder . . .

Suddenly she realised that this had to be Ellie's bag. Dora had given the poor woman a lift into Carmarthen days before her death. She remembered how Ellie had carried such a satchel after she had run from the Mini in the ditch by the road. She took a closer look at the drawings and suddenly everything became much clearer: those were sketches of Helena, Ian, Bebe, of Dora herself and of Christine. It seemed as though Ellie had hidden talent as an artist – and apparently she had staked out the hamlet for some time. Oh that silly girl. Dora almost had tears in her eyes. If only that woman had given up on that cheating bastard, she might never have come to Llangurrey and met her murderer.

Dora put the bag aside and planned on giving it to the policewoman on her next visit. She looked outside to see if maybe the detective was with Bebe, but her cottage was dark and all cars had gone. The hamlet was deserted. Dora could see the light switch on at regular intervals over at Ian and Christine's place, so they had to be both gone. Dora didn't like this. In her injured state she felt very vulnerable.

She was relieved when her daughter Julia arrived and helped her prepare a meal. They sat at the big oak table in Dora's bright kitchen and caught up on family news.

"Grandmother isn't taking her threats back," the daughter reported, while chopping vegetables for a ratatouille.

"I don't understand why she is so uptight," Dora said. "He is 57 years old, for crying out loud, and can do what he wants."

"Yes, but our new step-mom's going to be 25 – only six years older than me," Julia said. Dora nodded. She could understand that this was odd for some people, but her daughter was a very wise and mature girl: tall, dark, beautiful, intelligent and very balanced. Dora felt proud and protective at the same time and wanted to ease Julia's concerns.

"Stranger things have happened in the land of love," Dora said.

"Grandmother said if he gets married he'll be cut off and any children from the marriage won't get one penny of her money, either," Julia said. "I know it's blackmail, but I'm all for it. Let's see if Vera likes him without his cash."

"I don't understand," Dora said, perplexed. "How can Granny cut him off?"

"You don't know?" the daughter asked and put the knife down for a second. "His company went under before Christmas and she bailed him out. She's controlling his firm and paying his salary now."

Dora was surprised that nobody had told her this before.

"Daddy is naturally not giving in to her demands. He told Granny that he doesn't need her money, and I'm sure he means it. But the estate is hers, too. If she tells him to move out he'll have to downsize a lot."

"How is Vera taking the whole thing?" Dora asked.

"She never speaks a word."

"Probably the wisest thing to do in her situation," Dora said. "Your grandmother is hard to please."

After a short pause she added: "Do you think she'll make your dad happy?"

"I don't know," the daughter said. "I think it's gross. He's so old. Yikes. It really gives me the creeps."

"Do you think she loves him?" Dora asked.

"I can't imagine her being anything but a gold digger. He's more than twice her age. They're 32 years apart."

"We'll see what happens if Granny makes her threats real. I, for one, don't mind if the money passes her by and ends up with my gorgeous daughters."

"You say that now, but what if he cuts your alimony?" Julia asked.

"Then I'll move back to Portugal, of course," Dora said. "My money will stretch further there. I was always thinking of doing that when you're older. As long as Granny keeps her money so she can sponsor you two, I will be fine."

"I hope so," Julia said. "That could easily happen."

"The detective in the murder case once suggested that the shovel was meant for me," Dora said, grinning. "She seriously considered the possibility of your father or his new girlfriend coming here to kill me, so they could stop the alimony."

Julia fell silent.

"Vera has expensive tastes and he's is besotted with her," Julia said.

"Don't you start, too," Dora said. "The police even suggested the car had been tampered with, and that was an attempt at my life, too. Thank God they were abroad when all of this happened."

"Vera didn't go to on holiday with him," Julia replied. "She was in the UK."

"Don't," Dora said and held her good hand up to make her stop. "Enough said now. You're already prejudiced against your stepmother and that isn't right, and definitely not helpful."

Fortunately, Julia soon changed the subject of the conversation and discussed various plans for her gap year.

That night, after her daughter was picked up by the family chauffeur, Dora saw Bebe park outside her cottage, with that policewoman in tow. Those two were thick as thieves. Who would have thought? Dora was relieved, though. At least someone was in the hamlet now. It reassured her.

Chapter 23: Going It On Their Own

Bebe

Bebe was still high on all the admiration she had enjoyed over the last few days: from Fred and from the gig with Will Young. As a thank you, she had invited Beth back to Llangurrey to take the poor girl's mind off her job troubles and, to keep an eye on any in-official investigation of her daughter that the Detective Sergeant might carry out. She opened a bottle of vodka and began mixing Bloody Mary's while playing an Abba compilation CD, in honour of her duet with Will.

"Your friend is lovely," she said, passing a drink to Beth. "It's a shame you don't have chemistry with her anymore. You couldn't rekindle the spark?"

"Fred and I were great together but she has a wandering eye."

"Whatever went wrong with that pilot woman? Did she have a sweetheart in every port?"

"No," Beth said and drowned the drink almost in one. "She was never around, though. It was like having a long-distance relationship."

"Couldn't she take you with her to the exotic locations?" Bebe asked while working on the refill.

"Bebe, she worked in the Army," Beth said. "I didn't fancy going to Afghanistan with her."

"Oh, I see."

"I've got bigger problems than my love life, anyway," Beth said, pensive. "I've got to find myself a new role in the police force."

"What are you going to do?" Bebe asked.

"I wish I knew. I love what I do and I don't think I'm as bad at it as Warwick says. Many of his convictions are dubious, to say the least. Like this murder case here in Llangurrey, for instance. All circumstances suggest that Mrs Morris did it, but that doesn't make sense."

"Nothing that woman ever did made sense," Bebe said. "The clamping is only the tip of the iceberg. She makes a very likely candidate."

"It's all too obvious though, killing someone right outside her doorstep – who does that? And cutting through Dora's brake cable with her own tools? Psychopaths are usually a little cleverer than that and cover their tracks. But that's what my boss DCI Warwick, does: he makes a conviction and then lets everything that contradicts it disappear. We still haven't finished with that woman who stalked Dominic, nor has anyone seriously considered Ian Morris – solely on grounds of his swollen ankle. You should talk to the team and share your suspicion about the gravity of his injury. Warwick also missed the hole in Dominic and Helena's alibi. Why did they go to that posh restaurant after a night of food poisoning if not to round up the documentation of their every move? And, of course, maybe we are completely on the wrong with all of this and it has something to do with Dora and her ex-husband? After all, it was her car that got sabotaged, her ex is getting re-married and the victim was found close to her house. In my book this case is still wide open."

"You're right," Bebe said. "That Dora is a dark horse and she may have enemies we don't know anything about. She doesn't use diplomacy and riles people up, easily. Only last week she put up a scarecrow in her garden which looked remarkably like Christine as a parking warden."

"In that case I can understand better why one would think that Christine cut Dora's brakes, but shouldn't we also consider Dora as a suspect, who framed Christine by killing someone on her doorstep?"

"How should Dora have done that? Sneak across the lane, hit the woman from behind and then run back home, without anyone noticing?"

"It's a far stretch, I know," Beth admitted. "Everything in this case seems to be like that."

"You've watched too many *Midsomer Murders*," Bebe said. "People don't act like that in the real world."

"Wanna bet?" Beth said. "Work with me for a week and you'd be amazed at what people do to each other and why they do it."

"Maybe we should sound that Dora out," Bebe suggested. "Let's invite her over. She's had an accident; we have a pretext to check in on her."

"You told me that you don't really get on with her," Beth said. "Do you think she'll accept your invitation?"

"We can always try," Bebe said and put on her fur coat. "She's still got a light on."

"I don't know," Beth said. "I'm officially off the case. I shouldn't be snooping around."

"Darling, you clearly can't let go," Bebe said, on her way to the door. "And you're just here as my guest, checking in on my *dear, dear* neighbour." She winked and then put her boots on. "Come on!"

"OK," Beth said and finished her drink. "Let's do this."

Beth

Dora opened the door in her pyjamas. Even dressed like that, and bruised, she looked very attractive. Beth took a moment to collect her thoughts again.

"What can I do for you, detective?" Dora asked and then looked with confusion at Bebe.

"Dora, we were just wondering how you were," Bebe began in the sweetest voice she could muster. "How are you feeling after the accident?"

"I'm fine," Dora said, lifting her arm to show the sling. "A little handicapped right now but I'm alive."

"Would you like to come over to my place for a hot beverage?" Bebe asked.

"Thank you but I'm not really 'dressed for the occasion'," Dora said and raised her eyebrows.

"Darling I've seen you in fewer clothes than these many times over the years," Bebe replied. "There's no need to suddenly resort to formality now that you're injured," she added.

"Mrs Jenkins," Beth said, stepping between Bebe and Dora. It was time to take charge of the situation. "Bebe is right. You needn't worry about wearing pyjamas. You look great and after the trauma you've had it should do you good to have a little company. It must be a lot to take in, that someone made an attempt on your life."

Dora laughed: "You're too much," she said. "You and your conspiracy theory."

Beth looked at her surprised. What planet was this woman on?

"You know that your brakes were cut through, don't you?" she asked. "Your car was definitely tampered with. Our team searched the Morris residence and found a pair of pliers that matches the one used on your car exactly. Mrs Morris has been arrested and charged with both the murder of Ellie Seaborne and the attempt on your life. I can't believe you haven't been informed."

"You'd better come in," Dora said. "I think I need to sit down."

Bebe and Beth followed her into the house and they all sat in Dora's living room.

"Has nobody tried to contact you and tell you?" Beth asked after a few moments of stunned silence. She couldn't get over the idea that nobody had informed the victim of the new development. It wasn't just her who had messed things up. The entire investigation had been conducted in a chaotic manner. Had Warwick not interfered so much, maybe Beth would have had time to come on top of it and coordinate all the efforts in Carmarthen, Cardiff and London. She had messed this up, but it was Warwick's interfering that had stopped her from taking charge.

"I've had a message to call the police but I didn't think it was anything to do with my car," Dora admitted. "I wasn't in the frame of mind to speak to anyone, to be honest. This broken rib is annoying me so much."

"Someone attempted to kill you!" Bebe pointed out. Beth looked at her and shook her head. There was no need to make Dora feel worse than she had to already.

"If it was Christine, she'll be sorry," Dora said and looked angry for the first time. "I'm not convinced you got it right, though. Are you sure it could not have been a fox?"

"I'm afraid we are," Beth said. "Maybe it wasn't Mrs Morris but between Bebe's arthritis and Mr Morris' limp, she is the obvious choice and it fits with her obsessive streak about parking and cars. Of course, it could have been your husband's family framing them."

"An odd coincidence that would be," Bebe said.

"Why didn't you return my colleague's call?" Beth asked Dora. She never understood how casual and disobedient people could behave with the police.

"I thought it was only a formality and, frankly, I had gotten bored of this whole murder investigation."

"How can you get bored by a murder that happened right outside our doorstep?" Bebe asked. "You cannot be that cold hearted."

"You're one to talk," Dora said. "You were in London half of the time."

"Fair point," Beth said, grinning at Bebe.

"Of course it is a terrible thing that happened," Dora continued. "I'm appalled but I'm not Sherlock Holmes to solve it for you or to speculate. To me, it's always been blatantly obvious that this is a crime of passion, something to do with your daughter and that wastrel of a man."

"My daughter and that man have an alibi," Bebe said, looking nervously at Beth. "And if we're seeking obvious solutions then you should think hard about who really had a motive to cut your brakes, and that's your ex-husband. Believe me, it would suit me no end if we could prove Ellie's killer was Dominic," Bebe continued. "If he went to prison maybe Helena would go back to her sensible husband. Not that he might take her back, but anyone would be better than that underwear model she's dating now."

"That reminds me," Dora said suddenly. "I gave Ellie a lift to the station the day before she died. She left a small satchel in my car."

She got up and pulled it from behind the sofa. Beth grabbed the bag and looked through it.

"And you kept this to yourself all this time?" She heard Bebe say accusingly.

"I didn't know it was in my car until this afternoon," Dora defended herself. "A courier from the garage brought it to me, along with the rest of my things from the car. My daughter asked them to send me the contents because I had left some personal items in it."

Beth was stunned to find a bunch of sketches, clearly of the residents of the hamlet. This was incredible.

"I can't believe Warwick and his team missed this," she said. "There's clear proof that the victim has been stalking the area for over a week. It would even strengthen his case against Mrs Morris. And he has the audacity to call me and *my* methods unprofessional."

Bebe looked at the drawings and the receipts.

"Strange that she had a double room at the Lodgers Inn," she pointed out.

"Exactly," Beth agreed. She was both angry at Warwick and excited at the turn of events.

"Maybe she hoped that Dominic would come and stay with her," Dora guessed. "She didn't seem to be able to let go of him, the way she threw herself at him."

"I don't think so," Bebe said. "Look at the receipt from Burger King. Unless she was very hungry it suggests that two were eating there, as well."

"What's interesting is that she stayed at the Towy Valley Inn, according to our files," Beth said. "Nobody knew anything about her room at the Lodgers Inn. That's another thing that DCI Warwick dodged."

"You have to check the security cameras of both the hotel and the restaurant to establish who she was with," Bebe suggested.

"I'm off the case," Beth said and sank back into her seat. Reality caught up with her. "Warwick won't listen to me. If I investigate on my own and he finds out, it will only backfire and damage my career even further. Dora, you need to call the team and hand over the satchel and its contents. And Bebe, you should mention your suspicions to my boss."

"You lost your job already, darling," Bebe said. "You can solve the case and turn everything around. You've got nothing more to lose and everything to gain."

"You lost your job?" Dora asked.

"Yes," Beth said, embarrassed. She hoped Dora wouldn't get angry that she had come here and behaved as if she was still in charge of the investigation. "And I don't want to make it any worse by overstepping the mark. It's one thing to speak to you privately here, but to use my badge to demand access to camera footage might just send me over the edge of what my boss will tolerate."

"Not if you solve the case and find him the murderer," Bebe pointed out. "If you get damning evidence that helps a conviction he'll probably prefer it if the real killer is being charged, even if it doesn't change his statistics. You said that he has a weak case against Christine. The fact that Ellie had the bad assessment on her in the hotel room is only a weak pointer. He must be worried, too, that it won't stick."

"I for one am suddenly very interested in the case again," Dora said and laughed. "Can someone help me get dressed, so I can come with you?"

"I can't take you with me," Beth protested, blushing at the thought of helping Dora get dressed. That woman was too much.

"You must," Dora said, "or I'll call your supervisor and tell him what you're up to."

"You wouldn't," Bebe said.

Dora winked. "Try me," she said.

"What the hell," Beth said and got up from the sofa. "I'll help you change."

"You're such a sweetheart," Dora said and led Beth to her bedroom.

Beth wondered if Dora had any idea she was gay and fancied her. She coyly looked to the side throughout the process of taking the pyjamas off and finding trousers and a sweater.

"Darling, I went to art college," Dora said and giggled. "There were lots of lesbians. Don't feel self-conscious. I'm not a shy person as you might have gathered."

Beth blushed and said nothing. She was glad to get out of the house to move on with the investigation.

The Lodgers Inn didn't seem busy. There were few cars in the car park outside, she noticed, and the night manager sat on the front desk playing with his phone. He was in his mid-thirties, wearing a scruffy-looking and far-too-tight uniform, his hair stood up as if he had slept on his desk and there were empty crisp bags and sandwich wrappings all over his desk.

"Of course you can see the footage," he said after Beth had shown him her badge. "I'm short staffed, though," he explained. "I'll let you into the office and set the system up, then I've got to come back here."

"That's fine with me," Beth said. The less interference, the better.

"Who do you have with you here?" he asked.

"These are important witnesses in my murder case," Beth said. "I do need them with me."

"OK then," the man said hesitantly and let them into the office behind the desk. He opened the disk drive of the office computer and the drawer next to it.

"Here's the camera footage of the car park," he said, before pointing at a cupboard at the wall, "and in there are all the recordings from reception and from each floor. Everything is sorted chronologically and clearly labelled. Please don't mess it up, if you can. Every week we need to sort them. Tomorrow night it's my turn to wipe half of the old footage and re-label the tapes."

"Thank you," Beth said. "I'll do my best."

The manager nodded and then hurried back to the front desk.

"Just as well we came today then," Dora said. Bebe nodded.

"We don't really need to look at the footage of the car park for now," Beth decided. "According to the receipts, Ellie arrived on Sunday afternoon. Let's check her hotel floor first. I guess that's less busy than reception and we'll find what we need quicker that way."

She opened the cupboard and found the right disk. The computer screen showed an empty floor with only the odd movement between the static images. Beth began to awkwardly fast forward and rewind through the footage to hone in on the moments where people could be seen, but she was terribly clumsy with the mouse.

"We could be here for some time," she said, smiling apologetically.

"Give me that," Bebe said and grabbed the mouse off the police woman. "I work with modern sound equipment in my basement every day. I'm used to working with these things."

And indeed, Bebe proved very good at navigating through the footage.

"Here she is, on her own, getting into her room at 1:45pm," Bebe said, sounding like a real detective. "Someone write it down."

Beth did, as Bebe whisked through the next few hours.

"Here she is, coming out of her room at 6:47pm . . . returning to her room at 7:14pm . . ."

Within the shortest space of time Beth had recorded all of Ellie's movements for several days in her notebook

"Looks like she never had anyone with her," Bebe said, disappointed.

"So all this drama over a dead lead?" Dora asked. "That's very unfortunate."

"Wait!" Bebe called out suddenly. "Look," she pointed at the screen. "Here she is coming in with another woman, Wednesday evening, 8:44pm."

"Who is that?" Dora asked.

"I have no idea," Beth said.

Bebe forwarded through the footage.

"The woman stayed with her overnight," Bebe said, triumphant. "A lesbian twist?" she asked in the direction of Beth.

"It could be her sister," Beth said. "They look very much alike, don't they?"

"As much as you can tell from a security camera, yes," Dora agreed.

"If she expected her sister to stay, she would have booked a double room for the two of them, wouldn't she?" Bebe said. "It's weird that she didn't register the other guest."

"That is noteworthy," Beth agreed.

"Here they are coming out together at 9:13am Thursday morning," Bebe said.

"Freeze that frame," Beth said. "I'll take a picture of it on my phone."

"Ask the manager if he knows who the woman might be," Dora asked. "Maybe he's seen her."

"Good idea," Beth said and went to the front desk.

"Yes," the man confirmed between bites from his chocolate bar. "She's a regular here. I remember both of them now. Mrs Lackey, I think."

Beth froze.

"Not Lorraine Laffey?"

"Yes, that's her name."

He went to the computer and printed a sheet of paper.

"These are the dates she stayed with us in the last few weeks."

"Who is that woman?" Dora asked. "She sounds like a promising lead."

"One of Dominic's ex-girlfriends," Beth said and turned to the manager.

"Thank you," she said. "You've been very helpful."

"My pleasure," he said and unwrapped another chocolate bar.

"Let's go to Burger King, ladies," Beth said.

Chapter 24: The Final Trail

Beth

They weren't lucky at the restaurant, though. There was no manager around who had access to the security footage. They were told to come back at daytime when there would be more than just skeleton staff. How frustrating. She finally had something over Warwick and now this setback. Time was of the essence if she wanted to solve the crime for him and redeem herself in his eyes. If she didn't, chances were that he would get wind of her continuing the investigation and take her badge, too.

"Now what could the stalking ex-girlfriend and the cheated-on wife be doing in this area other than trying to cause problems for Dominic?" Beth asked when they were back in Bebe's car.

"Yes, and according to the print-out they were also here before Helena came to stay with me that week," Bebe pointed out. "Which is odd because my daughter hasn't seen me since Christmas. She only met that gigolo a few weeks ago, so why would they have been in this area?"

"All that leads us back to Mrs Morris," Beth said, "and it implies that the two women were here for her."

Then she had an idea. "It does, unless there is another connection to this area. Why did Helena and Dominic make the taxi drive the other way from your house, Bebe? They weren't going back to Carmarthen, they had a different destination."

"Can't you wave your police badge at the taxi company and ask that they give you the details of that journey?" Dora asked.

"I can always try," Beth said and grinned. "I called the taxi for them, so at least I know which company they used. I've gone beyond the point of no return as far as my career is concerned.

They drove to the office of the taxi company in Carmarthen and were lucky. A big lonesome middle-aged man with a potbelly stood in the door, smoking a cigarette. It was a slow night. He looked at the police badge, then at his wristwatch, rolled his eyes and then waved the trio in.

"I remember that call," he said. "They were going to the Millhouse Farm."

"That farm shut down over a year ago," Bebe interjected. "That can't be."

"Exactly," the man replied. "That's why I remember it so well. We've not had custom to there for ages. The clients made the taxi wait, picked up some luggage and then went to the station in Carmarthen. I wondered what they were doing there. I drove past it a few days ago to see what had become of the farm, it was still abandoned."

"Thank you," Beth said excitedly and headed for the door. "Come on ladies, we've got work to do. This sounds as if we have found our place of interest in the area."

She led the women back to the car. Beth couldn't wait to find out what was going on at that farm.

"This is so exciting," Bebe said. "I just hope it doesn't get my Helena into trouble."

"I hate to break it to you but you're about twenty years too late for that," Dora said and put her good arm on that of her neighbour.

Bebe turned her head, indignant at the insult, and removed her arm.

"I'm a mother, too," Dora said, trying to placate Bebe. "I know how little influence we really have on our children. I'm not saying you didn't try and do your best, but to pretend that Helena is an innocent child would be ridiculous. We have all seen her in action."

"Now, now," Beth interfered. She couldn't have her side-kicks arguing with such a promising lead to be investigated. They could sort out their issues later. "Let's just drive to the farm and see what the place is like."

Millhouse Farm appeared to be abandoned, just as the man from the taxi company had said. The windows were boarded up and the front door was locked. There were a few cars parked outside, although they, too, looked run-down and abandoned.

At first the women looked for a doorbell or another entrance. When this didn't bear fruit, they went round to the back of the building and saw that there were lights on in an extension to the main building.

"Now what?" Dora whispered.

"We knock on the door and make conversation," Bebe said.

"Aren't you worried?" Dora asked, her voice still low. "We don't know who these people are?"

"I'm surprised you should be scared," Bebe said. "You're the one who put a Christine scarecrow in the garden. If you were brave enough to do that, you should be ready for everything else."

"It's eleven o'clock at night," Dora pointed out.

"Don't worry," Beth said coolly. "Let me handle this."

She went to the lit window and knocked.

"Hello! Is someone in there?" she called out.

There were muffled voices inside.

"Hello!" Beth called again.

"Hello?" replied a timid female voice.

"That sounds like my Helena," Bebe whispered.

"Detective Sergeant Beth Cooper from the City of Cardiff Police," Beth called. "May I ask you a few questions, please?"

More muffled voiced from inside.

"Just a moment, please," the voice called through the window.

Beth heard chairs or tables moving and doors being shut.

"The entrance is on the other side of the extension," the voice directed them. "Walk around the building and I'll meet you by the door."

She did as she was told, Bebe and Dora following close behind her. Standing in the open doorway was Helena, holding hands with Dominic.

"Mother, what are you doing here?" she asked, almost oblivious to the detective and Dora.

"I was going to ask you that very question," Bebe replied.

"Since you kicked us out of your home we had to go somewhere. My friend Lucy told me about this place. She's seeing a married estate agent who brings her here when he has time. She told where the keys are hidden. Water and electricity are still connected. It's a good hideout place, only a bit cold and uncomfortable."

"Squatting is more like it," Beth said, "and trespassing and entering."

"Oh calm down," Dominic said and threw his hands in the air. "Be cool."

"You've got a nerve," Bebe started, but fortunately Dora took her hand and pulled her back.

"Let's just hear a bit more about this," Beth said. "Maybe, if you cooperate we can forget that we saw you here. Nobody needs to know you were trespassing."

"I like the sound of that," Dominic said and put both his thumbs up. "Cool."

"What do you want to know?" Helena asked.

"We've just found out that Ellie had been coming to this area a lot lately," Beth informed them. "We need to know if you two have met up here before last week."

Dominic gave Helena a questioning look. She nodded.

"Yes, we've been using this as our love shack," he confessed. "Quite a lot actually," he added and chuckled.

"We were here when the first big snow fell and got stuck," Helena explained. "Remember when I called you mother? I had to tell Aidan that I was with you since I couldn't get home. We had no idea that Ellie was already on our heels then."

"Did you know that Lorraine Laffey was helping your late wife to spy on you?" Beth asked. Dominic cringed at the mention of that name.

"Who's Lorraine?" Helena asked him, alarmed.

"So, you were aware of it?" Beth asked, more pointedly, but Dominic didn't reply.

"Who is this Lorraine?" Helena asked, her face flushed and her voice shrill. "You haven't got another girl on the go, have you?"

Bebe couldn't suppress a sigh. "Oh dear baby girl," she said.

". . . of course not," he stammered.

Beth smirked. "But you have an idea about her following you and cooperating with your wife?" she asked.

A heavy silence fell over the group. All eyes were on the underwear model who looked bedazzled from woman to woman. In the moonlight it was possible to see everyone's breath, and you could hear it in the quiet, too. Dora stamped her feet to keep the cold at bay and Bebe tightened the belt of her Babooshka coat.

"Well, I knew Lorraine was on my case," Dominic admitted at long last, looking at the Beth with his puppy eyes. "She showed up here one day while I was waiting for Helena. I don't know how she managed to follow me. Lorraine made a big scene about how she still loved me and never got over me. She said that we should give it another go. I told her that I was with Helena now and that I was still

178

married on top of everything else. Lorraine said she would tell Ellie she was pregnant with my child if I didn't break it off with Helena and start dating her again."

"Classy," Dora hissed under her breath. Bebe buried her head in her hands.

"You didn't?" Helena said and punched him in the shoulder, tears forming in her eyes.

"No, no, of course I didn't do anything with her," he said quickly to his lover. "Lorraine called me one more time when we were at your mother's house and gave me a last chance to change my mind. I hung up on her and later that Ellie appeared at the doorstep, tipped off about us by Lorraine no doubt. The rest is history."

Helena wiped the tears away and wrapped her arms around him.

"Oh, Dominic!"

Beth felt sorry for Bebe.

"And they say romance is dead," she heard Dora say and saw the injured woman put her good arm around Bebe. "

Bebe pulled herself away.

"I'm sorry you had to witness this," she said in a low voice. "I didn't raise her to behave like that. I never set her that kind of example, nor did her father for all of his other faults. From the day she was born she decided to do exactly the opposite of what I've told her. I don't know what to do with that child."

"She is no child anymore," Dora said. "But she will grow up eventually. Don't be embarrassed."

"We're veering off the investigation," Bebe said quickly. "What do you make of all this?" she asked Beth.

"It all seems to fit," Beth answered. "Lorraine was a regular guest at the hotel but only appeared one last time on Wednesday to meet Ellie, when she spills the beans about the affair with Helena and the hideout near Llangurrey."

"That doesn't make sense," Bebe contradicted. "Ellie had been here before that day, too. Either Lorraine had already told her, or Ellie was here for another reason?"

"Yes, we need to find out when Ellie and Lorraine actually connected," Beth admitted. "We need to speak to Lorraine, really. It's what I told my boss to do all along."

"Do you know her address?" Bebe asked.

Beth shook her head. "Unfortunately not."

That would have been too easy,

"I can give it to you," Dominic said and pulled his phone out. "So you see, I have nothing to hide."

"Alright then," Beth said.

A few minutes later they were in Bebe's car, the headlights flaring on snowbanks and highlighting silhouetted trees as the women headed towards London. Beth had considered dropping Dora back home but time was of the essence and nobody gave the slightest impression of being tired.

"I am sorry if I offended you earlier," Dora apologised to Bebe. "I know plenty of kids who are nightmares for the best-meaning parents. What I said all came out wrong, it seems."

"Dora, I'll stop you right there," Bebe interrupted her neighbour. "I'd be grateful if we could simply drop the topic. We've all seen enough, there is no need to comment any further."

"Oh you British and your pretence," Dora scoffed. "Never mind. I'm only trying to be nice."

"And I'm sure it is appreciated underneath all of this," Beth chipped in, trying to keep the peace. She couldn't have a fall-out now, when they seemed to be getting closer to solving the crime. "Now let's concentrate on the case. What do you think is Lorraine's real role in this? She was in the vicinity of Llangurrey on the day of the murder. Could she have killed her love rival?"

"It would make a hell of a lot more sense than Christine doing it," Dora said.

Bebe remained silent.

It was already 1:30am when they reached Lorraine's home. She lived on the ground floor of a Victorian house in Stockwell.

"We're lucky," Dora said. "The lights are still on."

"There's no rest for the wicked," Bebe said, coming a bit more alive.

"Let's hope she *is* the wicked," Beth said. "Else I can say goodbye to my police badge forever."

"That might not be a bad thing," Bebe said. "It is a dreary business to be in. You should do something more fun than dealing with criminals."

"Don't tell me you're not enjoying this," Dora said and nudged her neighbour. "I certainly am."

Beth pressed the doorbell.

"Who is it?" a woman asked through the intercom.

"Detective Sergeant Beth Cooper, from the City of Cardiff Police."

The door immediately buzzed open and they were let in.

Lorraine Laffey waited at the door to her apartment, wearing a bathrobe and holding a cup of coffee. She looked very much like Ellie: slim and well proportioned, the same short haircut, almost the same tone of henna red. She had dark rings under her eyes and her head hung low.

"What do you want from me?" she asked.

"Can we come in?" Beth replied.

"Of course."

She led the visitors to her living room and invited them to sit on the large leather sofa.

"It's come to our attention that you weren't actually staying at the Towy Valley Inn in Carmarthen, as you stated, but that you frequently stayed at the Lodgers Inn," Beth said, "including the night before the murder. Today we spoke to Dominic Seaborne, who told us you threatened to tell his wife about his affair with Helena Quinn and that you were pregnant with his child. You knew of their hideout at the Millhouse Farm and you were seen with Ellie Seaborne in the hotel the night before she was murdered. I think you have a bit of explaining to do."

Lorraine Laffey nodded slowly.

"Before Dominic went with her," she said, "we used to be good friends, Ellie and I. We knew each other from college. Obviously, we fell out when she started dating my ex, but recently we rekindled our friendship."

Dora coughed noisily.

"Shhh," Bebe hissed.

"I see you and Ellie spent a lot of time together in the hotel room, reminiscing; telling your alleged friend all the nasty details about Helena and Dominic; a fine way to reconnect with a long lost bosom buddy," Beth said. "Trying to steal her boyfriend and being pregnant with his baby."

"That's not what happened," Lorraine Laffey claimed. "And I'm not pregnant."

"That's a relief," Bebe said under her breath.

Lorraine shot her a warning look and pulled her knees up closer to her chest.

"I never wanted him back," she said. "I saw him snogging a girl after one of his concerts in London. I assumed this meant that he and Ellie were no longer an item, so I called her to see if we could be friends again. When it became apparent that Ellie was still with Dominic, I started to follow him and uncovered this hide-out and the scale of the affair with Helena."

"Mr Seaborne claimed you tried blackmailing him into getting back together with your 'pregnancy'", Beth said.

"Ellie and I wanted to make him nervous. We wanted to see how serious this affair was and how much lying he'd be capable off. I meant to smoke him out to see how he'd react, to show Ellie what a rat he is. She came to Carmarthen with me then and saw it all for herself. She had suspected it for weeks, anyway. Dominic isn't a great liar, as you can imagine."

"So, why the sudden drama when Ellie came to Llangurrey last week to confront Dominic and Helena?" Beth asked. "She was seen crying and making a scene of herself."

"Ellie expected the affair to die down. Dominic has gone astray many times but always came back to her. She assumed this thing with Helena wouldn't last, either. When it continued, Ellie followed Helena to her home address. We went together to tell Helena's husband, Aidan, about the affair. We were with Aidan when he called Helena during the snowstorm. When he heard that they had gone to stay with Bebe, he said it had to be serious between Helena and Dominic. Helena would never resort to involving her mother unless it was absolutely necessary. He packed his bag and took the next plane to stay with his sister in Greece."

"If you knew Ellie all this time," Beth said, "then she might have told you the story of Christine Morris and that awkward placement at the events management firm. Mrs Morris wrote a poor assessment of Ellie's performance and that very letter was found on Ellie's night stand in the hotel."

Lorraine Laffey cowered in her seat and said nothing.

"We also found sketches of the various people in the hamlet in Ellie's possession," Beth said firmly. "They were making it clear that she was aware that the woman who spoilt her career ten years ago was living in Llangurrey, the same hamlet as Bebe Bollinger, the mother of her husband's mistress. I believe that you never were friends with Ellie. You wanted her out of the way so that you could be with Dominic. You lulled Ellie into a false sense of friendship and planned her murder in cold blood. You persuaded her to confront the woman who had ruined her career, went to the Morris residence, planning to frame Christine for the murder you were about to commit yourself. All you needed to do was to accompany Ellie into the hamlet and then kill her on Christine's doorstep."

"No," Lorraine Laffey screamed. "I didn't kill Ellie."

"I find this hard to believe," Bebe said. "She was your love rival!"

"We were like sisters, burnt by the same man," Lorraine Laffey retorted. "We both had had enough of Dominic by now. But we wanted revenge. During our stakeout we were hiding in the empty cow shed past the Morris residence. One night, we saw a woman clamp a neighbour's car. We laughed so hard, we nearly gave ourselves away. When the woman returned to her house, Ellie recognised her immediately and she wanted to pay her back for that nasty reference she wrote."

"Didn't Mrs Morris help Ellie to get a career in publishing?" Beth interrupted.

Lorraine snorted.

"A 'career'. Ha, ha! Lorraine became an assistant, paid next to nothing. Her parents topped up the salary to allow her to have a decent living. And there was no reason to be so nasty in that reference, either. If Mrs Morris thought she was being helpful, she is even more condescending than I thought."

"So what happened that night?" Beth asked.

Lorraine sighed and drew her knees closer to her chest.

"We bought a big pair of pliers the next day, so that we could cut through the brakes of another car and then leave the cutter by Mrs Morris's garage. Dominic used to be a mechanic and had described to Ellie exactly how you do that. The timing was perfect with all the heavy snow. In those conditions the car would crash long before it got to a main road and nobody would come to serious harm. In the stormy weather conditions the suspicion would fall no doubt on Mrs Morris and Ellie would have her little revenge. It was freezing cold, and lying underneath the car in those temperatures was not much fun for Ellie, believe me. But she beamed with excitement when she came back out from underneath the car."

"Thank you very much," Dora said and pointed at her arm. "That prank could have killed me and as if it that wasn't enough the little minx then proceeded to hit me."

Lorraine Laffey was sobbing uncontrollably now.

"We didn't think that far ahead," she said. "We were like school children, high on revenge."

"So who killed Ellie, if it wasn't you?" Beth asked. "Was it Christine after all?"

"It was her husband," Lorraine Laffey said. "He must have heard us and came out of the house with the shovel in his hand, just when we tried to plant the pliers. He didn't see me behind the recycling bin but he saw Ellie. I recognised him. When she did that work placement with Mrs Morris, Ellie had had an affair; I had no idea it was with him. It had to be the reason why Mrs Morris kicked her out and why Ellie bore such a deep grudge. Ellie shouted she would make him pay for it. She meant, of course, because of what we had done to the neighbour's car but he flipped out, shouted and lifted the shovel."

"How did he manage to creep up on you with his limp?" Beth asked. "The man can hardly move."

Lorraine looked puzzled.

"He didn't limp as far as I could see. Ellie was retreating but he hit her before she got away. It was terrible. I keep reliving that moment every night. I couldn't leave my hiding place beside the bin for fear he'd kill me, too. Mr Morris checked the body. When he realised that Ellie was dead, he buried her body beneath the snow, opened the garage and brought out a second shovel. He placed the bloody shovel near the road and the fresh one next to the door. He was so calm. I was lucky he never spotted me, the bin being so close to the garage door. I threw the pliers behind his Land Rover in the garage and then waited by the bin until he went back inside the house via the garage. He behaved as if nothing had happened. I was in such a state but I still had to walk all the way back to the hotel in Carmarthen."

"Why didn't you tell us about Mr Morris?"

"I thought I would never be implicated. To be safe, I'd already prepared an alibi by leaving my phone back in London. The Lodgers Inn was booked in Ellie's name. The key card in the Towy Valley Inn would give me a secondary alibi all night, if you found out about that. Nobody could have linked me to Llangurrey, not in the storm."

"You went to great length to cover your tracks," Beth pointed out. "Almost as if you thought you would be caught. Wouldn't the truth have been much easier?"

"I knew if I owned up to being in Llangurrey and been a witness to the murder, I'd be done for cutting through those brake cables and possibly attempted manslaughter. I didn't want to get a criminal record or go to prison. I thought I could do it. Only, since that night I haven't been sleeping. Every time the phone rang I thought it was the police. Every time I spoke to your colleague Warwick, the Detective Chief Inspector, I thought he'd arrest me. I figured he fancied me and I was beginning to feel safe. When you came here tonight I knew my number was up. I can't lie anymore and protect a murderer. I need to clear my conscience and move on with my life."

"I think that's very wise of you," Dora said. "I won't be pressing charges, darling. There is no point in ruining your life with this but you must be more sensible in the future."

Lorraine Laffey smiled through her tears. "Thank you."

"So what happens now?" Bebe asked Beth.

"I think I'm going to wake up Warwick and tell him my news," Beth replied with a smirk. "It's time for me to point out the flaws in *his* investigation for once and then take it from there."

"He must reinstate you after this," Bebe said.

"You'd think so," Beth said, although she wasn't too sure. "I'm keeping my options open."

"What do you mean by that?" Bebe asked, puzzled.

"I'm considering a transfer to somewhere else."

"I thought you liked your job?"

"Exactly," Beth replied. "I love it, but I hate working with him. I'll look for a similar job somewhere else in the police force."

She turned to Lorraine Laffey.

"I need to bring you in to a police station to take an official statement. Please, get dressed."

185

"Of course," Lorraine said. "I'm ready to face the consequences of my actions."

"Then we need to sort out the practicalities of all this," Bebe said. "We've got a long drive home ahead of us. Can we take her with us to Wales?" she asked Beth.

"Since Mrs Laffey has been so cooperative that would be the perfect solution," Beth said. "Are you sure you can stay awake and drive another three hours?"

"Of course," Bebe replied. "I don't think I'll be sleeping a wink after all that excitement anyway."

Chapter 25: Back in the Driver's Seat

Beth

Warwick took Beth's news stoically. He neither scolded nor applauded her over the phone and only told her that he'd be in the police station in 20 minutes. Once she got there he still kept his cards close to his chest. Beth guessed that he was thinking of a way to take full credit for her findings and still sack her.

After they had the written statement from Lorraine Laffey, Warwick called his colleagues in Carmarthen to have Ian Morris arrested. He threw his car keys in the air a few times and caught them again. Then he turned to Beth and almost smiled.

"Are you coming, Cooper?" he asked, putting his jacket on.

"Do you need me for this?" she asked, tired and reluctant.

"Turns out for once I do," he said, sounding friendlier than he had been to her in a long time.

"Cool," she said and followed him down to the car park.

"I won't beat around the bush, Cooper," Warwick said on the drive to Carmarthen. "That was excellent police work. That really redeemed you. I wish you had been so focused from the beginning of this investigation."

"Thanks, I guess," she said.

"Maybe I haven't given you enough credit," he continued, to her astonishment. "Maybe I need to let you work more independently. Trying to fix your cases and my own at the same time has made me very resentful towards you."

"You don't say," Beth said. She tried to sound sarcastic but his changed attitude unexpectedly got to her, and she couldn't help feeling pleased, and smiled.

"First thing tomorrow morning I'll make sure that paperwork about your transfer is destroyed and nobody will ever know that you weren't authorised to continue with your investigation. Carla in personnel owes me a big favour. You'll stay on my team, but I'll let you have more freedom. What do you say?"

"I'll think about it," she said.

"What's there to think about?" he asked, irritated. "I'm being exceedingly generous. What about a little gratitude, Cooper? You've broken a lot of rules."

"You've been quite annoying to work with," Beth spurted out. "The thought of a transfer away from you is actually quite appealing."

"Nonsense," he said. "Everyone is annoying in the police force. A different boss is not going to solve your problems. Stick with the devil you know."

"Is that why you want to keep me, to save yourself getting used to someone else?"

"That's a big part of it," he said and smirked.

"I was sure you'd sack me for breaking the rules," she said, still genuinely surprised that she had been so wrong about his reaction.

"Results are what counts," Warwick said. "I thought you knew me by now."

In Carmarthen police station Ian Morris was ready for them in the interrogation room. Confronted with the witness statement he didn't put up a fight.

"I'm relieved in a way," he confessed. "It's been killing me to know that my wife is accused of a crime I've committed. I should have come clean a long time ago."

"You move me to tears," Warwick said from across the tiny table that separated them.

"It's true," Ian protested. "It's hard to tell what is worse for her: the worry about herself or me. Worrying is all she does."

"Why didn't you think of that before you killed Ellie Seaborne?" Beth asked.

"I didn't think at all," Ian said. "I went outside to put some shredded paper in the recycling bin and to see how bad the weather was getting, and there she was. I panicked. She had come to ruin my life."

"All she had done was cut Dora's brake cable and plant the pair of pliers in your garage," Beth informed him. "But you couldn't have known that. How did you think she was going to ruin our life?"

"Oh my God! You mean that I killed her for nothing? I thought she would tell Christine about our affair," he said.

"Your wife didn't know?" Beth asked. "According to Mrs Laffey, Ellie thought she had been sacked because of the affair."

"No, no, no," Ian corrected her. "Lorraine was fired for being useless at her job. If Christine had found out about the affair at the time she would have divorced me immediately, and she probably will do so now. That's why I didn't bail Christine out from prison. I would have lost her for good if I had implicated myself. I hoped she would be released due to lack of evidence and we would stay together. I didn't think I'd be caught."

"That was a risky gamble," Warwick said. "Leaving the dead body outside of your house and claiming you knew nothing about it."

"You played that part very well," Beth said. "You nearly got away with it."

"Good job, Cooper," Warwick said. "Good job."

She wasn't so sure of that. She had blundered badly all the way through. She should have suspected Ian much earlier on and not let herself be blinded by his kind manners and fake limp. Even the originally not so interested Bebe had thrown more suspicion his way. Had it not been for the singer, Beth would not have known that Ian's ankle wasn't as bad as it was made out to be. Beth also wouldn't have continued with the investigation on her own, had Bebe not pushed her to meet Dora, where Ellie's lost satchel provided vital last clues. Coming to think of it, in her casual way, the *Diva* had been incredibly helpful. The professional way in which she had searched the surveillance camera footage alone showed just how crucial Bebe had been to the investigation.

But she wasn't going to tell Warwick that.

Epilogue

Bebe

Bebe parked outside her cottage in a new cabriolet sports car for the first time. After suddenly finding herself in the public eye again, she had felt it necessary to use some of her savings to build up a hip image. She wasn't used to the car's dimensions yet and regretted that Dora had erased Christine's yellow markings from the road. As annoying as the strict rule had been, it had actually given Bebe, a less confident driver, guidance on how to make best use of the limited parking space.

Christine hadn't been seen in the hamlet since she was released from police custody two months previously. Bebe felt sorry for her neighbour. She knew all about scandals and bad press, and could only imagine what is felt like to have your own husband convicted as a murderer, let alone finding out that he had cheated on you, even if that was some ten years ago. The two remaining residents of Llangurrey doubted they would ever see Christine again. It was a shame to lose the handy man of the hamlet. Ian had been such a nice and useful neighbour.

It was a huge relief that Helena's name had been cleared, though. Bebe had come close to a scandal there, with her daughter's alibi being called into question, and Bebe had begun to doubt just what that child was really capable of. Thank God, it wasn't murder after all. With everything that was happening in Bebe's career right now, that would have been most inconvenient.

Helena split from Dominic after only two weeks after Ian's arrest when she found him with his trousers down in her marital flat with another woman. She had immediately flown to Greece to persuade Aidan to give their marriage another go, but to no avail. It was only a matter of time before she would be coming knocking on her mother's door again.

The *Comic Relief* event had gone tremendously well. The murder in Bebe's hamlet and her involvement in solving it had become a minor news item and the nation assumed that this was why Bebe had been invited onto the show. She received a lot of attention even before the show aired. The sketch written by Jennifer Saunders was very harsh on Bebe and she cringed when she saw how old she looked. On the other hand, it was hailed as very funny and, according to the high number of views on YouTube, she was rated as one of the highlights of the evening. She adored what they had done with the Abba video between her and Will. It really rocked the crowd that night and had given Bebe the biggest buzz of her career. She would never forget that night and the way the audience had been on her side.

Bebe's willingness to be made fun off, especially in combination with her recent crime solving, created a very positive buzz on social media. *#Bebe* was even trending on Twitter. The newspapers wrote plenty of nice things about her and her community and charitable spirit. The BBC made some offers, and a big record label was interested in releasing a 'Best-of' album if her proposed duet with Will was successful. The label was currently negotiating with her ex-husband about the rights to her songs. It looked as if he was prepared to cut her a deal.

Bertie had been so full of himself when he called Bebe with the offer from the record label that she had no qualms about firing him that instant. The way he sold this success as his doing – she had had enough. Fred was doing the negotiations with the record label on her behalf and she proved to be a tough cookie.

There was a little scare when Alison Moyet announced she would be recording a new album with Guy Sigsworth and that it would be released in 2012, but then her rival stated on a radio show: "I appear to have forfeited my recording deal because I won't do reality TV. No-one needs to make an album that badly."

For once, Bebe agreed.

As Fred had feared, Engelbert sadly sank at Eurovision and came second-last. Dora and Beth had come round to Bebe's to watch the show together and had a great time. Even Dora enjoyed herself, despite the fact that Portugal failed to qualify that year and her husband's alimony payments had stalled in May.

Engelbert's song peaked at No. 60 in the charts but Bebe actually still liked the song and felt sorry for him. She'd had a lucky escape there.

Bebe was shortly about to sing on Will Young's new album, with a good chance that the track might even get a single release. Opportunities to tour with Will were naturally in the offing and the

West End stage had also been in contact with her new agent. Things were looking up for Bebe Bollinger, not even a body in the snow could stop her comeback, she vowed as she headed down to her basement to start work on some new material.

The End

Did you like the book?

Please take a moment and let everyone know by posting a review on Goodreads, Amazon.com or Amazon.co.uk to tell others about it. Reviews – however short - and word of mouth are the best way to support an author. Thank you…

… or read on. Here is the first chapter from THE HEALER

The Healer - Chapter 1

The tired, small hatchback hit a rock next to the edge of the road and came to an unexpected and abrupt stop. Erica had not seen the bulky thing hidden underneath the uncut grass. She switched off the engine and got out. There seemed no significant damage to her old banger but she couldn't care less right now, to be honest, and decided she would leave it parked here anyway. She must be close.

Quite frankly, she considered herself lucky to have made it this far; the roads had been bumpy and her car was in a dire condition, too. It wouldn't be much longer before it would have to be scrapped. Living in London she rarely needed it and had often been tempted to sell it anyway.

This was deepest Wales, the countryside - something that the Londoner in her had not seen for years and certainly hadn't missed. Poor phone reception, miles to the nearest supermarket with its supplies of cigarettes and bubbly: that's what the countryside meant to her.

She guessed the car was sufficiently off the road and out of the way. Who would come here, anyway? It was unlikely that two cars would find this remote corner of Wales at the same time, she reckoned. Erica looked around: not a living soul in sight, no houses or vehicles; she was totally off the beaten track. She could see no significant landmarks; all views were blocked by large trees and hedges. It was drizzling a little and although it was past lunchtime, there was mist that reminded her of early mornings. The wind had made the spring temperatures drop more than she had anticipated and she was chilly in her inadequate city clothing.

She searched her purse for the map, which her assistant Hilda had drawn for her. It seemed as if she was in the right place; there was the small path at the foot of the hill, and the two opposing gates leading to fields with horses and sheep. Since leaving her nearby B&B, all the road junctions she had come to had been easy to recognise and here was the little shoulder by the side of the road, where Hilda had recommended she should park the car.

She assured herself once more that it was the right path and then she psyched herself up for the walk up the steep hill. The tricky part, Hilda had explained, was finding the hidden gate, which would lead her to the man himself. However, Hilda didn't have pancreatic cancer and was not recovering from a course of chemo and so she had no idea how difficult it would be for Erica to walk up that hill. It seemed by no means the easy climb her assistant had called it. For all her recent goodness, that woman could drive her mad.

Erica looked at herself in the outside mirror of her car before getting ready to face the man. Her hair had not fallen out from the chemo but it had turned grey and made her look much older than she was. There were still crow's feet and wrinkles despite being facially bloated – it really wasn't fair; the worst of both worlds. People used to think of Erica as at least five years younger than she actually was, but now people thought she was five years older. Overnight it seemed, she had aged from 40 to 50 but given her current situation she would be lucky to reach 45. Additionally, she had lost a lot of weight, despite the effect that the steroids had had on her. With her mere 5' 4" frame, she looked tiny and felt thin and weak.

Only this man might be able to improve her chances and she desperately hoped the trip here would be worth it. If the man really was who Hilda thought, there was a slight chance for her. If she could make him speak to her, then she was sure she could persuade him to help - if he still possessed *those* powers. There suddenly seemed a lot of ifs.

She locked the car and began the climb up the tree-covered hill. Her trainers slid on the moist moss, her jeans too tight for some of the big steps she had to take. There was only a tiny trodden path, which seemed easy to lose sight of, curving its way upwardly through the trees. She was glad she had the map. Hilda deserved an award for organising this; if Erica ever made it back to her position at work she would make sure to find a way of compensating her, if she had anything left after she had paid the man.

Her assistant had come here a few days ago and had scouted the place out in the manner of a gifted detective. Hilda had been an angel the last few months with an uncalled for loyalty and devotion which Erica felt she didn't deserve. Erica cringed when she thought of the numerous times she had blown a fuse in the office and let out her life's frustrations on this woman: she had complained about the coffee being too milky, the memos being too floral or the diary too busy. If only she had known how her life would play out, she would have made many decisions in different ways and definitely would have treated Hilda with more respect and humanity. Well, it was too late for regrets, she could only hope to make it right in the future, if she had one. For now it was time to keep going and move forward and rescue whatever she could.

A chicken wire ran parallel to the path, then some strong wooden fence panels replaced it that were so thickly overgrown with ivy that Erica would have missed seeing the gate itself, had it not been for the directions on the map.

To her surprise the gate was unlocked. A dog barked and howled from afar but it stayed at a safe distance. The noise was not very aggressive anyway and her guess was that this was a companion rather than a guard dog; a further indication that she was at the right place. She doubted that this spiritual guru called Arpan would have aggressive attack dogs around for protection: that would not be the style of someone so ostentatiously non-violent and serious. What she remembered about the man was admittedly extremely vague and distorted by what Hilda had told her.

He had made some headlines a long time ago and at the time, Erica had often seen his picture; if only she had paid more attention to current affairs. Her personal circumstances at the time had kept her pre-occupied and now she was unsure how the press had handled him. Hilda was of the opinion that this was a good thing, since Erica should meet him and find out for herself anyway. Arpan would probably not like to give such an unfavourable impression; Erica thought she remembered him as being very image orientated. He'd either maintain a soft and gentle outward image or would be far too cocky and confident; since the beginning of mankind, gurus had behaved as if they were invincible.

She reminded herself that she had to keep an open mind about this and that it was better to think the best of the man. After all, she had nothing more to lose.

Erica had to navigate between some very overgrown bushes until she came to a small clearing at last. A dome structure was at the other end of the clearing, made of wood and concrete and what looked like parts of camping tents. Solar panels, vegetable beds and free range animals populated the clearing: goats, chicken and sheep. She should have expected that. Green and new age living, she supposed.

"Arpan?" she called out. "Hello?"

An Alsatian came jumping out of the dome full of excitement and began to sniff and lick Erica's hand. He did not look like a puppy but he certainly behaved like one. She knelt down to stroke him gently. The dog wagged his tail excitedly and lay down on the ground, inviting her to rub his belly, and Erica happily obliged. What a happy little dog. She'd forgot how much fun dogs could be.

"Ashank, come back here!" a male voice called from inside the dome. "Come here!"

"Arpan?" Erica repeated shyly. "Hello, is that you, Arpan? I need to speak to you… please."

A young man, maybe 20 years old, slim, spotty and dressed in baggy, red and pink clothes, came briefly out of the dome and called the dog back. Ashank rolled on his side, jumped up and ran to his master. Before Erica could engage with him, the man had zipped the entrance to the dome shut. From what she had seen, his was not the voice she had heard, Erica was sure of it. The person who had called the dog from inside the tent sounded mature and older, much more like that of the Arpan she had heard about. Exactly how she had imagined him to be.

"I need to speak to you, Arpan. It's urgent," Erica called out again, unsure how best to proceed. She wished he would come out of the dome, so she could read his body language and figure out how to best 'work' him. Years in the advertising business had taught her how to handle these situations and she prided herself for her skills in that department. Him not coming out of the dwelling was its own kind of body language and dictated the rules of engagement; she would have to change them, break him down and transform this into a more intimate conversation.

196

"Go away. You're in the wrong place," the voice called out, sounding tired and slightly annoyed.

"Arpan, I need your help. Please talk to me!" she pleaded. "Hear me out. A few minutes of your time is all I ask of you. Please listen, and then I will go away."

"Who are you anyway?" the man asked, still not showing himself, but she thought she had seen a piece of the tent move. Perhaps he had seen her now and in her current fragile state that had to work in her favour. She looked positively ill and maybe this would appeal to his charitable side. To have done all the good things that he did in youth, he had to have some feelings and a heart. Even if he was a changed man now – as the abrupt stop to his healing practice implied - there had to be a little of his old self beneath the icy exterior, and she would try her damnedest to get to it.

"I'm very ill. You are my only hope now," she said calmly, eager not to overplay for sympathy.

"As I said: you've come to the wrong place," was the curt reply. "I can't help you."

"You have a gift, Arpan, I know you do. And I know you cannot let me die like this. You have a good heart, don't you? They once said that you were an 'Offering' to the world, that is the meaning of your name Arpan, isn't it? Even if you hide yourself away now, you have a responsibility to the world to share this gift. Save me, please!"

"I have responsibilities alright, but they are not to you or anybody else out there," Arpan replied in the manner of a sulky child. "You need to leave now."

"I beg you," Erica said, and sank to her knees. The sudden plunge hurt not only her knees but every other of her joints too. The muddy floor drenched her jeans, but she hardly cared.

"You seem familiar. You're not some journalist, are you? What did you say your name was?"

"Maria Miller," Erica lied. "So you really are Arpan," she added relieved and hopeful. She had found the right man, or rather, her assistant Hilda had. If she were religious, she would bless the Lord.

"I said no such thing," the man shouted back angrily. "I call myself Amesh. A different name altogether, a different man and a different life. One more suited to me. Please get up and leave."

"It doesn't matter what name you have. I'm dying, Amesh, so I don't have much time left to persuade you to help me."

"The man you're looking for is no more. I wish I could help you, but I simply can't. He disappeared with the name. Go home and do the only thing you can do: make peace with your enemies, tell your loved ones how much they mean to you and sort out all of your affairs in a manner that will make you proud. If it is your time to die, you should not waste the gift of time by looking for miracles that didn't find you on their own. Not many have the opportunity to right their wrongs. Use it wisely."

"Maybe you're right," Erica said, after a few seconds of deliberation. "If it really is my time to die, I will. I have already begun the process of righting my wrongs, as you call it. I had given up all hope and had resigned myself to die. But then I found you and I seriously believe that found you for a good reason. Many others must have tried to find you and didn't succeed. If things are meant to be, then this meeting between us now might not be a coincidence, so please let's talk. Let me at least look at you. Let us stand face to face. Maybe it will help me so I can bury the illusion that you would have been the one man left on the planet able to save me."

She heard a whisper in the tent, then the young boy came out from under the dome and looked her up and down. He was slim but more muscled than what she had initially thought, not as tall as he had looked just moments earlier, blond dreadlocks and a beard hiding some of his spots, piercings, tattoos and a cocky walk. Although he had a young face, he carried himself like someone who had been through a lot and knew how to handle life. He was focused but not quite calm enough to carry it off completely convincingly.

"You don't have a microphone or anything, do you?" He asked and frisked her. He was not shy touching her. "Let me look into your backpack," he said and rummaged through it when Erica offered it to him without hesitation. All Erica had brought with her were pen and paper, some snacks and her purse.

"She's clean," he called out to the man still hiding inside.

"What does Amesh mean?" Erica asked. "If Arpan meant 'Offering', then surely Amesh must have a meaning. What is it?"

"Coward Boy," said the old voice.

She was shocked at that and fell silent.

At last the man himself stepped out of the tent, with the Alsatian dancing around him. "The name represents what I have become."

Amesh looked nothing like she had expected. He had shaved his beard off and also his long, dark, Jesus-like hair. Bold and haggard he was a shadow of his former self. At least 60 and looking every bit of it, his face seemed deflated, his shoulders were hunched and there was nothing left of the charismatic persona Arpan had once been. She could see why he had chosen Amesh as his new name, there was something timid about him. It suited him better than Arpan, 'the Offering', as he had been known.

"You see," Amesh said shrugging his shoulders. "Stripped off all the glamour and of all power! I'm just your regular woodland hermit, growing vegetables and talking to the trees."

A hint of recognition slipped across his face.

"You remind me of someone," he said, but Erica shook her head. "Well, maybe it is the disease you have that makes me think I know you," he added. "I spent years with it and have seen it in all of its shapes and forms. Are you sure we haven't met before?"

"I know we haven't," she said quickly.

"How did you even find me?" he asked, looking intensely at her as if scanning her thoughts while he was doing it. "It's quite worrying," he added. "I'll finally have to succumb to necessity and install security again. Can't you people simply leave me alone? It's been years since anyone has taken notice of me. I thought I was at peace at last."

"I'm sorry," she replied sheepishly. "I guess it was the right amount of desperation and luck. For what it's worth, I can assure you that the people who helped me wouldn't give out your secret easily."

"I should hope so. Not many have any clue as to where I live these days. Trust me, I will silence them myself as soon as I can," he said forcefully, but Erica didn't think he meant it.

"Well, now that you've seen me in my new earthly incarnation I hope you can go back to your life in peace, knowing that you didn't miss out on some miracle that was meant for you. You can tell that I'm not the man you're looking for." He opened his arms in a gesture of disclosure and even turned around for her to have a good look.

"What happened to Arpan?" she asked, hoping to play up to his vanity. As long as she kept him talking, she was building a rapport. The more he knew about her, the more likely he was to feel sorry and change his mind. If he ever had the powers to heal pancreatic cancer with his hands, then that ability had to have stayed with him. As long a shot as this was, if he had done it once he had to be able to do it once more for her.

He shook his head. "As I've said, Arpan is no more. The world has transformed him and his gift, and it put me in his place."

"That's very cryptic. What's that actually supposed to mean?"

"You know, you sound just like a journalist," he said with a grin. "If I didn't see the disease in your face I would say you're here only looking for a scoop. Either way, what I said means simply that I don't have the powers that you seek."

"You healed hundreds of people," Erica insisted.

"That wasn't me; it was Arpan, 'the Offering'. He was something else, entirely. I cannot heal you, however much I wish I could," Amesh said resigned.

"You could at least try."

"Maria, you know nothing about me, about Arpan or about the so-called miracles. I indulged you by letting you see me, as you requested but I beg of you to leave now and to keep my location a secret. Arpan has given enough to the world, now it is time for Amesh to live his life to suit his needs."

"You can't give up on a calling like yours," Erica said with growing desperation.

"Amesh can and Arpan did, too. If you knew more you would probably understand."

"I have money, plenty of it, and I can get more, if that's what it takes," Erica blabbered in panic. She knew it was the wrong approach but she just couldn't help herself.

"Do I look like I need money?" Amesh said, shaking his head and pointing around him. "This is not the life of someone who wants lots of money - that should be very obvious to anyone."

"Actually, if I'm honest, it looks like the property of someone who could do with quite a lot of money." Erica contradicted. "It could buy you more living space, better isolation against rain and wind, to say the least, and security or a receptionist to help you out."

"I don't want any of that," Amesh said dismissively, "and I really don't need or want your money, thank you very much."

"Arpan took 50% of everything his patients owned," Erica said accusingly. "How does that fit in with what you are saying? For all his spirituality, Arpan did like the cash. Has it all gone? Looks like Amesh could do with a topping up his bank accounts to improve this place. At least get it safe for the next winter. I can help you if you help me."

"Arpan didn't 'like' the money, but the payment was an important and a very necessary part of the process," Amesh replied. "If the people who came to him weren't prepared to give this much for their life, then Arpan wasn't able to help them, just as western medicine couldn't help them. You need to value your life and the cost of keeping it."

Erica had to bite her tongue. Her natural distrust for miracle healers and un-scientific claims was ever-present but she mustn't alienate Amesh with her critical thoughts.

"If someone values their wealth above their health, then western medicine or *any* alternative measures can only slightly prolong their life," Amesh lectured her. "They are doomed, and nobody can stop the course of their destiny. People cheated Arpan and paid him only a fraction of what they were worth. When the disease then indeed didn't go away they asked for their money back, and Arpan returned all of those monies, without even charging them for his time, which they wasted. Every single person who didn't get cured was reimbursed. Many brought it onto themselves, I hasten to add."

"I get that you are retired for some reason or another and bitter with the world about something it did to you, but that doesn't necessarily mean that you're suddenly incapable of healing," Erica said. "Whatever it was that stopped you practicing at the height of your fame doesn't justify throwing away your gift. You mustn't let the newspapers and their hate campaigns get to you. You must at least try. Try on me to see if your powers are back. Please."

"You are so naïve," Amesh replied and sneered. "The work Arpan did was more complex than you will ever be able to comprehend. The newspapers and their treatment of him were not what stopped him; they were simply a symptom of the all underlying evil that stopped him: human nature and society. I don't want to get into the whole thing. As Amesh, I'm happy now and I lead a life that suits me just fine. I have a right to enjoy it."

"But…" she began, but he interrupted.

"Enough said. I have asked you to leave on numerous occasions and you have refused to comply. You are trespassing on my property and I wish for you to leave now. Anuj will escort you of the premises," he said and, as if on command, the young man came towards her, followed by the excitable Alsatian; he took her by the elbow and led her away.

"Please, Anuj," Erica pleaded on their way to the gate. "Put in a good word with him for me. I'm desperate and I don't have much time. Here is my card. I'm staying at Woodlands B&B, which is not far from here."

Anuj took the card and put it in his pocket.

"Don't get your hopes up," he warned. "As Amesh, he is hurting and as Arpan, he hasn't seen a client since he retreated from the limelight years ago. We also don't have a phone or computer and I doubt that you will hear from him. Do as he says and get on with your life, or what is left of it. He doesn't play games and this is not a case of 'playing hard to get'. I agree with him, that your time is a gift to get your life in order. I can tell there is a lot for you to do. Trying to be saved is a selfish use of the little time you have left when there are many things you should be doing instead. Think of the things you have to do before your time is up. Think of the people around you and what they need: goodbyes, sorting of affairs… there is so much. When you come to think of it, I doubt that you really have time for us, don't waste it by holding out for an unobtainable miracle. Think of the things you need to do and the people that need you."

"Those people need me alive," Erica said. "If they care, they need me alive."

"You need to trust what he said. Amesh might only be a shadow of what Arpan was but he can still see into people's souls. It's like a psychic X-ray; he gets people with only one look. I'm only his apprentice but I too can see the disorder in your life that needs to be rectified. You carry hurt and anger with you. Your disease has prompted you to fast track those issues and requires you to sort them out. Look into your heart and you will find this to be true."

"Tell him I'll be waiting for your call," Erica said stubbornly, "Amesh must have seen my determination," she added just before Anuj closed the gate behind her.

Angrily she walked down the hill, slipped twice and fell over the root of a tree. She had a few scratches and skinned one of her knees. Since the chemo, her skin was so fragile and seemed to rip open at the slightest touch. She got into her car and tried to start it, but the engine would not spring to life. She tried and tried but gradually realised that she was stuck. Here, of all places. This couldn't have happened anywhere worse. There was nobody, no sign of civilisation, people, houses or even mobile phone reception. For a brief moment she contemplated going back up the hill but she feared Arpan and Anuj would see it as a fake excuse and that would in no way help her cause with those two, of that she was sure. They would help her with the car but it might put them off for good and then he would never agree to help her with her illness.

Her body was aching badly and her painkillers made her terribly tired, so she decided to take a little rest before making any further plans. She quickly nodded off in the driver's seat and slept for several hours. It was late afternoon when a knocking on her car window woke her. It was Anuj with the Alsatian.

"Nice try," Anuj said dismissively when she explained her predicament to him. "Don't think we'll be changing our mind because of a broken down car."

"I wouldn't dream of such a thing," she said. "Just tell me what you suggest I should do."

He nodded and said with a hint of sarcasm: "It's only a two mile walk from here to the next farm. I'm sure they'll let you call the rescue services. I'll draw you a map how to find them."

"Thank you," Erica said as gracefully as she could. "I'll do that then."

She took her backpack and followed his directions. The walk was definitely much longer than the two miles Anuj had promised. The thought occurred to her that she mustn't get lost or she would never get out of here alive. The lush green Welsh countryside here started to grow on her a little: the constant rain had at least one upside. She had heard her fanatic hiking colleagues say that one could go days without meeting anyone else in some of these 'off the beaten track' locations. Obviously that was what Arpan or Amesh had gone for and what had brought her into trouble. She had tempted fate by driving here in such an old banger, she knew that.

She had to sit down and rest several times as she kept running out of breath. The farm was abandoned when she got there. After what seemed like an eternity of resting on a garden bench, she was getting concerned. At this time of the year, the sun would set soon and she had to consider all of her options. She began to worry that no-one would come home to the farm and she had to make use of the little daylight that was left to get back to her car. She would rather sleep in her car than somewhere here as an intruder in a farm outbuilding. At least, she had some food and a blanket in her car, here she would be nothing but a trespasser again. When she got back to her Fiesta it was already pitch dark. It didn't take much for her to fall asleep again and despite the wildlife noises that she was unaccustomed to, she slept all the way through to sunrise…

More books by Christoph Fischer:

The Healer

When advertising executive Erica Whittaker is diagnosed with terminal cancer, western medicine fails her. The only hope left for her to survive is controversial healer Arpan. She locates the man whose touch could heal her but finds he has retired from the limelight and refuses to treat her. Erica, consumed by stage four pancreatic cancer, is desperate and desperate people are no longer logical nor are they willing to take no for an answer. Arpan has retired for good reasons, casting more than the shadow of a doubt over his abilities. So begins a journey that will challenge them both as the past threatens to catch up with him as much as with her. Can he really heal her? Can she trust him with her life? And will they both achieve what they set out to do before running out of time?

Amazon: http://ow.ly/J4Wt6
Facebook: http://ow.ly/J4Wun
Goodreads: http://ow.ly/J4Ww4
Book-likes: http://ow.ly/J4WxU
Rifflebooks: http://ow.ly/J4WzY

The Gamblers

Ben is an insecure accountant obsessed with statistics, gambling and beating the odds. When he wins sixty-four million in the lottery he finds himself challenged by the possibilities that his new wealth brings.

He soon falls under the influence of charismatic Russian gambler Mirco, whom he meets on a holiday in New York. He also falls in love with a stewardess, Wendy, but now that Ben's rich he finds it hard to trust anyone. As both relationships become more dubious, Ben needs to make some difficult decisions and figure out who's really his friend and who's just in it for the money.

Amazon: http://ow.ly/S5tJC
Facebook: http://ow.ly/S5tcQ
Goodreads: http://ow.ly/S5tmE
Booklikes: http://ow.ly/S5sU9
Rifflebooks.com http://ow.ly/S5t2W
Createspace: http://ow.ly/S5txM

Ludwika:
A Polish Woman's Struggle To Survive In Nazi Germany

It's World War II and Ludwika Gierz, a young Polish woman, is forced to leave her family and go to Nazi Germany to work for an SS officer. There, she must walk a tightrope, learning to live as a second-class citizen in a world where one wrong word could spell disaster and every day could be her last. Based on real events, this is a story of hope amid despair, of love amid loss . . . ultimately, it's one woman's story of survival.

Editorial Review:

"This is the best kind of fiction—it's based on the real life. Ludwika's story highlights the magnitude of human suffering caused by WWII, transcending multiple generations and many nations.

WWII left no one unscarred, and Ludwika's life illustrates this tragic fact. But she also reminds us how bright the human spirit can shine when darkness falls in that unrelenting way it does during wartime.

This book was a rollercoaster ride of action and emotion, skilfully told by Mr. Fischer, who brought something fresh and new to a topic about which thousands of stories have already been told."

http://www.audible.com/pd/Mysteries-Thrillers/The-Healer-Audiobook/B01G62A7MQ/
http://bookShow.me/B018UTHX7A
http://smarturl.it/Ludwika
https://www.goodreads.com/book/show/28111001-ludwika
https://www.facebook.com/LudwikaNovel/
http://www.barnesandnoble.com/w/ludwika-mr-christoph-fischer/1123093504?ean=9781519539113

The Luck of the Weissensteiners
(Three Nations Trilogy: Book 1)

In the sleepy town of Bratislava in 1933 the daughter of a Jewish weaver falls for a bookseller from Berlin, Wilhelm Winkelmeier. Greta Weissensteiner seemingly settles in with her in-laws but the developments in Germany start to make waves in Europe and re-draw the visible and invisible borders. The political climate, the multi-cultural jigsaw puzzle of the disintegrating Czechoslovakian state and personal conflicts make relations between the couple and the families more and more complex. The story follows the families through the war with its predictable and also its unexpected turns and events and the equally hard times after. What makes The Luck of the Weissensteiners so extraordinary is the chance to consider the many different people who were never in concentration camps, never in the military, yet who nonetheless had their own indelible Holocaust experiences. This is a wide-ranging, historically accurate exploration of the connections between social status, personal integrity and, as the title says, luck.

Amazon: http://smarturl.it/Weissensteiners
Goodreads: http://bit.ly/12Rnup8
Facebook: http://on.fb.me/1bua395
B&N: http://ow.ly/Btvas
Book-Likes: http://ow.ly/J4X2q
Rifflebooks: http://ow.ly/J4WY0
Trailer: http://studio.stupeflix.com/v/OtmyZh4Dmc

Time to Let Go

Time to Let Go is a contemporary family drama set in Britain. Following a traumatic incident at work stewardess Hanna Korhonen decides to take a break from work and leaves her home in London to stay with her elderly parents in rural England. There she finds that neither can she run away from her problems, nor does her family provide the easy getaway place that she has hoped for. Her mother suffers from Alzheimer's disease and, while being confronted with the consequences of her issues at work, she and her entire family are forced to reassess their lives.

The book takes a close look at family dynamics and at human nature in a time of a crisis. Their challenges, individual and shared, take the Korhonens on a journey of self-discovery and redemption.

Amazon: http://smarturl.it/TTLG
Goodreads: http://ow.ly/BtKs7
Facebook: http://ow.ly/BtKtQ
Book-Likes: http://ow.ly/J4Xu0
Rifflebooks: http://ow.ly/J4XvR

Thanks

A big thank you to 'crime fiction junkie' Ryan, without whose enthusiasm I would never have fallen in love with the genre and written the book.

A huge thanks to my editor David Lawlor for his invaluable contributions and suggestions, his honesty and diplomacy in the process, and to my excellent beta readers: Sharon Brownlie, Pam Lecky, Giselle Marks, Fran Lewis, John Hazen, Sarah Mallery, Chris Westlake, Pat Zick and again, Ryan. Thanks to my amazing friend and cover designer Daz Smith for getting it right once again and for pushing me into publishing in the first place.

Last, but not least, to Celeste Burke and Dianne Harman, two professionals in the genre, for their inspiring body of work and lending support.

Disclaimer

This book is a work of fiction. Except for some real singers and TV personalities, the characters of this novel are all fictitious.

Although my story, hopefully playfully, involves some public figures (such as Jennifer Saunders and Engelbert) and TV shows they have taken part in (such as "Absolutely Fabulous", "Comic Relief" and the "Eurovision Song Contest") their interactions with my fictitious characters are naturally ficticious. Any similarities with their actions in connection to said shows are coincidental, too.

I have the deepest respect for all artists mentioned and that is the reason that they are in the book. I have not intended to portray them in any negative or dubious light, especially the team behind Jennifer Saunders and Engelbert's Eurovision entry.

A Short Biography

Christoph Fischer was born in Germany, near the Austrian border, as the son of a Sudeten-German father and a Bavarian mother. Not a full local in the eyes and ears of his peers he developed an ambiguous sense of belonging and moved to Hamburg in pursuit of his studies and to lead a life of literary indulgence. In 1993 he moved to the UK and now lives in Llandeilo in west Wales. He and his partner have several Labradoodles to complete their family.

Christoph worked for the British Film Institute, in Libraries, Museums and for an airline. His first historical novel, 'The Luck of The Weissensteiners', was published in November 2012 and downloaded over 60,000 times on Amazon. He has released several more historical novels, including 'In Search of A Revolution' and 'Ludwika'. He also wrote some contemporary family dramas and thrillers, most notably 'Time to Let Go' and 'The Healer'.

For further information you can follow him on:

Twitter:
https://twitter.com/CFFBooks
Pinterest:
http://www.pinterest.com/christophffisch/
Google +:
https://plus.google.com/u/0/106213860775307052243
LinkedIn:
https://www.linkedin.com/profile/view?id=241333846
Blog:
http://writerchristophfischer.wordpress.com
Website:
www.christophfischerbooks.com
Facebook:
www.facebook.com/WriterChristophFischer

Made in the USA
Charleston, SC
22 September 2016